S0-AJU-979

DEATH OF A
DEBTOR

DEATH OF A
DEBTOR

JENNA HARTE

W☉RLDWIDE™

TORONTO • NEW YORK • LONDON
AMSTERDAM • PARIS • SYDNEY • HAMBURG
STOCKHOLM • ATHENS • TOKYO • MILAN
MADRID • WARSAW • BUDAPEST • AUCKLAND

If you purchased this book without a cover you should be aware
that this book is stolen property. It was reported as "unsold and
destroyed" to the publisher, and neither the author nor the
publisher has received any payment for this "stripped book."

To Jay—Thank you for supporting this crazy dream of mine.

W🌐RLDWIDE™

Recycling programs
for this product may
not exist in your area.

ISBN-13: 978-1-335-73638-3

Death of a Debtor

First published in 2019 by Camel Press, an imprint of
Epicenter Press, Inc. This edition published in 2021.

Copyright © 2019 by Jenna Harte

All rights reserved. No part of this book may be reproduced or
transmitted in any form or by any means, electronic or mechanical,
including photocopying, recording or by any information storage and
retrieval system, without permission in writing from the publisher.

This is a work of fiction. Names, characters, places and incidents
are either the product of the author's imagination or are used fictitiously.
Any resemblance to actual persons, living or dead, businesses, companies,
events or locales is entirely coincidental.

This edition published by arrangement with Harlequin Books S.A.

For questions and comments about the quality of this book,
please contact us at CustomerService@Harlequin.com.

Harlequin Enterprises ULC
22 Adelaide St. West, 40th Floor
Toronto, Ontario M5H 4E3, Canada
www.ReaderService.com

Printed in U.S.A.

ACKNOWLEDGMENTS

Writing is a solitary activity, but getting a book into the world requires the help of countless people. Thank you to my family, especially my husband, Jay, for his support and encouragement. Thank you to my agent, Dawn Dowdle of the Blue Ridge Literary Agency, for liking the idea of a mystery involving coupons and airplane repos, and encouraging me to write it down. Huge thanks to Jennifer McCord at Camel Press for taking a chance on the book and helping me make it even better. I'd also like to give a shout out to my virtual assistant, Melissa Caldwell, who takes such great care of me. And finally, hugs and kisses to all the SweetHartes who read and enjoy my books.

ONE

"WE DON'T HIRE people like you, Miss Sophie Parker."

At the mention of my name, I looked up from my résumé I was reviewing. I needed this job, so I wanted to make sure I covered all the salient points in the interview. Not that there were many. I had two things going against me: a useless college major, and no marketable job skills. I hoped my ability to learn fast would get me the job at Denny Coker's bail bondsman business. That hope quickly faded as I looked into the pinched-faced middle-aged woman wagging a bony finger at me.

"Like what?"

"That look like you. Or criminals."

I blew out a breath. The criminal comment wasn't anything new. I'd been hearing it ever since I moved back home to Jefferson Grove, Virginia, six weeks ago. But in the few other job interviews I'd gone on and not been hired because of my family's criminal history, I hadn't been screened out because of my appearance.

I glanced at my wardrobe. Yes, my clothes were mostly used, but I bought them at the thrift shop closest to the affluent Monticello Heights neighborhood. The black, one-size-too-big skirt was Anne Klein, and the white Talbot blouse, while a little snug around the girls, wasn't risqué.

"What's wrong with how I look?" I glanced toward

the very pregnant receptionist for help, but all I got was a shrug and a bored expression.

The woman wearing a drab olive-colored dress that hung loose over her stick-thin body glowered at me. It occurred to me that if her face was the same color as her dress, she could pass as the Wicked Witch of the West. "We run a Christian establishment here," she said. "This is a bail bondsman place. You work with criminals."

"They're clients, not employees. And Mr. Coker doesn't need a temptress like you luring him into sin."

I chanced a look at the pregnant receptionist and wondered if she'd lured him. Or maybe Mr. Coker was a frequent visitor to Booty Burgo, a pirate-themed sports bar where I currently worked as a wench waitress until I could find a real job.

"I need a job. I'll wear baggy clothes and no makeup."

"And what will keep you from robbing us blind?"

"I'm not a crook." It was true, even though it wouldn't matter.

"The fruit doesn't fall far from the tree. Does your brother share a cell with your father?"

Having had this discussion more times than I could count, I stood. "Sins of the father, I get it. But I'm not sure Jesus would agree."

"Well!" The woman blustered. "You can't talk to me like that."

"I can because you're not the boss of me." There was no sense in trying to be polite anymore.

The receptionist snickered. The muscles and veins on the witch's forehead and neck throbbed to the point I worried she might explode. I took a step back, just in case.

The door opened behind the receptionist and a portly disheveled fiftyish man appeared. He had barely any hair, but what he did have, he apparently didn't think needed care, as its greasy strands clung on his shiny head. "Ms. Parker? Ready for the interview?"

"I was, but I don't think I'll be a good fit."

Immediately his eyes went to the old witch. "Madge, what did you say to this poor girl?"

"You know what I said. I told you I was going to say it."

Mr. Coker rolled his eyes and looked toward me. "You'll have to excuse my wife. She's under the mistaken assumption she works here."

Wife. That made sense. He moved closer to me, his eyes scanning me from head to toe. Perhaps the wife was right about the temptress thing. His leering made me want to gag and take a shower.

"Why don't you come into my office? We'll talk. I knew your dad, though I was smart enough not to invest with him. There was something shifty about him. But I can see you're not like that."

A tug-of-war battled in my brain. I needed this job. I didn't want to spend my life schlepping burgers and beer in a wench uniform. But I didn't want to work for a lecher or his mean wife, either. On the other hand, what was the difference working for a lecher versus serving them in a pirate-themed sports bar? It might be easier to avoid one man's attempt to grab my butt versus a whole bar of them. Still, Madge was part of the deal, and I didn't need a hostile workplace on top of everything else I had to cope with.

"Thank you so much, Mr. Coker. I appreciate the opportunity, but I'm going to have to pass."

His jovial demeanor dropped a notch. "There isn't anyone else in town, besides the Booty Burgo, who'll hire you. Not after what your father and brother did."

So far, that was true. I interviewed for the job at the local bank and, while sympathetic to my situation, Mr. Bryson couldn't hire me. "It would make our patrons uncomfortable to have a member of the Parker family around their money." The public school never responded to my applications as a substitute teacher and classroom assistant for the upcoming school year. Dax Hampton, the local big wig real estate broker laughed and hung up the phone when I followed up on my application for an administrative assistant position. I wasn't qualified for the other job openings in Jefferson Grove. I didn't have a social work or accounting degree, so that eliminated the child welfare job at the county Department of Social Services or an auditor with the County Treasurer. Going to another town wasn't viable either. Jefferson Grove was the metropolis compared to all the tiny Virginian Blue Ridge towns surrounding it, which meant a significant commute to find work in a larger town. So, the smart thing would be to interview with Mr. Coker.

"I appreciate your considering me. I really do." I glanced at Madge. "But I just can't."

Because I didn't want to be talked out of it, I turned and left the bail bondsman's office as quickly as possible. I sat in the Brown Bomber, the name of my poop brown Volvo wagon, which, at thirty, was three years older than me. It was ugly, beat up, and big enough to live in, which might be a real possibility if my luck continued to tank.

The car had air-conditioning, crucial for Virginia's humid summers, and it ran, most of the time. Although lately, there was a slight delay between when I turned the key to when the engine turned over. It was long enough to have my stomach clench and make me wonder if I was driving on borrowed time.

I steered the Brown Bomber back to the center of town. Jefferson Grove was a wonderful place to grow up but not a great place to come back to when your father and brother were doing time after running a Ponzi scheme. My mother was never arrested because she ran off with her personal trainer to Nicaragua or some South American country that didn't have an extradition treaty with the United States. I received a postcard about a week after she left telling me she was fine, but I might not hear from her in a while. I was a daddy's girl, but that didn't stop the sting from being abandoned by my mother especially with my father and brother in jail. Even so, I wasn't surprised she'd left. I'd known ever since I'd learned the word "selfish" that everyone, including her family, came second to her own wants and needs.

I'd grown up in the lap of luxury and, as far as I knew, all my father's business dealings had been legitimate. But when the economy tanked, apparently so did my father's business and he engaged in some creative, illegal, and hurtful money-making schemes. At least that was what the FBI explained when they were interrogating me about my knowledge and participation. Fortunately, being daddy's little princess meant I knew nothing.

But it didn't change the fact I was the sole non-criminal in my immediate family. Well, me and my great-aunt Rose on my father's side, who escaped the sting of being shunned because she didn't give a rat's butt about what others thought. She'd been labeled a crazy mean old lady long before my father stole his first million.

Given the choice, I wouldn't have returned to Jefferson Grove, but with my father and brother in prison, and my mother MIA, I was the only family left to watch over Aunt Rose, who, in her eighties, was physically healthy as a horse, but mentally, a few wires had come loose. She lived independently, but needed someone to check on her. It was a job my father had until his incarceration and he'd asked me to take over the duties since there were no other Parkers able or willing to do it. At first, it seemed like an ideal situation. I needed to get my life together and how hard could it be to watch over her? But last week I came home and found piles of packages from a home shopping television show totaling nearly a thousand dollars on the doorstep. They were addressed to her, but she fussed at me for ordering so much stuff that would clutter her house. I sent them back and then blocked that channel from cable service.

I'd have preferred to live somewhere else and checked on her, as my father had done, but my finances were in bad straits, so living with Aunt Rose was my best option. She balked at first; worried I'd get in the way of her card parties or mess up her kitchen. She acquiesced when the situation was presented as she was taking care of me, instead of the other way around. I suppose it wasn't far off the mark. I needed a place to stay until I could get my life in order. Plus, it gave my father some relief knowing someone was watching out for her, and I was glad to help ease his conscience about that.

I paid rent, plus half the utilities and for all my own groceries. It was a fair deal, but the Booty Burgo didn't pay much, so I was usually running out of money before the end of the month. Especially since I'd accumulated a lot of debt when I first became financially independent after the government seized my father's assets and he could no longer help support me.

Since I had no food, my next stop was the grocery store. I pulled into the parking lot of the local IGA and found a spot near the shade of a tree. Normally I shopped at the chain grocery store on the edge of town because it had a larger selection and better deals. But the IGA was having a sale on soup, buy three get two free, and I had a save seventy-five cents on three cans of soup coupon that would double to $1.50 off. If I did the math right, I'd get five cans of soup for 60 cents each.

I opened my coupon binder to get my list and coupons. The women in my couponing group always brought their binders in the store, but I already had to suffer through the looks and snickers of the locals who knew my family members were crooks and I was broke. I didn't want to highlight how dire my situation was by lugging around a two-inch-thick binder containing what few coupons I'd been able to gather or trade at my weekly group.

That had been the worst part about coming home from New York City. You wouldn't know it now from the way people whispered and looked at me sideways, but I was once well-liked in Jefferson Grove. I had lots of friends in high school, and they weren't just the other kids from well-off families like mine. I'd never been one of those mean girls you saw on TV and in the movies. My friends came in all sizes, shapes and socioeconomic backgrounds. I even had friends from Cooters

Hollow. You didn't get any lower on the social totem pole than that.

But coming home, nearly everyone forgot I'd been nice. No one wanted to hire me for fear I was a thief like my father. The few friends from high school that still lived in Jefferson Grove avoided me, except Lani Lafferty. She was the one who introduced me to the coupon group. As an administrative assistant in the local county sheriff's department, she was about as broke as me. The coupon group was a mixed blessing because, while most of the ladies were nice enough and I was learning to shop for less, my high school nemesis, Vivie Danner, was in the group, and she was as mean as ever.

I put my shopping list and coupons in my Prada purse, left over from when I had money, and double checked my wallet for the twenty dollar bill I'd withdrawn from the ATM that morning. God, I hoped I'd done the math right. The coupons should cover everything but $19 and a few cents. They better, because that twenty was all I had.

I made my way through the store, keeping my head down as I gathered the few items on my list before going to the checkout. Once the items were scanned, I handed the young, bored-looking checkout girl my store rewards card and then my coupons, in the order the ladies in the coupon group told me to give them.

"Twenty-four dollars and fifty-seven cents."

I handed her my twenty. "Wait. What?" *No, no, no!* "Did you get all the coupons?"

"Yes, ma'am."

"Are you sure?" Panic built. The embarrassment was as bad as when my credit card was denied trying to buy fifteen dollars' worth of clothes at the thrift store.

The checkout girl, whose name tag said "Amber," stared at me for a moment before huffing out a breath and pointing to the register screen. "They're all there."

I'd never been one to swear, but I was seriously considering taking it up. "What about the deal on the soup? That's supposed to be buy three get two free."

Amber rolled her eyes, scanned the screen and then pointed. I couldn't read grocery tallies very well, but the two items with minus $1.50 in front of them had to be the soup discount.

I swallowed my humiliation and lifted my chin. It was one thing to feel embarrassed. I didn't need everyone noticing it. "I guess I'll need to put something back."

Amber stared again, her expression saying, "Duh."

I surveyed my items, trying to decide what I could live without until I got paid from the Booty Burgo. All of a sudden, the air around me changed in a way that made my spirits rise and drop in quick succession.

Taking a deep breath, I turned my head and starred into the sapphire eyes of AJ Devlin. Good criminy, he was even better looking than the last time I'd seen him, which should have been impossible, because he'd been perfect ten years ago. Looking at him took me back to high school in the same way the scent of paste brought back memories of kindergarten. I swallowed as all those teenage feelings of love and lust swirled in my gut, along with mortification that made me want to run.

He'd never returned my feelings of love back then, but he'd been my friend. Of course, now things were different. It was possible he'd feel the same way about me and what my father and brother had done as many people in town did.

He gave me a lopsided smile, making my belly do another looptyloo, as he handed money to Amber. "I got here just in time. I would've gotten an ear full later for taking money out of her wallet if I hadn't. She always says, 'AJ, if I ever get stuck at the store and don't have enough money to pay the grocery bill, I'll be so mad.' While you're at it, add these too." He slid two sports drinks and two deli sandwiches toward Amber.

The humiliation remained, but I smiled in gratitude. He was helping me save face.

I'd always wondered what it would be like to see my teenage crush again, now I was all grown up. In my fantasy-filled world, I'd imagined it much differently. For a long time, the dream involved him seeing me and instantly falling in love, confessing he'd always loved me and then, like a hero, whisking me away. Now that I'm older, and know fairy tales aren't real, I knew that wouldn't happen. Still, never in a million years had I conjured up this scenario. Then again, in many ways, even in this situation, he was my Prince Charming, rescuing a damsel in distress. Not romantic, but I'd learned firsthand from my riches to rags life that beggars couldn't be choosers.

At seeing AJ, Amber's mood improved. I couldn't blame her. AJ was good looking, with his crystalline blue eyes and dark auburn hair he kept short, but not so short it masked the thick waves. Even more attractive, he had an amazing smile, which he turned on me and I nearly swooned.

I watched, unable to say or do anything as AJ paid for the difference in my groceries and his food. A part of me wanted to run and hide, but that would be bad manners. And let's face it, it was AJ Devlin.

Once our items were bagged, he motioned me to the exit.

I picked up my bags and started toward the door. "Thank you."

"You're welcome."

Then I didn't know what to say, which was crazy. I'd known him well during high school when he worked odd jobs around the house for my family. It was no accident I was by the pool when he was there to clean it, or laying in the sun on the deck when he was there to cut the grass. I'd had a crush on him from the first time I saw him as a freshman in high school. He was a junior, and if he knew how I felt, he never let on. He never showed any romantic interest in me, but he was always friendly, and by the time I'd graduated from high school, and he'd finished community college and decided to join the military, we were friends. Good enough friends that at one time, I'd have given him a hug at seeing him again. In fact, I'd probably have run and jumped in his arms. But I wasn't a teenager anymore and nearly ten years was a long time.

"I didn't know you were in town." I managed to choke out as I put my groceries in the back of the Brown Bomber.

"I'm passing through."

My heart sank. Coming home might not be so bad after all if AJ was around.

"I'm surprised you're here." AJ closed the hatch of my Volvo for me.

"I had no choice. Someone needs to look after my aunt." I opened the driver side door and got into the Bomber. I wanted to spend more time with him, but what good would that do? "Thanks again, AJ."

For a minute, it looked like he might say something, but then he nodded and shut my door.

I turned the key in the ignition and nothing happened. I swallowed and tried again. This time my stomach clutched and my heart stopped. *No, no, no!* Of all the times the Brown Bomber could die, this was the worst. I turned the key one more time, and when nothing happened, I did the only thing I could, I burst into tears. I don't cry easily, but apparently, I'd hit my frustration threshold and I couldn't stop the wail of despair.

The door opened. "Hey, Soph?"

I waved my hands as if that would stop the tears. But having AJ see me cry was the last straw. "It's just been a bad day. I'm tired and frustrated…"

"Let me take a look. Maybe you just need a jump. My car is over there. I'll be right back." He turned and walked away.

I used the time to heave in deep breaths and pull myself back in control. He drove back in a nondescript blue sedan. It wasn't what I would have imagined for AJ. He'd always been a country boy, so a truck would have been more appropriate. This looked like a rental or company car, which reminded me he was just visiting. Probably his mother in Cooters Hollow.

I pushed the lever to pop the hood and got out of the car. Fortunately, I had jumper cables. When I'd visited my father in prison and told him about the car I'd bought with my last $500, he warned me to always be prepared for a breakdown. So, I'd stocked the car with tools I didn't know how to use, along with blankets, protein bars and water.

I handed the jumper cables to AJ. He connected the cables, started his car and then told me to start mine. I waited a minute, giving a silent prayer, and then turned the key. The Brown Bomber roared to life. Hallelujah!

AJ exited his car and removed the cables, tossing them in the back of the Bomber. Then he came over to me. "You should get a new battery."

I wondered if there were coupons for car batteries.

He reached out and pushed away a piece of dark hair that had been plastered to the side of my face with sweat and tears. It was a gesture he'd made once before on my eighteenth birthday, the day before he left for boot camp. I'd always wanted it to be romantic but, in reality, I was like a goofy kid sister to him.

"Thank you. Again." I sighed and reached to pull the door shut.

"Wanna go flying?"

"Huh?"

He grinned. "I'm delivering a plane for a friend of mine. It's at Twin Oaks airfield."

AJ had always had a fascination with planes, so I wasn't surprised to hear he was a pilot. I wondered if he flew jet planes in the military.

"Where are you taking it?"

"Richmond."

"How will I get home?"

He shook his head in amusement. "I won't leave you stranded, Sophie."

"I know, but I have a thing tonight at seven. Will I be back?" A part of me told me to forget my couponing meeting that night. After all, AJ Devlin had invited me to fly with him. But if the incident in the store had taught me anything, it was that I had a lot to learn about couponing.

"You used to love adventures." He grinned, the cocky one that had me forgetting everything.

So, of course, I was going flying.

TWO

AN HOUR LATER I'd changed out of my interview clothes into white capris and a sleeveless top, and I sat on the back of the hideaway bed in my room at Aunt Rose's watching out the window for AJ. He'd said he had one more errand to run and then would pick me up at home. He also told me to watch for him because there was no way he was coming up to Aunt Rose's door.

I couldn't blame him. Aunt Rose was cantankerous with her strong opinions about life and people, but she could be especially scary on her canasta days. She was currently ranting to her card buddies about her no-good crook of a nephew and how difficult it was to take in his daughter. I worked hard to stay out of her way. In fact, unless you looked in my bedroom closet, there was no indication I lived in the house or even in the guest room. Every day I closed up the hideaway bed and put away my personal effects.

I considered going over my coupons and failed shop, except I'd recalculated all the numbers twice since returning home and I kept getting the same answer. I wasn't a numbers genius, but you didn't get into college with remedial math. The only way I was able to get Amber's sum was if I didn't double my coupons. But why didn't she double them? They were less than a dollar. My "Coupon Rules" guide Lani created indicated the IGA doubled coupons up to ninety-nine cents.

Did Amber rip me off? Was she pocketing the extra few dollars? Eventually I gave up, determining I could ask the more experienced ladies of my coupon group later that evening.

Instead, I pulled out the leather-bound book of *Grimm's Fairy Tales* AJ had given me the last time I'd seen him on my eighteenth birthday. I'd always loved fairy tales and, even though I already had a copy of Grimm's tales, the edition AJ gave me was the only one I'd kept after having to cull my book collection when I moved back to Jefferson Grove.

My eighteenth birthday had been my favorite one ever. And it wasn't because of the bash my parents had thrown that would have rivaled any debutante ball. It was because AJ had surprised me by showing up. Although I was clearly in the friend-zone with him, my crush had never quite gone away. So, his surprise arrival fed all my teenage fairy tale fantasies.

He hadn't actually come to the party but sent a message to me through one of the caterers that he was on the back terrace. The dark late summer night was illuminated by lightning bugs and round paper lanterns. The humid warm air was cooled by a light breeze that ruffled AJ's wavy hair. The cicadas chirped in a symphony.

He'd given me the book and touched me, pushing my hair back when the breeze loosened a tendril. In my memory, he looked at me in more than a friendly way. It was my fairy tale come true. The next day he was off to boot camp and a week later, I left for college.

People never know quite how to respond when they learn my bachelor's degree is in Folklore. I love a good story, but as it turns out, it isn't a great major when you needed a job in a small rural town in Virginia. Aunt Rose said my father should have put more sense and practicality into me, and on that point, I agreed. Although, if I hadn't come home to watch over her, I could probably live somewhere else and get a job that didn't require wearing a wench uniform. Unusual degree or not, a liberal arts education was useful. Still, there wasn't a vast array of jobs that required knowledge of Celtic Folklore or Russian fairy tales.

I loved my father. He was the best dad ever, except for the Ponzi scheme, and his lack of guidance on encouraging me to studying something practical. We'd never discussed what I might do with a degree in Folklore. I pursued it because I loved fairy tales and folklore, and my father supported me in studying something that gave me meaning. He had me believing I could do or have whatever I wanted because the money would always be there. Except, it wasn't.

For a time, I thought I'd continue my education and get a master's in folklore. With that I could teach at the college level. But as graduation approached, I needed a break from academics. Instead, after college, I moved to Sleepy Hollow, New York, where I volunteered with the historic society, living off an allowance from my father. Two years ago, I moved to New York City and took my first real job with two of my former college classmates, who were developing a new video game and needed me to develop its mythology and lore. In hindsight, I think they expected me, or more accurately my father, to invest in their fledgling gaming company, but by then, things were going south for my father. The company failed, my father went to jail, and now I was hiding in my great-aunt Rose's guest room.

A flash out the window distracted me. AJ's car pulled up to the curb. I put my book in the closet, checked the room to make sure Aunt Rose wouldn't be upset about anything being out of place and then headed up the hall toward the front door, where I hoped to escape unnoticed.

"Where are you running off to, Sophie?" Aunt Rose had never had children, but she still had eyes in the back of her head.

"I'm meeting a friend."

"What friend? Since when do you have a friend?" Aunt Rose stood from the card table where she and her friends played cards, drank watered-down bourbon, and ate peanuts. Like all Parker women, Aunt Rose was petite with thick curly hair. At one time, her hair had been dark like mine, but now it was a really cool shade of purple-tinted silver that had help from a bottle on her once a week trip to the hairdresser for a wash and style. She wore pink Capri pants with a matching floral top, accented by a string of pearls that all southern women of a certain age seemed to wear.

"Sit down, Rose. It's your go." Fiona Simpson waved her cards impatiently at Rose.

My aunt ignored her and made her way to the front window. I glanced outside, hoping AJ would stay in the car. No luck. While he wasn't meeting me at the door, he was leaning against the car, waiting for me.

Aunt Rose's brows knitted together. "Who's that?"

"Just an old—"

"Is that a Devlin? You're not taking up with him, are you?" Aunt Rose thought everyone with ginger hair was a Devlin. She was usually wrong, but, of course, in this case, she was right. She pursed her lips and turned her disapproving scowl on me. Aunt Rose might have been a small woman in stature, but her personality filled the room, and to be honest, she intimidated me.

My dad told me she was more bark than bite, so taking a chance, I blew out a breath and explained. "He's an old friend who's in town for a day."

"It doesn't help your situation, Sophie, to waste your time with people from the Hollow."

"Great day." Tilly Watson drew out the southern expression of dismay. "Rose, let her go and play cards."

Aunt Rose planted her fists on her hips as she turned her attention toward Tilly. "I've been charged with taking care of Sophie, and clearly, she needs direction. It's hard enough to get any respect in this town after what your father did. What are people going to think?"

"Since when do you care what people think, Rose?" Betty Bealeton finished off her drink then standing, she walked over to my aunt's 1950s bar cart to refill her glass.

"Well, I don't. But Sophie does. At least she should." Aunt Rose turned back toward me.

"It's just an afternoon." I felt like I was a teenager again.

"Let her go, Rose. We aren't getting any younger." Betty carried her drink back to her seat.

When Aunt Rose turned her head to glower at her card buddies, I saw my chance to escape and hurried out the door toward AJ. As I approached the car, I saw he wasn't alone. In the backseat sat a hulk of a man.

"I was beginning to think she had you locked up in there." AJ opened the passenger side door for me.

"Would you have come to save me?"

"I'd send Bull." AJ nodded to the man in the back-seat. "Bull, this is Sophie Parker. Sophie, this is Bull."

Sitting in the front seat, I turned to say hello to Bull. He was the size of a tank and looked like a biker, with a faded metal band T-shirt, a leather vest and tattoos from his neck down to his wrists.

"Sophie." Bull's voice was deep and scary. "Gordo isn't gonna like you bringing along a friend."

"I'm doing him a favor, so he'll just have to accept it. Besides, he doesn't have to know." AJ strapped on his seatbelt. "Bull is taking the car back after we get the plane."

"I see. Was he at the store with you?"

"Nah, Bull had me drop him off at the florist." AJ sent Bull a teasing grin through the rearview mirror.

"Florist?" I turned back toward Bull, wondering if he was a wise-guy extorting protection money from local mom-and-pop businesses. It wasn't that far-fetched. During the 1920s, Jefferson Grove was filled with or-ganized crime types running moonshine to Washington, D.C., and north. In fact, many moonshiners continued the tradition. Some of them were AJ's kin in Cooters Hollow.

Bull scowled at AJ.

AJ ignored him. "It's his mother's birthday."

"Oh. That's nice." I smiled at Bull.

His scowl lessened, reducing the scary factor.

"My mom had a birthday not long ago, but I didn't send her anything."

"Why not?" Bull frowned. "Mothers are important."

"I don't know where she is. She ran off with her per-sonal trainer."

Bull's features softened into sympathy. It made him look a little like a teddy bear.

"Besides, Sophie is more of a daddy's girl." AJ pulled the car from the curb into the quiet residential street. "Did you get your dad a present?"

"Yes. I made him lemon bars."

"Where's your dad?" Bull asked.

"Prison."

Bull's eyes widened. "Your pop's doing time?"

I nodded. "Along with my brother."

"No kiddin'? Would I know them?"

AJ shook his head. "White collar crime, Bull."

"Oh. What do you do, Sophie?"

"I'm a waitress at Booty Burgo."

"What?" AJ's head turned so fast it was a wonder it didn't fly off.

"It's the only place that will hire me."

"Why? You went to college."

"You smart?" Bull asked.

"Only about some things. It doesn't matter in this town, though. Everyone who has a job opening is afraid I'll rob them or probably they're just getting back at my dad and brother."

"People suck."

I was beginning to like Bull. "Today, the wife of Denny Coker, the bail bondsman, said she couldn't hire me because I was a crook *and* a temptress." I shook my head at the ridiculousness of that. "I'm too short to be a temptress."

"Height has nothing to do with it." Bull spoke with authority. "Do you know how to dance? I know a club in Richmond looking for a dancer."

"Really?" I craned my head to look at him.

"It's exotic dancing, Sophie." AJ cast a warning glance back at Bull.

I rolled my eyes. I might not be worldly, but I wasn't completely naive. "I know what he meant. Do you think I'm pretty enough?"

"Well, sure," Bull said. "You remind me of the old cartoon bombshell, what's her name... Betsy... Bessy..."

"Betty Boop." AJ snorted.

"Yeah. That's her."

It wasn't the first time I'd been compared to Betty Boop, but it had been awhile. During my freshman year of college, I considered growing out my short, dark curls, just so the comparison wouldn't be made. The problem was, the longer my hair got, the more unwieldy it became. Plus, there wasn't much I could do about the round cheeks and wide eyes. Now I wondered if maybe I could turn this small annoyance into an asset. "Does dancing pay well?"

"The girls I know do pretty well."

"Sophie." AJ's voice was tight. "Men will leer and grab at you."

"They leer and grab at me at the Booty Burgo, but they don't give good tips."

"You got that right," Bull agreed.

"You're not seriously considering dancing?"

I glanced at AJ, curious to his negative reaction. What did he care what I did? "No. Although I might have to if Aunt Rose kicks me out for seeing you."

"Your family is messed up," Bull said.

AJ shook his head. "Why not go to Charlottesville? There are more jobs and less people who care about what your father did."

"My father asked me to watch over Aunt Rose. Plus, I'm broke and I'm not sure the Brown Bomber would be able to make the drive on a regular basis."

AJ snickered. "You named your car?"

I glowered at him. "Yes."

"So, you're going to live with Aunt Rose and serve burgers and drinks at the Booty Burgo the rest of your life?"

My heart thumped hard in my chest because more and more I was afraid that was exactly what was going to happen. "I don't know. I hope not."

"Well, if you change your mind about the dancing, let me know. I've got an in with the manager."

"Thank you, Bull."

AJ passed the entrance to the small county airport sitting in the middle of rural Virginia.

"Where are you going?"

"I want to drive the perimeter to see where the plane is."

"Might be in a hangar." Bull scanned the airport from his window in the backseat.

AJ made a left and drove along the side of the airport.

"Oh, wait, there's a Cessna. That might be it." Bull's bulky arm pointed between the two seats out the front window.

"That's good. It's out." AJ slowed as the car neared the plane.

"Not a lot of people around, either," Bull added.

Why does that matter?

AJ made another left and drove along the backside of the airport. It was all very odd.

"What's back here?" Except for a car and a truck parked along the chain link fence encircling the airport, there was nothing. Just road, airport and, on the other side, the woods.

"Just looking."

About a half-mile in, the pavement gave way to gravel. AJ turned around and started back.

"Do you suppose that red Audi is him?" Bull asked as we approached the car and truck.

"Yes."

"Him who?" I craned my neck to look at the car. It did seem odd to have such a nice car parked in a place that would make it easy to strip or steal. Jefferson Grove was a nice town, but that didn't mean there weren't bad elements.

Neither AJ nor Bull answered me. Instead, AJ drove to the front of the airport, pulling the car into the lot and parking in the farthest spot from the building entrance.

"Let's go." AJ exited the car as did Bull.

"I thought you were taking the car back?"

"I am. But I help AJ check the plane. Don't want to fly something that won't stay airborne."

I hadn't considered any danger. I assumed AJ knew how to fly, otherwise, why invite me. I knew it had been his dream to fly planes in the military. But now, as I walked with the two men toward the plane in question, I had an unsettling feeling deep in my belly. The military flew jets or cargo planes, didn't they? Did AJ know how to fly other planes?

As if he knew what I was thinking, he said, "If it can get airborne, I can fly it, Soph. Don't worry." He took my hand. "It'll be fun. Like old times."

We'd never flown during our old times, but I liked that he was holding my hand and decided not to mention it.

"Yep, that's her." Bull pointed to a set of numbers on the tail of the plane.

AJ opened the door to the plane and motioned for me to board. He followed me in. "Take a seat while Bull and I check her out."

The plane was narrow but had comfortable-looking leather seats. Despite my family having money while growing up, I'd never flown on a private plane before. When we traveled, we flew commercial first class.

I sat in one of the lush seats and was reminded of two perks of being rich. Comfort and luxury. AJ sat in the cockpit, poking at buttons, flipping switches and every now and then calling something out to Bull.

I settled in to enjoy the flight until AJ let out an expletive, left the cockpit and headed out the door. "You stay here."

I nodded and looked out the window. A lean, well-dressed man with silver hair stalked toward the plane. His mouth moved, but AJ had shut the door so I couldn't hear what was being said. Even so, it wasn't hard to tell the man was angry. His red forehead bulged with veins along his tanned temple. Every now and then spittle shot from his mouth. His hands flailed through the air, occasionally making a threatening gesture.

Where's Bull? I worried the man would attack AJ, even though AJ didn't act worried. He approached the man with his hands up and out, as if he was being robbed at gunpoint. Although he'd taken a surrendering stance, AJ never the let the man pass him as he tried to get to the plane. After several attempts, the man grabbed AJ and then just as quickly backed off as Bull finally entered the scene. AJ held a hand up toward Bull who, with both meaty fists up, appeared ready to flatten the angry man. Instead, Bull stood, looking like a bouncer, as AJ talked to the man.

What's going on? I was dying to find out but didn't dare exit the plane. Bull had said someone wouldn't be happy AJ was bringing me along, so I stayed put. Still, that initial unsettled feeling when we were skulking about was growing. It was like in high school, when I dated Randy Danner for a week and he took me up to Jefferson Lake. There was something about the gleam in his eyes that should have had me saying, "No," and breaking up with him then and there. But in the middle of such situations, it's hard to tell if the this-isn't-a-good-situation vibe is legit. I should have listened to my intuition then. Fortunately, AJ had taught me how to protect myself. After a quick knee to Randy's groin, I called AJ on my cell phone to come pick me up and Randy didn't ask me out again.

But AJ wasn't Randy. I had so few friends, and AJ was right, I could use a little fun. So I sat, watching the strange altercation out the window.

Eventually, the angry man's fists rested at his sides, and his head dropped as he shook it side to side. Then he turned and started back toward the hangar. AJ said something to Bull, his head gesturing toward the plane. Bull nodded and AJ followed the man into a door to the right of the larger hangar opening.

I hoped Bull would check on me so I could ask what was going on, but he disappeared under the plane. I glanced at my watch, wondering how much longer AJ would be and if he was in danger. It seemed like eons, but a quick check of the time when AJ emerged from the building showed it had only been ten minutes. He strode toward the plane, carrying a large white binder.

Just outside the plane, he met Bull. They shook hands and then Bull left in the direction of where we'd parked the car. The door of the plane opened and AJ entered the cabin.

"Let's fly." He put the binder in a cabinet between the cockpit and cabin. "Come up here."

"In the cockpit?"

"Sure. You don't have to do anything. It's a nicer ride up front."

I shrugged to act nonchalant, but inside my brain was screaming in excitement. I followed AJ to the cockpit, climbing into the seat, careful not to bump any of the gadgets on the center console. "Why was that man so upset?"

"Just a misunderstanding." AJ poked a few buttons and made a few marks on a checklist. Then he turned to me. "Get your seatbelt on." He reached over to help me. "Ready to roll?"

"If you are." I couldn't help the silly grin that bubbled up from the excitement inside me.

He flashed a smile that reminded me of when we were teenagers and he was getting ready to fly into Jefferson Lake with the help of a rope swing.

"Here, put this on." He handed me a headset. "It gets loud. We'll be able to talk through these."

When he turned his attention back to the instruments, his features became all business. I felt the vibration of the plane as it whirred on and then settled into a loud purr. The plane rolled, turning enough so I could see Bull getting into the car in the parking lot. Then AJ turned the plane again, and my body was pressed back against the seat as the plane picked up speed.

"Let's fly, Sophie." His voice came through the headset.

My stomach did a looptyloo as the speeding plane lifted from the ground. This time I laughed in delight as the ground dropped away.

I turned to AJ. "You did it. Your dream was to fly and here you are. This is real."

"As real as it gets. I'm glad you like it."

"I love flying."

We flew for several minutes, the ground getting farther away. The plane turned, and we headed back toward the way we'd just come. I could see the airport underneath us as another car pulled up behind the two vehicles already parked there. I craned my head to see what was back there that had so many cars parking in that spot, but we moved too quickly for me to watch what the driver would do.

We continued parallel to the road to Jefferson Grove. The car I suspected was Bull's looked like an ant as it drove toward the town where he'd be able to catch the main highway east to Charlottesville. From the sky, Jefferson Grove was an idyllic town with its tree-lined streets, centuries old brick buildings lining the main town and spire of the Baptist church towering over it all. It was the type of town that showed up in Norman Rockwell paintings and that many people escaped to for friendly neighbors and a slower way of life.

As Jefferson Grove drifted out of view, AJ took one hand off the controls to point out the window in front of me. "Look there."

My gaze followed the direction of his finger. The lush Blue Ridge Mountains sloped and curved like a blanket across the ground. In between two ridges sat a lake. "Is that Jefferson Lake?"

"Yep."

Immediately, all my memories of spending time with my friends at the lake rushed back. We swam, water-skied and tubed and, of course, made out. All the things teenagers did. The lake disappeared, as the hills gave way to the piedmont. The James River flowed below us, and I remembered tubing and kayaking with my family and friends during summers there as well. The memories were bittersweet now that my life was upended.

He said something into his radio. The response was a code I didn't understand.

"Is everything okay?"

"No worries, Sophie." The plane's direction shifted slightly as we headed east. We flew a few moments before AJ said, "I was sorry to hear about your dad."

I turned to gauge the sincerity of his expression. It appeared genuine.

"Why? He broke the law."

His lips twitched upward slightly as if amused by my comment. "Well, I feel bad what his being gone has done to you. I know you're close to him and being forced to move back here after what he did and to watch over your aunt can't be easy."

"I'm doing alright." I wasn't going to have much time with AJ. I didn't want to waste it lamenting over my downfall.

He slanted a look at me, as if gauging my sincerity. I smiled. He shook his head slightly as he turned his attention back out the window. "What's the deal about the coupons?"

"I'm broke and have to save money."

"Do they really work?"

I shrugged. "I'm not sure."

He laughed. "Then why do it?"

"My coupon group says it works, but so far I haven't had much luck. It's harder than it seems."

He glanced at me, one auburn brow arched in a "you can't be serious" expression. "What's so hard? Fifty cents off. It's basic math."

"No, it's not. It's more like algebra. There are a lot of variables. There are manufacturer coupons you can stack with store coupons. There's the face value plus whether or not the store will double it and if it will double both a manufacturer coupon and store coupon in the same deal. Plus, you have to match the coupons to sales so you can get them for free—"

"Free?"

"I haven't managed that. Vivie said she has, but I'm not sure I believe her."

Vivie was the queen of one-upmanship.

"Are things that tight?"

I groaned inwardly. Hadn't I just decided he didn't need to know my woes? "Actually, I kind of like the challenge."

"So, going from rich to poor hasn't been hard?"

"No, it's been hard, but the money isn't the thing that has been the most difficult change. In some ways, I'm glad because it's forcing me to learn to take care of myself, although some days it's harder than others to see the self-reliant silver lining."

He laughed. "No doubt. But good for you looking at the world as a glass half full."

My glass was nearly empty, but at least I had a glass and I was hopeful I'd fill it someday. "Where are you stationed?" In the military, he had to have travelled to interesting places.

Before he answered, there was static from the radio and someone spoke to AJ in a code I didn't understand.

He responded back and then there was a slight change in the plane as it began its descent.

"That's it?" I looked at my watch. It seemed like we'd only just taken off but, in fact, we'd been airborne for nearly fifty minutes.

"It's not that far to Richmond."

I tried not to appear disappointed, but it was hard. Not wanting to distract AJ, I turned my attention back out the window and watched the city of Richmond get closer and closer.

"Strange," AJ said, after rattling off several words and numbers in his radio.

"What?"

"Different runway than expected." But he didn't seem concerned, so I watched as the runway sped toward us. There was a bump and bounce of the wheels hitting the ground and pressure on my seatbelt as AJ applied the brakes. About halfway down the runway, the plane slowed enough that AJ was able to turn it toward the area for private planes.

Movement ahead had me squinting out the window. Several police cars with lights flashing sped toward us.

The excited feeling in my belly quickly dissolved. "What's that about?"

AJ blew out a breath and swore. "Probably a misunderstanding."

"Probably?" That was the same thing he'd said about the man who nearly punched him. "What's going on?"

AJ stopped the plane. "Put your hands up where they can see them, Sophie."

AJ's hands were already up, but I was a step behind.

Why were the police treating us like criminals? And why was he acting like this wasn't the first time the police were after him?

"Up, Sophie!"

I jumped in my seat. "Yeah, okay. Can you tell me what's going on?"

"When they get here, just do what they say. Don't tell them anything."

"What if they ask me something?"

He shot me an annoyed glare. "You don't know anything, so you don't have anything to tell them."

My heart rate shot up. What didn't I know? What had he gotten me into? After my disastrous job interview and failed couponing attempt that morning, I didn't think the day could get any worse. Clearly, I'd been wrong.

Policemen exited their cars. A few had their guns drawn. They demanded AJ and I get off the plane. It took a few minutes, but then I was following AJ down the few steps of the plane.

"I have all the paperwork—" AJ started.

"Down on the ground!"

"Okay. But I have the paperwork. I'm in control of this plane—"

"You too." One of the cops waved at me. I looked at the dirty, oily pavement. I wanted to tell them I couldn't afford to ruin my clothes, even if they were secondhand cropped pants and a tank top, but decided they'd remedy that by giving me an orange jumpsuit if I didn't listen.

"Ooh ouch!" The ground wasn't just oily and dirty, it was scorching hot too.

AJ was already prone on the ground. "Check the plane. All the repossession paperwork is there."

Repossession? From the hot asphalt, I craned my head to where AJ lay a few feet away. "Repossession? You repoed a plane?"

"Quiet." The cop assured my silence by grabbing my arms behind my back and restraining them with plastic ties.

I'd watched a video on YouTube once on how to get out of this type of restraint but decided now wasn't a good time to test it. When the cop was done, he rolled me over and helped me sit. AJ was already sitting and trying to get the attention of the cop who was searching the plane.

"Hey!" A burly cop that could give Bull a run for his money kicked at AJ's shoe. He squatted down and looked AJ in the eyes. "We don't care about your repo. We're here about the murder of Joseph Cullen, the man you just repoed this plane from."

THREE

I CHECKED MY WATCH. For almost three hours I'd been sitting in the tiny interrogation room. Long enough to wonder if the bland beige paint on the walls was chosen on purpose to make people feel depressed and as void as the color, or maybe the paint had been on sale. Did cop shops use coupons? Thinking of coupons, if I didn't get out soon, I wouldn't make my coupon group. How would I find out where I'd gone wrong on my calculations during my shop this morning?

"Am I boring you?" Sergeant Scowl, as I'd named him, tapped his fingers on the table.

Yes. Fortunately, I was smart enough to keep my mouth shut. While the Richmond cops had asked a few questions when they'd brought me to the interrogation room, for the most part they'd left me alone. While both boring and nerve-wracking, it was better than dealing with Sergeant Scowl, who arrived fifteen minutes ago from the Jefferson County Sheriff's department. It was nearly a two-hour drive to Richmond, which suggested Joseph Cullen, the dead guy, had been found not long after we'd left Jefferson Grove. I didn't know a lot about crime and police work, but even I understood things didn't look good for AJ and me, since we were the last ones to see Cullen. Except for the killer, of course. Since I didn't kill him, and I was pretty sure AJ didn't kill him, I was biding my time until they let us go.

The fact that he kept asking the same questions, with only slight variations, suggested he didn't believe the answers I was giving him. Pre-father-getting-arrested-for-a-Ponzi-scheme days, that would have scared me. But after spending thirty-six hours over two and a half days being interrogated by the FBI over my father, mother, and brother's illegal activities, it took more than a clichéd bull-dog-faced detective to make me squirm. And just like three years ago, when I was on the verge of being arrested then too, it was the fact I was clueless that helped me. Actually, I liked to think it was that I looked innocent but, in reality, it was probably because I didn't look savvy. No one ever thought Betty Boop had the smarts to pull off a crime.

"I'm just tired." I decided that was a better response to Sergeant Scowl's question about whether or not I was bored.

He studied me with bulging bloodshot eyes for a long moment, probably hoping his piercing glare would make me pee my pants and spill my guts. I considered telling him I survived the FBI so his tactics only annoyed me.

"Do you play golf, Ms. Parker?"

Huh? Now he had my attention. What did golf have to do with anything? "Not anymore."

"But you did?"

I narrowed my eyes, studying the detective for some clue as to where this line of questioning was going. What did Mr. Cullen's murder have to do with golf? "I used to play with my father. When I was younger."

"Where are your clubs now?"

I bit my lip. *My clubs?* I shrugged. "I suppose they were sold along with all my father's other assets."

"You don't have them?"

"No. Why?" Was Mr. Cullen killed with a golf club? Was that even possible?

"What about your father or brother's clubs?"

I shook my head. "I don't have my clubs. Why would I have theirs?"

"When was the last time you played?"

"I told you, it was a long time ago. High school." I wanted to ask if I was right about Mr. Cullen being killed by a golf club but wasn't sure how Sergeant Scowl would interpret my question.

He pulled out a photo from a folder and pushed it toward me. "Do you recognize this?"

I studied the picture of the gold and platinum golf club and my stomach sank. I looked at Sergeant Scowl. One dark brow rose as he waited for my response.

I swallowed. "It's a golf club. A wedge, to be precise."

The scowl returned to his face. "Is it yours or someone's you know? I'm told this brand is expensive."

"Yes, it is."

He let out an exasperated breath. "Do you recognize this club, Ms. Parker?"

"I can't say it's the same club, but my father owned a set of these." I tried to keep my expression and body language nonchalant, but I knew this didn't look good. Sergeant Scowl was right in that this brand of club was expensive and not many people in the United States owned a set.

"Just a couple celebrities and me own these clubs," my father had boasted when he bought the Japanese-made gold and platinum golf set.

"What are the odds someone else owns these clubs?" Sergeant Scowl asked.

"Pretty good, actually. Even if this once was my father's club, either he or the government sold it to someone else. Maybe Mr. Cullen bought the clubs from my dad. He sold off a lot of his assets before he was arrested."

"Assets?" He looked at the clubs. "How much are these things worth?"

"I don't know about now, but my dad paid over thirty thousand for his set."

Sergeant Scowl choked. "Thirty grand?"

"If Mr. Cullen bought them, he'd have paid significantly less. My father was desperate to liquidate and get some cash. It also means my father would have no reason to want Mr. Cullen dead, since he'd helped him out financially."

"You're speculating. We don't know this club belongs to Mr. Cullen."

I shrugged, conceding the point. "It's an odd and expensive murder weapon. It's not something you'd bring to kill someone, so it had to be at the scene."

Sergeant Scowl's mouth curved into a Cheshire grin, and only then did I realize my mistake. "I never said it was the murder weapon. But it's interesting you'd think the club had already been there."

I tried to remain calm, even though on the inside I was wondering how bad I'd made things for AJ and me.

Sergeant Scowl sat forward, tapping his fingers on his notebook. "Why do you suppose Mr. Devlin was repossessing Mr. Cullen's plane?"

I shook my head at the switch in questions. "I guess he wasn't making his payments."

"Why do you suppose that is?"

A tingling sensation niggled at the back of my neck. He was leading me somewhere. Somewhere I felt certain I didn't want to go. "Perhaps he lost it in online gambling or to a gold-digging mistress."

The slight flare of a nostril was all he gave to let me know he didn't like my attitude. He flipped back a few pages in his notebook. "Maybe he made bad investments. And maybe he told the Feds about it."

I flinched as I realized he was suggesting the dead man was broke because my father had swindled him out of his money. I studied Sergeant Scowl, trying to determine if he was bluffing. I'd learned the hard way that law enforcement had a lot of leeway when it came to wrangling information from people.

Going with the worst-case scenario, I contemplated what it would mean for me if it was true. My father would provide a link between the deceased and me. But I knew, even if it was true, it wouldn't mean anything except what Sergeant Scowl wanted it to mean. It didn't take a genius to figure out the detective thought I might want the guy dead for putting my dad in jail. And apparently, I used Dad's golf club to do it. That was ridiculous. I wasn't a murderer. And if I was, I wouldn't use a golf club. I'd want something more reliable, like a gun or poison.

Or maybe Sergeant Scowl thought my father wanted the guy dead and I was the person to make it happen by hiring AJ. But that was just as nuts. My dad might be a crook, but he wasn't a murderer.

I'd already told Sergeant Scowl I'd never heard of or seen Joseph Cullen before today. I didn't have golf clubs, and I had no idea why someone wanted him dead. Realizing my interrogator would be happy to continue the conversation indefinitely, reframing my statements to fit his agenda, I decided to do the one thing that would put an end to it. At least for now.

"I'd like to talk to my lawyer."

His clenched jaw told me he didn't like that. "Why do you need a lawyer? That just makes it seem like you have something to hide."

"No, it doesn't. The fact that I've told you the same thing, and yet, you still keep asking the same questions suggests you don't believe me. At this point, I'll do better having a lawyer." Of course, I didn't have a lawyer. I didn't have the money for one. But I knew, from the crime shows I sometimes watched on TV with Aunt Rose, I would be assigned one if I couldn't afford one.

Sergeant Scowl's beady eyes bored down on me, as if he was going to use a mind trick to make me talk. I figured he either needed to arrest me or let me go. I prayed he couldn't arrest me. After all, I didn't kill anyone. There was no way my fingerprints or DNA or golf club were anywhere near Mr. Cullen. Plus, who'd be left to take care of Aunt Rose? She was a difficult woman, but I was certain dealing with her would be a whole lot easier than dealing with people in prison.

Fortunately, the door opened behind him before he could respond. An older cop poked his head in. "You're free to go, Ms. Parker."

Relief washed through me, but I tried to mask it. "Well then." I stood. "Where's AJ?"

"He's busy," Sergeant Scowl said. "And with someone not as nice as me."

I ignored his comment, knowing it would irritate him that he couldn't ruffle me. "I want to see him."

"I'm sorry, you can't." Nice cop stepped out of the way to let me pass into the hall. "It's best if you just go."

"But he's my ride." How the heck was I going to get back to Jefferson Grove?

"I'm here, Miss Sophie." Bull made his way like a... well, a bull...across the police station.

I didn't know how he knew to come, but I didn't care. I was glad he was there. He was so imposing, even Sergeant Scowl took a step back when Bull wrapped an arm around me, putting his meaty hand on my shoulder and escorting me toward the exit.

"What about AJ?"

"Let me get you home."

I tried to stop him, but it was like trying to stop a train and I was stuck in the cow-catcher. "You can't just leave him here."

"AJ will be fine."

"But—"

"Now, Miss Sophie, I'll pick you up and carry you out if need be. AJ said I might have to."

"You spoke to him?"

"Everyone gets one call."

One call? Did that mean AJ had been arrested?

I didn't fight Bull as he dragged me out of the Richmond police station, but once we were outside, I wanted answers. "AJ needs a lawyer."

"AJ is fine." Bull tugged my arm toward a motorcycle. It looked like the type of bike associated with bikers with the low seat and long handle bars.

"Where's the car?"

"What car?"

Did I just fall through the looking glass? "The car you had this morning."

"I turned that in." He thrust a black helmet covered in scratches toward me. "The car was part of the job.

The job was over, so I turned it in. The bike's more fun anyway."

I tentatively took the helmet. "Why didn't you get it again to come get me?"

"Because Gordo doesn't know you were with AJ."

He said it like it made total sense. When I didn't respond, he let out a breath. "Gordo wouldn't like it that AJ brought you along on a repo."

"I see." Except I didn't.

"I was turning in the car and keys when cops stopped by Gordo's asking about AJ. AJ didn't want Gordo to know you were with him, which he would have if I asked for the car to come get you. So, I hopped on my bike and came down."

"Thank you."

"You're welcome. Now let's get out of here."

"What about AJ?"

Bull growled under his breath. "You're like a dog with a bone. Becca is taking care of AJ."

"Who's Becca?"

Bull stared at me with a wide-eyed, annoyed expression that said, *Do you ever stop asking questions?*

My placid stare back told him, *No, I don't.*

He sighed. "Gordo's daughter, who's also a lawyer. Can we go, Miss Sophie? Otherwise we'll be stuck in traffic."

I tugged the helmet over my head and Bull helped me onto the bike. He straddled the bike, leaning slightly to the side, forcing me to grab onto him. Then, with one foot, he kick-started the motorcycle. It roared to life and I nearly let go of Bull to cover my ears, but then the bike shot out of the parking lot. I screamed, squeezing my eyes shut and tightening my grip around him. I didn't grow up in a religious family, but I started to pray. Better late than never, right?

It seemed like forever we weaved through traffic until finally entering the interstate. The ride was smoother, but still loud, so I simply clung to Bull. About thirty minutes later, Bull exited onto a rural road, pulling into an old-time soft serve ice cream shop.

He turned off the engine and glanced at me over his shoulder. "Vanilla, chocolate or swirl?"

I nearly tumbled off the bike, and my legs wobbled as they got used to standing again. "Ah…swirl."

"Dipped?"

"Sure."

"Wait here."

I hobbled to a picnic table under the shop's red and white awning while Bull ordered our ice cream. I wasn't sure where we were, but I was glad for the respite from the roar and vibration of the motorcycle.

"I love soft serve." Bull handed me the chocolate dipped cone.

"You don't look like an ice cream kind of guy."

"Everyone loves ice cream."

"My mom doesn't. Or maybe she just doesn't eat it because it's fattening." I took a bite of the sweet cold confection and felt better.

"You've got gumption, Miss Sophie, standing up to those cops."

"Yeah, well, I've had a little practice. What's going on anyway?"

"All I know is that after y'all took off, the debtor was found dead. Pretty fast, too, because by the time I got back to Gordo's after taking care of some business for AJ, a cop was there asking questions about AJ."

Some business for AJ? That sounded ominous. Did AJ ask Bull to kill Mr. Cullen?

"Bad bit of luck for AJ. He wasn't even supposed to be doing the repo. Patch was."

"What?"

"Patch was supposed to do the repo, but something came up, so he asked AJ to do it."

If AJ wasn't supposed to be there, then certainly he didn't ask Bull to kill Cullen. I still couldn't figure out why AJ was there. "Why was AJ doing a repo in the first place? He's in the military."

Bull shook his head. "Not anymore. Not for a while. You didn't know?"

"Know what?"

AJ and I had been close friends when I'd known him before. But in that instant, I realized I didn't know anything about his life since he left for the military and I left for college. Ten years was a long time. A lot of growing and changing happened since I'd last seen him.

"He left a few years back. His momma isn't well—"

"She's never been well." I was never sure if AJ's mom was a scatterbrain or just irresponsible, but from the way he'd talked about her, it didn't seem like she had all her faculties.

"Well, she got worse. AJ moved her into a special home in Charlottesville."

"Why aren't Ally or Adam taking care of her?" I asked about AJ's siblings.

"I think they did for a while, but the sister is in the military somewhere in California and the brother is in medical school in Chicago."

I wasn't surprised AJ put his life on hold for his siblings. He'd practically raised them when his father left.

But I felt bad for him having to put his dreams aside. "So now he's a repo man?"

"You make that sound bad, but it's a pretty good life. You only need a few repos a year to make a decent living. AJ spends most of his time fixing up a hovel of a house he bought at Jefferson Lake. Becca helped on it for a bit—"

"Becca? The lawyer?"

"Yeah. She and AJ had a thing for a while. But... well, it didn't work out."

My teenage self did a little happy dance at that news. My adult self wondered when my hormones would grow up.

"The house and area suit him, although he always said he'd never step foot in Jefferson Grove again, and yet, there we were today. I wonder if it had anything to do with you?" Bull's narrowed gaze suggested he was curious to my response.

"Why would you say that?"

"You don't think AJ just happened to be in that grocery store at the same time you were, do you?"

Ten years ago, I'd have read something more into AJ's actions. Now I knew better. AJ had only ever been my friend. A friend who looked after me like a big brother. If he was in town, it wouldn't have taken long for him to hear the gossip I was back too. He had to feel sorry for me, learning I was living with Aunt Rose, and enduring the snickers of the townsfolk.

"I don't know. You tell me."

Bull grinned, his white teeth peeking through his dark beard. "It's not for me to tell."

"That's no answer. You can't say something like that and then not explain yourself. It's just wrong."

He laughed. "You're a tiny little thing but don't take no guff. I like you, Miss Sophie. Eat your ice cream then I'll take you home."

I rolled my eyes. "You're not going to explain?"

"Nope." Bull finished his ice cream in two bites. "Eat up and let's get you home."

I frowned but began enjoying my ice cream. After all, it was the first good thing that hadn't gone wrong all day.

When Bull turned up the tree-lined street toward Aunt Rose's, I tapped him on the shoulder and pointed to the side of the road, hoping he understood I wanted him to pull over.

"Problem?" he asked when he stopped.

I pulled the helmet off my head. "Aunt Rose wouldn't like me riding up on a motorcycle."

He grinned. "You don't think she'll appreciate my charm?"

"Aunt Rose doesn't appreciate much of anything. Thanks for coming to get me, Bull. I know it was out of the way."

"Nah. I'm always happy to get the bike out on the open road."

I said my good-bye and hoofed the half a block to my aunt's house, which was easier said than done because after nearly two hours on a motorcycle, my legs felt like Jell-O. As I walked by the Brown Bomber sitting in the driveway, I noticed papers in the front seat. Opening the door, I picked one up. A receipt for a battery. Huh? Across the top was a note. *Drive safely, Miss Sophie.* Bull had bought me a new battery? And installed it? How had he done that without Aunt Rose knowing? I shook my head. Didn't matter. I had a new battery, thanks to Bull. Was that the bit of business for AJ he mentioned before? I owed them both a big thank-you, even if they got me into trouble.

I turned the doorknob slowly, hoping to sneak in undetected to avoid having to answer a bunch of questions by Aunt Rose. I had just enough time to clean up and get to my coupon group if I wasn't waylaid by her.

"Sophie?"

I stiffened and stopped in my tracks. "Yes. It's me." Did she know I just spent the afternoon being questioned by the police? Accused of killing the man who put my dad in jail with a golf club? Probably as she had a network of townsfolks who kept her up on people in town.

"Since when do you have enough money to hire a mechanic that makes house calls?"

I hadn't expected that question. Relief washed through me as I realized she must have seen Bull replacing my battery. "It was a favor, Aunt Rose. It didn't cost me anything."

"Nothing's free, Sophie." Her squinty eyes glared at me. "You look like you rolled in oil."

"What? No." Of course, I couldn't explain why I really had oil on my clothes. "I fell."

"Um hum." She wasn't buying it. She was taking this role of watching me pretty seriously. I wondered if my father was giving her the same pep talks about me as he was giving me about her. I'm not sure how. She never visited him. And she didn't have a computer to email him. Did she send him letters?

Then again, maybe under her gruff exterior she really did care about what happened to me. I remembered my father once telling me that a long time ago, she'd been a lovely, charming woman. He wasn't sure, but he thought someone broke her heart.

"I've got my coupon group tonight," I told her.

"Bah." Aunt Rose waved her arm and turned away. "Coupons just make you spend money on stuff you don't need."

Always happy to have the last word, she walked towards the kitchen. I made my way to the shower and hoped my coupon group would go much better than the rest of my day had gone.

FOUR

I PARKED THE Brown Bomber in front of Aggie Parnell's home. For the first time that day, I felt like I was back to my regular life. No witchy jealous wives. No leering potential employers. No murder interrogations. No AJ. The last thought made me sad. It had been good to see him again. A reminder of when my life was easy and uncomplicated. I wondered if he'd been able to talk his way out of the police station. Bull said he had a lawyer, so hopefully AJ wasn't spending a night in jail.

I pulled my coupon binder out of the car by the strap and slung it over my shoulder. I wondered what, if anything, the ladies tonight knew about all the goings ons. Jefferson Grove was a small town. Nothing happened without everyone knowing about it within a few hours. I steeled myself against the bombardment of questions bound to come my way about spending a day flying with AJ Devlin, a man questioned for murder.

I made my way up the tidy walkway to the small brick ranch. Most of the homes on the street were built in the 1950s and all looked the same. In fact, the only way I knew I was at the right house was seeing Aggie's old red Pontiac Bonneville convertible in the driveway.

I rapped on the door and heard the familiar, "Come on in." That was another thing about Jefferson Grove. People didn't worry about locking doors or strangers attacking them in their homes. Although, after the murder at the airport today, that might change.

I opened the door and stepped into the cold, air-conditioned home. Aggie's husband, Earl, sat in his recliner, a beer in one hand and a remote in the other, watching baseball on TV.

"Is it that time already?" He turned his head toward me, his friendly brown eyes hooded by giant gray caterpillar-like brows smiling at me.

"Almost. How are you, Mr. Parnell?"

"Well, I'm doing alright for a man my age." He clicked off the television and, with a rocking motion, launched himself forward. He stood, but his legs never quite straightened all the way. "Aggie! I'm goin' to George's to watch the game." Then he winked at me. "Don't let her take advantage of you, Miz Sophie. Those coupons are like gold."

"I heard that!" Aggie appeared in the doorway between the living area and dining room. Her mocha skin was accentuated by the thick puff of white hair that made me think of a cotton swab. She had the highest cheek bones of anyone I'd ever met, and when she smiled, there was a little hint of mischief, as if she knew something I didn't. "Don't pay him no mind, Sophie."

Aggie always reminded me of Madea. She was large in size and personality, not afraid to speak her mind and never took any guff. But she had a sweeter side that often made me wish I could live with Aggie and Earl instead of Aunt Rose.

Aggie and Earl made faces at each other as he shuffled to the door. But I could see that underneath it was love and playfulness.

"You can help me set out the food." Aggie turned back and I followed her to the kitchen.

When the other ladies hosted the coupon group, they usually set out chips, dip and maybe some veggies. Aggie was old school. When we gathered at her home, she set out plates of deviled eggs, Vienna sausages baked in crescent roll dough, a Crock-Pot full of meatballs and homemade cookies.

"I brought soda." I set my bag of generic brand liter soda bottles on Aggie's kitchen table. I was going to get grief about not buying name-brand, but my Pepsi coupons expired yesterday and I didn't have enough money to let vanity or avoiding hassle get in the way.

"I've got some sweet tea and fresh lemonade as well." Aggie nodded toward the old yellow refrigerator. "You can get the pitchers from the fridge. If all goes well, we can add a little something to our drinks later."

Aggie was old school in that respect too. Every day at 4 she had a drink with Earl. But drinks weren't allowed at coupon group until the deals were made and done. Although I was pretty sure Aggie had already had a little something in her drink.

I got to work helping Aggie put the food and drinks on the kitchen table, listening as Aggie chatted away about who was doing what to whom in Jefferson Grove, yet interestingly, there was no mention of AJ or me or murder. I was setting the Crock-Pot of meatballs on the table when there was a knock and the door opened.

"Hello?" In walked Vivie Danner and her sister, Tracy Simpson. I went to high school with Vivie, while Tracy had graduated with my older brother, Will. Neither woman liked me, not then, and not now. But at least Tracy had outgrown juvenile teenage angst and could be civil. Vivie, on the other hand, reverted to a classic mean girl whenever I was around. Probably because I'd won the attention of Randy Danner for a week in high school. Of course, Vivie got the final word, as she married Randy and had their first baby seven months after they graduated. Vivie liked to rub it in, along with all my other woes.

But gloating over Randy wasn't any great feat. In the ten years since high school, he'd lost most of his hair and his athletic build. Vivie was a part of turning him into that, if she bought all the stuff on the coupons she always coveted. I wondered if Vivie and Randy had a single piece of fresh produce in their house. Maybe they did, because while Randy was turning into a dough boy, Vivie actually looked good. Her expensive blond hair was pulled back in a ponytail and bangs wisped over her brows, giving her a youthful appeal. She liked to brag about the two hours she spent at the gym every morning and it showed in a trim, firm body.

"Oh, hello, Sophie."

"Tracy, Vivie."

Tracy was a duller version of Vivie, but not unattractive. She'd kept her brown hair, opting for less expensive highlights over dying it a completely different color. She didn't work out as much but blamed her mother's genes on her inability to be as trim as Vivie.

Tracy and Vivie set their giant coupon binders on the table. That was the one thing I did envy about them. They were truly extreme couponers. Had they been friendlier, I'd have asked to watch them in action in the grocery store and checked out their stockpile.

"What can we help you with, Aggie?" Tracy stole a meatball from the Crock-Pot.

"Sophie's got it all covered, I think. We can grab something to drink and sit a spell waiting for the others."

Aggie made the best lemonade, so I filled my red plastic cup.

"Did you hear about the murder at the airport today?" Tracy chose sweet tea.

"I did. Wasn't surprised, though. There was always something shifty about Joseph Cullen." Aggie's face pinched in disgust.

"Rumor is AJ Devlin did it." Vivie glanced over at me with her I'm-going-to-make-you-miserable stare. "You still crushing on him, Sophie?"

All sorts of retorts, some that were acceptable in mixed company, but most that weren't, ran through my mind. Fortunately, there was a knock and the door opened. Lani Lafferty stepped in, along with Gwen Stevens. Saved. Although I didn't know Gwen well, Lani was my one true friend since returning to Jefferson Grove.

"Come on in, girls." Aggie waved them in. "We're having cold drinks before we start."

Lani and Gwen set their couponing binders on the dining table and then sat with us at the kitchen table.

"Where's Mr. Aggie?" Lani always had a soft spot for Aggie's husband.

"He's off carousing with the menfolk."

"Better the men than another woman." Gwen poured herself a glass of lemonade.

"He's a smart man." Aggie stood. "Why don't you help yourself to some food? You'll need to fuel up. I got some good coupons this week."

I picked up a plate and took my turn selecting my

food. It would be my dinner for tonight, so I tried to pick the healthiest options, which wasn't easy.

"Hey, rumor is AJ Devlin was in town today." Lani said it with a waggle of her brow toward me. She also knew I'd had a crush on him, but her words weren't meant to be hurtful.

"Yes."

"Ah, poor Sophie. Your one chance missed. And now he's in jail. You'll end up a spinster."

"You keep that sass outside," Aggie chastised Vivie.

"I'm just teasing you, Sophie. You know that, right?" The voice was sweet. The tone wasn't.

"Oh, he's not in jail." Lani poked a meatball with a toothpick. "He was questioned and he's a person of interest, but there's not enough evidence to arrest him."

"How do you know?" Gwen picked up a deviled egg, ate it and then added one to her plate.

"Lawson Davis is the investigator on the case here, and he told Dwayne about AJ being picked up and questioned in Richmond, but there was nothing to keep him on. He had a woman with him in the plane." Lani's voice was sympathetic, indicating she had no idea I was the woman on the plane with AJ. So, Lawson, my buddy Sergeant Scowl, hadn't told Dwayne or maybe Dwayne hadn't told Lani it was me. Perhaps he wasn't allowed to tell her, even though she was his wife.

"Double ouch." Vivie's eyes gleamed at me.

Well, those where fighting words. "It was me." I said it nonchalantly as I headed to sit at the dining room table.

"You killed Mr. Cullen?" Tracy nearly did a spit take.

I shook my head. "No. I was on the plane with AJ." Vivie's meatball fell off her toothpick. It was quite satisfying. Even Aggie's brows made wide arcs over her dark eyes.

Only Lani seemed intrigued by my statement. "How did that happen?"

"I ran into him in the IGA. I was having a crappy day and he noticed, so he invited me to fly with him."

Recapturing her inner-mean girl, Vivie said, "How did you know he didn't mean drugs? Everyone knows Cullen was smuggling drugs with that plane of his."

I shot her a when-are-you-going-to-grow-up glare, but Lani again intervened, before I could retaliate. "How'd he look?"

I smiled and licked my lips. "Like the old AJ, only more. Better."

"Yum."

"I can't believe you're going all gaga over a murderer." Vivie repoked her meatball.

"I don't think he did it."

"Oh my God. You were there!"

As if everyone only just realized what flying with AJ meant, they gawked again. "I saw the man too. He came out to talk to AJ. If anyone had murder in their eyes, it was him. But AJ was calm, cool and collected. They talked, we left and that was that."

"Why was he mad?" Gwen asked.

"Probably because AJ was repossessing his plane."

"He's a repo man?" Vivie's face distorted into distaste.

"He repos airplanes."

"That's a thing?" Aggie asked. "I've seen ads for a TV show but didn't think it was real. Almost nothing on TV is real anymore."

"So…is he back in town?" Lani's eyes shone with excitement.

It was nice to have a friend who was hopeful for good things for me. Not that AJ had any interest in me, but Lani knew of my interest in him in high school and wanted to see me happy.

I shook my head. "He's got a place at Jefferson Lake but works out of Charlottesville. Apparently, he's moved his mom there."

"You know what they say, you can take the Devlin out of Cooters Hollow, but you can't take the hollow out of a Devlin."

I wondered if I'd go to jail for poking Vivie's eyes out with a meatball sauce-laced toothpick. "Do you come by that attitude naturally, or is it work?"

There was an audible snort from Gwen. She recovered by covering her mouth with her napkin.

"Well, if anyone was going to get out of the Hollow, it was AJ." Aggie stood. "Now, enough of this chitchat. Let's get couponing."

Saved again. I cleared my plate without saying more. Fortunately, Vivie kept her vile trap shut too.

"You know, AJ is on my deserted island list." Lani sat next to me at the dining room table.

The table was large, with extra leaves in it, but once all the binders were opened and the exchanging began, it was tight. It made me think of a Vegas blackjack table. On the buffet against the wall, there was a large wooden cutting board I suspected Aggie lifted from the elementary school where she retired as a teacher.

"What do you mean?" I opened my binder and tried not to be embarrassed by how scrawny mine was in comparison to everyone else's. After all, I'd only been couponing a couple of weeks.

"You know, who would you want with you if you were stuck on a deserted island."

"And you want AJ? It's supposed to be a celebrity, you know, like Daniel Craig." Vivie's lips pursed and gave a look like she thought Lani was an idiot.

"Oh, Bond. I like him." Gwen waggled her brows.

"I know and I have a few celebrities. Idris Elba, Will Smith. But Sophie wasn't the only one swooning over AJ in school."

"Does Dwayne know you didn't pick him to be on your island?" I asked.

"Yes. The whole point is fantasy. You're not supposed to pick your significant other."

"It's a good game for Sophie. You're not seeing anyone, are you?" Once again, Vivie's tone didn't sound mean, and yet there was an undercurrent that made me want to punch her in the throat.

"Dwayne picked Beyoncé." Lani happily chatted on, but I knew she was doing it to stop my response to Vivie.

"Just one?" Gwen asked.

"Well, Beyoncé is worth like ten."

"That's true. Beyoncé for President." Gwen whooped.

"He didn't pick Rihanna? I'd have thought he would since you look a lot like her."

Lani was the most beautiful and exotic person I knew with her light coffee skin and green cat-shaped eyes.

"See, that's why you're my bestest friend." Lani bumped my shoulder with hers.

"I'd have MacGyver. The old one, not this new one." Aggie joined in the fun. "He's handsome and handy.

Imagine the things he could do with coconuts and palms."

We all laughed.

"I know the Devlins have a reputation, but I still don't get why people would think AJ killed Cullen." Gwen turned the conversation back to murder.

"He was there, dummy."

"Vivie, you're about to wear out your welcome and since you're my ride, I'd appreciate it if you'd rein in your nastiness."

I wanted to clap and cheer at Tracy's comment. Vivie gave her the stink eye, but Tracy didn't seem to care as she pulled out a stack of coupons.

"Rumor has it AJ got his mom a place in Charlottesville and his brother and sister are living out of state." Lani tossed a coupon in the expired pile. Once a month, the coupons that were expired less than six months were sent to a military coupon exchange overseas, where families serving abroad could still use them.

"Cullen had plenty of other people who'd want to see him dead. That's for sure." Aggie made stacks of her coupons just above her binder.

"Like who?" I had nothing to do because I didn't have many coupons to trade.

"Well, there's his estranged wife, who's estranged on account of he can't keep his willy in his pants." Aggie pointed her scissors at no one in particular to make her point. "A wife can put up with a lot, but cheating ain't one of them."

"Speaking of willies, Vivie, your name has come up as one of Cullen's…friends."

"Shut up, Gwen!"

Okay, now I was having fun. I bit my lip to keep

from blurting something that would have us in a cat fight. I was more interested in learning about Vivie and Cullen's willy.

"Oh come on, Viv. Everyone knows. You grew up here. How you can think something like that doesn't get out, I'll never know." Tracy sat back, apparently waiting for the trading to begin.

"That gives you motive." It was out of my mouth before I could stop it.

Everyone looked at me and I thought I'd be the one asked to leave.

But after a moment, they turned their curious gazes on Vivie.

"I didn't kill him." Vivie looked and sounded indignant, but there was a quiver to her voice. "He and I had a little thing months ago. To be honest, he's not very skilled with his…willy."

Her statement resulted in snorts of laughter. Even from me. Vivie's features relaxed some, but not quite all the way.

"Maybe it was Randy," Lani said. "Most husbands don't like their wives playing with another man's willy."

"Fffttt…like he'd care." Vivie waved the comment away. "He doesn't have the guts to discipline the kids. There's no way he'd kill anyone."

So, there was trouble in paradise. I felt satisfaction in that, even though it was petty.

"I wouldn't put anything past Maggie, either." Tracy stood and went to the buffet to cut coupons from the weekend circular.

"Who's Maggie?" It was weird not knowing who someone was, considering I'd grown up in Jefferson Grove.

"Cullen's wife. She's a mean one." Aggie stood. "I want more tea. Anyone else?"

Everyone shook their heads and Aggie went back to the kitchen.

"Tea?" Lani whispered. "Maybe with a little bourbon."

"I can hear you!"

"Oh!"

But the group laughed.

"Did you see anyone else there, Sophie?" Gwen asked.

"Now you're *CSI*?" Vivi scoffed.

"Just curious." Gwen cast Vivie an annoyed glare. "Think about it. If they arrested AJ when he landed in Richmond but Sophie saw the dead guy alive when they left, then he was murdered in a small space of time. Small enough they think AJ did it."

"AJ was there with another man, Bull. He's scary enough looking, but…" Bull didn't strike me as a murderer, unless he had a good reason. Then again, he scared me when I first saw him. And he looked like he'd take Joseph Cullen's head off when he was threatening AJ.

"Bull? What kind of name is Bull?" Tracy looked intrigued.

"He's built like one."

"Maybe he's AJ's enforcer." Vivi sneered.

"Not everyone from the Hollow is a criminal." I rolled my eyes.

"No. Some of them are from Monticello Heights."

Vivie's retort was a slap at my father and brother, but since it was true, I couldn't respond. Still. "I don't remember you being so mean to everyone when we were little. What happened to you, Vivie?"

"I'm not mean, Sophie. I'm just telling the truth."

"No. You're mean," Lani said. "Or at least your tone is mean."

Vivie glared.

"How was he killed?" Gwen's attention was on me, clearly more intrigued by murder than coupons.

"I'm not sure. But they asked me several questions about golf clubs."

"What?"

"It's true." Lani nodded. "Dwayne told me the killer whacked him on the head with a golf club. It knocked him down and stunned him enough that the killer was able to straddle him and choke him with it."

There was a collective "ooh" from the group. After I got the image of Cullen being killed by a six thousand dollar golf club out of my head, questions zoomed through my brain, the biggest one, aside from who was the killer, was why kill with a golf club? If you were going to kill someone, wouldn't you bring something more substantial, like a bat or a tire iron? Unless the club was already there, but why would there be a golf club in an airport hangar? Most golfers I knew kept their clubs at home or in the trunk of their car. So maybe the killer brought his from the trunk of his car, but again, why not the tire iron, which, in my mind, seemed a better choice.

"Aggie, you said a lot of people would want Cullen dead. Why?" I decided the how wasn't as crucial as the who at this point.

Aggie returned to her seat, drink in hand. "He's an arrogant weasel, for one. And rumor is that he's the source of all the drugs coming into this area. He uses that plane of his to get 'em here."

"Wouldn't he do better in Richmond?" I asked.

"Selling them, yes. But he probably has an easier time bringing them in through a small county airport than through a large city. At least that's what Dwayne says." Lani started to set a coupon on one stack and then opted for another one.

"If he's bringing in drugs using his plane, wouldn't that be easy to get proof on?" I felt like Nancy Drew sorting out the clues of a mystery.

"You'd think so, but the investigators haven't gotten anything except rumors, and apparently you can't get a warrant to search based on rumors." Lani finished stacking her coupons and sat back.

"So a competing drug dealer could have killed him," I said, thinking out loud.

"Or a scorned mistress or jealous husband," Gwen added.

"I still think his wife is a good candidate," Aggie tossed in.

"He was a hound dog." Gwen scrunched up her nose. "He sniffed around me some, but I sent him packing."

"Who *are* you seeing?" Tracy asked.

Gwen sighed. "No one now."

"Really? I saw you with Jacob Landry at the Jefferson Inn." Vivie was back to her accusatory tone.

"He's a bore." Gwen waved Vivie's comment away.

"Is there anyone in town you haven't gone on a date with?" Vivie turned her mean girl snark on Gwen.

"AJ Devlin." Gwen waggled her brows.

I liked Gwen, but I didn't like that. As nice as Gwen was, I didn't think she was AJ's type. Or maybe I just hoped she wasn't. For one, at six feet three, she was at least two, maybe three inches taller than him. And two, well, I couldn't think of a good second reason. She was pretty enough with a dark bob that had purple along the tips and stunning blue eyes I suspected were contacts but was too polite to ask.

"You're not very discriminating." Vivie sat primly in her chair. It was quite a statement, considering she'd had an affair with a possible drug smuggler who wasn't very talented with his willy.

"You know what they say, you have to kiss a lot of frogs to find your prince." Gwen grinned.

"Actually, you have to throw the frog against the wall." I studied Lani's coupons, hoping I could get the fifty cents off bagged lettuce. When there was no response, I looked up to see all eyes on me. "What?"

"You have to throw him against the wall?" Lani asked.

"In the original story, *The Frog Prince*, well, it's actually *The Frog King,* the girl gets mad and throws the frog against the wall and he turns into a king."

"Do they get married?" Gwen sat forward.

I nodded. "Yes."

"Even after she hurled him against the wall?" Aggie mimicked throwing the frog against the wall.

"Yes."

"I guess I've been doing it all wrong." Gwen laughed.

"How do you know this?" Tracy asked.

"I read it. It's a Grimm's Fairy Tale."

"You read fairy tales?" Vivie sported her usual smirk.

"I read lots of stuff, but I like fairy tales. I took a class on it at school."

"They teach fairy tales in college?" Vivie's tone was dubious.

"Yes. I took it for my major in Folklore."

Everyone had various expressions of puzzlement. I couldn't blame them. Most people had similar expressions when I told them my major.

"I thought college was for smart people. Why would they have a class on fairy tales?" Vivie asked.

"It's not different from any other literature class, like British lit."

"Oh, I love Jane Austen." Lani sighed.

"Me too." I grinned.

"So, what sorts of jobs use folklore and fairy tales?" Tracy asked.

"None in Jefferson Grove."

"So, she throws the frog against the wall and it becomes a prince?" Aggie eyes narrowed in puzzlement, and I was glad she was changing the subject. "Why was the story changed? I kind of like that."

We all laughed.

"The original story isn't appropriate for children. In fact, most of the original stories aren't."

"There are more stories?" Aggie asked. "Like what?"

"Well, in Cinderella, one step-sister cuts her toe off and the other cuts off part of her heel to get the gold— not glass—shoe on. And at the end, birds peck their eyes out."

"Eww." Vivie scrunched up her face in disgust.

"Cool." Gwen and Lani chimed in together.

"Does Cinderella still marry Prince Charming?" Aggie asked.

"Did you know that the name Prince Charming isn't in any of the original tales? But yes, she marries the prince."

"No Prince Charming?" Aggie looked disappointed.

"Not as a specific name, no." I enjoyed discussing fairy tales and other stories. At least my major wasn't a total waste. I could entertain, even if I couldn't make a living. I wondered if there were any storyteller street performers.

"Fairy tales should be banned."

"What? Why?" I was horrified by Vivie's comment.

"Because they lead little girls to believe a man will whisk them off their feet and make their lives perfect. Reality is different."

"That's true." Gwen pointed toward Vivie.

Everyone nodded in agreement.

"You could say the same about Jane Austen," I pointed out.

"Yes, but in her time, women needed a man to survive." Lani defended her beloved Jane.

"When do you think fairy tales were written?" I argued. "I agree that women don't need a man today, but fairy tales are fiction stories of their time. Many have moral messages that can apply today."

"Like throw men against the wall?"

We all laughed at Aggie's comment.

"All this chitchat is nice, but I need me some coupons. Let's get trading, ladies." Tracy picked up one of her coupon stacks.

Once each of our stacks of coupons were organized, they were compiled together in the middle of the table by category. All produce coupons went in one pile, soup in another, and so on. Store coupons were piled by store, and there was one pile for specialty coupons, such as from a restaurant or hair salon. Once all the coupons were in their proper piles, we started going through to find the ones we wanted. Usually, we were polite and took turns if more than one person went for a single pile. One time, Tracy threatened to shave off Vivie's eyebrows in her sleep if she didn't stop grabbing at all the piles at once.

Sometimes, we negotiated directly with another person for highly coveted coupons. For example, one time Gwen traded three toothpaste coupons to Vivie for one Edy's Ice Cream coupon.

Along with swapping, the ladies shared about successful shops, hidden sales they'd found, or, in my case, asked for help.

"I need help with something." I handed my receipt to Lani. "It should have come out to less than twenty dollars."

Lani frowned as she scanned the receipt. "Did you think the coupons would be doubled? Because the IGA doesn't double. Not anymore."

Oh, yeah. Duh.

"College gal, huh?" Vivie said under her breath.

ONCE WE WERE DONE, I stayed behind after the other ladies left to help Aggie clean up. It was the polite thing to do. It also kept me out later, which meant I might miss Aunt Rose when I got home.

"AJ did alright for himself and his mama." Aggie handed me a plate to dry.

"Yes." I glanced at her, unsure why she said that.

"But that doesn't make him husband material."

I laughed. "The last thing on my mind is finding a husband. And even if I was, AJ sees me as a kid sister."

Aggie stopped washing and gave me a pointed look. "You're no kid and you're not his sister."

I frowned.

"You're a smart, pretty young thing. But you're not very worldly. A man like AJ, any man, might get you to thinking they'd be a good way to escape your current situation."

"Prince Charming."

"That's right. He doesn't exist. My Earl comes close, but sometimes I'd like to knock him against the wall just like in your story."

I couldn't stop the image of a frog with Earl's face being hurled against the wall.

"God bless him, he does the best he can, but trust me on this, Sophie, men can be more work than they're worth sometimes."

"I appreciate your concern. I really do. But you don't have to worry about me falling for a man's charms. First, there would have to be a man. Assuming there was a man in Jefferson Grove I was interested in, which there isn't, he'd have to be interested in me too. We know that's not happening because everyone is afraid I'm like my dad—"

"That will pass in time."

"Plus, I promised my dad I'd take care of Aunt Rose, and I need to learn to take care of myself. I'm trying, but good golly, Aggie, it's really hard."

"Well, bless your heart." The phrase could have so many meanings, including mean ones. But I believed Aggie said it as a term of pity.

"You'll get your bearings. Your pa did you wrong by not raising you to be more independent and using your smarts to get you a high-powered career. But you're no dummy. You'll figure it out and then you'll have men lining the streets to be with you."

I laughed. All of a sudden, it sounded like Aggie was promoting love. "From your mouth to God's ears."

"That's right. And I talk to him every night, so I know he's listening."

FIVE

I TIPTOED INTO the house. It wasn't too late, and I heard the TV blaring, which meant Aunt Rose was watching one of her shows. It didn't take much to set her off, so I opted to sneak in rather than interrupt.

I must have made a noise, because Aunt Rose's head turned. Her scowl had me inhaling a breath to steel against whatever angst she was going to heap on me. My luck hadn't been good today, so I didn't hold out that Rose would spare me from complaint or insult. Fortunately, luck was with me at that moment, as Aunt Rose turned back to her show.

Now I had to decide if I should say good night. Saying something could be construed as rude, as it would interrupt Rose's show. But not saying anything could be rude too. I opted to keep quiet. Rose hadn't said anything when she saw me, so I figured she was rude first. Keeping my mouth shut, I made my way up the narrow hall to my room.

I changed into pajamas, which, in the hot humid summer, consisted of cotton knit shorts and a tank top. I carried my toiletry bag across the hall into the single bathroom I shared with Aunt Rose to wash my face and brush my teeth. Once back in my room, I opened the hideaway bed and pulled the pillows from the closet.

Turning out the light, I climbed into bed and willed my brain to shut up, which wasn't easy. My days in Jefferson Grove had become monotonous, but today was a roller coaster ride, making me second guess the desire for more excitement in my life. It started with the disastrous interview with the witch and the letch. Then there were the miscalculations on my coupons, leaving me unable to pay for groceries, and then my car didn't start.

The frustration of the morning was lessened by seeing AJ again. I wasn't kidding when I told the coupon group AJ was the same but more. Even if I hadn't already spent my teenage years crushing over him, I'd have been affected by him the minute he smiled at me. But, of course, I recognized now that having a crush on him was a waste of time and energy. Not because he was a Devlin from the Hollow. I had never cared about that. He might have been poor and rough around the edges, but he'd always been nice to me. Nicer than many of my polite, rich friends.

And it wasn't because he was currently suspected of committing murder. I didn't believe for one second that AJ killed Mr. Cullen. Of course, that might be naïve, but still. In some ways, AJ *was* my Prince Charming. Today wasn't the first time he'd come to my rescue. When I was younger, he saved me from embarrassment, grabby boys, and discipline from my parents on a few occasions.

Allowing any interest in AJ now was a bad idea because I'd spent my whole life relying on others to take care of me and look where it had gotten me. College was a piece of cake compared to the lesson I was learning now about how to take care of myself. I wasn't very good at it, although it wasn't from a lack of trying.

I frequently reminded myself that change took time. I wouldn't work at the Booty Burgo and live with Aunt

Rose forever, except I couldn't see how I'd escape them. I flung an arm over my face as the idea I might be a wench forever crossed my mind. If AJ showed up right now and offered to take me away, I'd go, and that annoyed me because it was wrong to rely on a man to save me. It didn't matter how handsome and funny and nice he was.

Of course, lying face down on a tarmac and being taken to the police station for questioning about a murder put a damper on all the warm fuzzy feelings I had for AJ. Plus, he hadn't called to see if I got home okay or was upset about being taken away in handcuffs. Lani said he hadn't been arrested, so maybe his not checking on me was a sign he didn't care. Maybe he blamed me for today's fiasco. While timing had to be a factor in the interest in him, Sergeant Scowl also hinted that my father's connection to Cullen gave AJ a motive through me.

At least the coupon group had gone as usual, with Vivie spitting piss and vinegar my way whenever she had the chance. The one interesting bit was learning that Vivie had had an affair with Mr. Cullen. Not that I didn't think Vivie wouldn't ever cheat. But it was intriguing to know more people connected to the victim.

I supposed AJ had as much motive—a big payoff upon delivery of the plane—and he had the opportunity to kill Joseph Cullen. But I couldn't see happy go-lucky AJ as a murderer. Vivie, on the other hand, was as mean as a snake. I suspected I wasn't the only victim of Vivie's venom.

It was interesting that Vivie said Randy wouldn't care about her affair. Was that true? It was hard to believe a man wouldn't be upset at his wife's cheating ways. If Randy didn't care, maybe it was because he was having one too. I hadn't heard any rumors about it, but then again, I hadn't heard about Vivie's, or Cullen being a drug smuggler, either. I knew why. As much as possible, I stayed away from public because I was certain I was the topic of their conversation. The only time I heard gossip was at coupon group or when Aunt Rose's card buddies were over.

I winced in the dark as I realized I'd be the center of talk again when it got out I was with AJ when he was taken into police custody. In fact, how was it that Rose wasn't tossing me and my clothes into the warm night? Surely there was something on the news about the murder and AJ as a suspect.

If she didn't know now, she'd know soon, which meant I might be homeless tomorrow. Thank goodness Bull and AJ got the Brown Bomber fixed. It might be my new home.

I blew out a breath. This was no way to live. I had a job at the Booty Burgo, but I couldn't make it on my own by working there. So maybe I needed to go back to Denny Coker to see if he'd give me a job after all. My stomach roiled at the idea.

I needed to beef up my efforts to find a better paying job that didn't involve jealous witches and lecherous men. Not that I hadn't been diligent in searching for work. The problem was there weren't many job openings in Jefferson Grove. And the few there were didn't want the daughter of a crook or I wasn't qualified to do.

But Bull and AJ fixed my car, so maybe now it could make the commute to Charlottesville. They'd still know about my dad and brother's incarceration, after all it was big news throughout the Commonwealth. But maybe they wouldn't hold it against me.

Or there was Bull's idea of being an exotic dancer in Richmond. Even if I did it for a little while, maybe I could make enough to break free from the Booty Burgo, Aunt Rose, and Jefferson Grove.

You're not seriously considering dancing? AJ's words came back to me. Why would he care? It wasn't like he would be jealous. He didn't think of me like that. He was like a big brother. I had a big brother, and I wasn't sure he'd care if I flaunted my booty, which I already did as a wench waitress at the Booty Burgo.

Still, I didn't have faith in my ability to make money as a dancer, as Bull seemed to think I did. Not that I was ugly, but I was short and rounder than most dancers. I was athletic at one time in my life, but not necessarily graceful or seductive. So, dancing was probably out. But places like that needed waitresses, didn't they? In a bigger city, waitresses probably got paid more than the Booty Burgo offered. But I had to watch over Aunt Rose, which meant I couldn't move. And Richmond was far enough away that any extra income I might make would be burned up in gas expense. So, I was stuck where I was for the time being. Deciding there was nothing more I could do right then, I sought to quiet my mind and go to sleep.

I WOKE TO the sound of my phone playing "Let It Go" from *Frozen*. "Hullo?" I glanced at the phone to see the time. Eight thirty.

"Good morning, Miss Sophie."

"Who is this?" I pulled the covers around me and

considered going back to sleep. I had nowhere to be until dinnertime.

"It's Bull. You haven't forgotten me already, have you?"

"Bull." My eyes opened, now wide awake. I scooted up to sit. "No, of course not. You're unforgettable. Is AJ okay?"

"Yep. He's home. He asked me to call to make sure you're okay. I guess there's some concern about your aunt."

He asked Bull to call? "Why didn't he call?"

"Well, his mama heard about his problems and went off her rocker. She's not right in the head, so he needed to see to her last night. Plus, just because the cops can't arrest him doesn't mean they don't think he did it. He's got a lot on his mind."

I was selfish to expect AJ to call. It wasn't like he hadn't thought of me if he asked Bull to call. I hadn't thought once of his family. His mom had always been one waffle short of a full breakfast plate, and I'd known AJ had always been the one to put things right for her. Bull was right. Just because they didn't have enough to arrest him didn't mean they wouldn't continue to look at him. "Is he in trouble?"

"Hard to tell. Doesn't appear the cops are looking at anyone else."

"But lots of people wanted Mr. Cullen dead. All the ladies in my coupon group said so. One of them had an affair with him."

I couldn't see him but, in my mind, Bull shrugged. "I imagine his lawyer is looking into all that."

"I guess it's good he did that repo because lawyers cost a lot of money." The only money the government hadn't taken from me and my family had been spent on lawyers.

"He won't get paid for that. At least not in a long time."

"Why not?" That didn't seem fair.

"Well, the plane is evidence now. The cops think AJ was one of Cullen's pilots flying drugs into the area."

"He wouldn't do that!" *Would he?*

"No. But with the plane confiscated, the bank can't auction it to get its money, which means Gordo doesn't get his money, which means AJ doesn't get paid."

"Will Gordo's lawyer be able to help him?"

"Now, all this isn't for you to worry about, Miss Sophie. Is your car running right?"

"Yes. Thank you for fixing it."

"You're welcome." In the background, I heard talking. "I need to go now. You call me if you need something. You're a friend of Bull's now, so when you need a Bull, you've got one."

I showered, dressed, folded up my bed, hid my pillows in the closet and then walked to the end of the hall, poking my head around the corner like a spy to ascertain where Aunt Rose was and her mood. She was futzing around in the kitchen.

I considered going back to my room, but then I heard, "Is that you skulking around, Sophie? You come in here. I have to talk to you."

I wished I'd packed and hoped Aunt Rose would give me enough time to gather what meager items I owned before she kicked me out for being picked up by the police with AJ Devlin.

I stepped around the corner and, with my head high,

despite low spirits, I entered the kitchen. "Good morning, Aunt Rose."

I got a grunt in response. "There's coffee."

"Thank you." I intended to get a cup and retreat back to my room, but Rose told me to sit at the yellow Formica table I got my finger stuck in on the underside when I was five.

"That was a Devlin yesterday."

"Yes, ma'am." My palms turned clammy and my heart started to race. I was more nervous about an interrogation from Aunt Rose than the police yesterday.

"Were you with him when Joseph Cullen was killed? Are you the woman they're talking about in the news?"

I wondered why the news hadn't revealed my name. It would make for a better story. Daughter of a scam artist stealing a plane with a murderer.

"Yes, but—"

"The news says the cops think he killed Cullen."

"But he didn't."

Aunt Rose's face pinched. "Are you sure?"

"He's not the type."

Aunt Rose waved the comment away. "Everyone is the type if they're pushed far enough. The news said they argued."

"Yes. But AJ was calm and cool. When he came back, he didn't act like he'd just killed someone."

"You've been around murderers before to know how they act?" Aunt Rose rested one hand on the back of a chair and the other on her hip as she glared at me.

"Well...no...but he wasn't nervous or sweaty or bloody. I just don't think he did it."

"The man deserved what he got."

"Huh?" I was certain Aunt Rose was planning to

kick me out, except she sounded almost disappointed AJ hadn't killed Cullen.

"Vile man. No respect for anyone. I was getting ready to rethink my opinion of Devlin, but if you said he didn't do it."

"Wait. Are you saying you'd like AJ if he'd killed Mr. Cullen?" Maybe I wasn't really awake. Maybe I was dreaming.

"It was about time someone stood up to him. No one but his killer had the guts."

I decided I must still be sleeping. There was no way my aunt was telling me AJ would no longer be persona non grata if he was a murderer.

"Some of the ladies were even talking about taking up a collection to pay for his legal fees."

Now I really was in the netherworld.

"But since you say he didn't do it—"

"The sheriff's investigator doesn't believe me. And I didn't see him not do it."

Aunt Rose's brows grew together in a single line. "What are you saying, girl?"

"I'm saying I didn't see anything that proved he was innocent."

"So, he could have done it?"

As much as it pained me to say it, I admitted it was possible. I hoped I was never asked to reveal what I'd just said in court, as it would contradict my belief AJ was innocent. But if it kept me from being kicked out and maybe pulled together some money for his legal fees, it was worth it. "I suppose."

"Well then, why didn't you say so?"

I took a deep breath, feeling like I'd betrayed AJ. "Why do you think Mr. Cullen deserved to be killed?"

"I told you. He was vile. Had no respect for anyone. He'd brought only destruction to Jefferson Grove."

"Can you be more specific?"

"He called the cops on your crook of a father, for one. Then bought up all that real estate your family owned after it was taken by the government and raised rents, forced businesses to close, evicted families."

"What? How could he get away with that?"

"It was his property. He could do what he wanted. Poor Alice Jenkins nearly starved to death before we finally got her over to the old folks' home."

"Did you know he had affairs?" I asked, happy in a weird sort of way to be conversing with my aunt.

"Sure. Everyone did. Except you. Thank the Lord you have some sense."

"If he was so vile, why did the women want to be with him?"

"Power. Money. To put one on his nasty old wife, Maggie. She's no prize, either."

Jefferson Grove wasn't the idyllic town I'd remembered. Or maybe it had always had scandal and crime but I'd never seen it behind the gates of Monticello Heights.

"Plus, all them drugs he brings around here. We didn't have much of a crime rate until he began getting everyone hooked on the devil's candy." Aunt Rose's beady eyes scrutinized me. "You're not on drugs, are you? I can tolerate a lot, but I won't have that stuff in my house."

"No, ma'am. I'd never."

"You're not selling yourself, are you? I see what you wear to work."

I shook my head like a six year old trying to convince

Mom it wasn't me that misbehaved. "It's the uniform of the Booty Burgo. I hate it, but I have to wear it."

"Booty Burgo. Another one of Cullen's dens of sin." *Cullen owned the Booty Burgo?* "It's a restaurant."

"A restaurant that forces you to show off your boobs. No one needs that in their dinner."

I had to stifle a laugh, which was funny in and of itself because Aunt Rose was never funny. "I agree. I've been trying to find other work, but no one wants to hire me."

"Because of your daddy. Doesn't help that all you know about from that expensive highfalutin education of yours is useless stories."

I opted not to defend the importance of stories to understanding culture and history. They weren't useless in the grand scheme of things, but, at the moment, they were useless in helping me find work.

"I've been thinking, maybe I can find work in Charlottesville. My car might be able to survive the commute."

"What sort of work? What can you do besides tell stories?"

That was a good question. But I knew just because I didn't have practical everyday skills, it didn't mean I couldn't be a good worker. I was smart and a quick learner. The problem was, because I was small and looked like a Kewpie doll, people didn't think I had a brain. And Aunt Rose was right. Having a degree in Folklore didn't help my case. Few jobs required my knowledge.

I was saved from having to answer when Aunt Rose's phone rang. Unlike my phone, Aunt Rose's was attached to the house by a cord. It wasn't even a cord you could plug in or out of the wall. The hookup was inside the wall. Another symbol of the age gap between us.

"Thank you for the coffee." I took my coffee to my room to give Rose privacy on her call. It was probably one of her card friends calling to get the scoop about AJ and me. I wondered if their opinion of AJ would be improved if they too thought he killed Mr. Cullen.

Back in my room, I went through my coupons while reviewing the weekly grocery sales on my smartphone. Supposedly, Wednesdays were the best days to shop because that was the day most retailers put out their sales circular, and also when they marked down food getting ready to expire. I hadn't yet been able to coordinate my shopping needs so I could shop on Wednesday. Usually I ran out of food sooner than that.

But that didn't mean I couldn't plan and match up the coupons I had to this week's sales. I scrolled through the sales circular of the other grocery store than the IGA I'd visited yesterday. I preferred the national chain store over the IGA, especially since it turned out the IGA didn't double coupons anymore. When I had money, I was a big believer in supporting local business. Now that I was broke, I couldn't justify paying more for local when the chain stores had significantly better deals.

While the phone apps for checking sales and saving digital coupons were convenient, it was tedious after awhile to work with such a small screen. Unfortunately, I didn't have a computer anymore since it died the blue screen of death shortly after arriving back in Jefferson Grove. I didn't have the money for the repair or to buy a new one. This put me at another coupon disadvantage in that I couldn't print online coupons. I considered using the library's computers, but with printing costs of ten cents a page, the coupons had to be great deals to make it worth the expense.

I'd just matched a fifty cents off shampoo coupon with the sales price of $1.49 when my phone rang. That was another annoyance of not having a computer. I couldn't multitask online activities and phone calls.

The caller ID indicated it was Lani.

"Hey, Lani."

"Hey, girl. How's it going today after yesterday's excitement?"

"Everything is back to normal. Aunt Rose didn't kick me out, yet. Actually, she was disappointed when I told her I didn't think AJ killed Mr. Cullen. She was organizing a group to pay his legal fees."

"Is she sick?"

I laughed. "It's always hard to tell."

"So, have you talked to him today?"

"Who?"

"Ugh. AJ, you dummy. He must have checked on you by now."

"No. He had Bull call and check on me."

"So call him. What are you waiting for?"

Lani, like most women I knew, always got into matchmaker mode when the possibility of romance arose.

"He's got a lot going on now. He doesn't need me pestering him."

"I bet he could use a friend."

That was true. I'd been so focused on my lousy day yesterday, I hadn't considered his situation. I supposed he was more used to being looked at with sideways glances than I was. Everyone from Cooters Hollow was looked on with suspicion. Still, even if it was the norm, it couldn't be fun. So, maybe for once, I could help him. I didn't need to go to work until dinnertime, so I had some time.

"I don't have his number."

Lani made a noise that usually went along with an eye roll. "Check the phonebook. I'm sure the Jefferson Lake resident association has that information on their website too."

"Yeah, okay. I'll get in touch with him."

"Good. Then call and tell me all about it. I've gotta run. Break is over and I've got a stack of reports to file."

"Talk to you later." I hung up with Lani, opened a new browser on my phone and searched how I could find AJ.

It took a little research, but I eventually found an old online directory for the lake. Lucky for me, his number and address were listed. I was getting ready to call when I decided I'd visit instead. It would get me out of the house and have the added benefit of being able to see AJ in person again. I noted the address, adding it to my phone in case I needed GPS help getting there.

"Where are you running off to?" Aunt Rose's tone suggested I was sneaking out.

I suppose I was. "I'm going to visit a friend at Jefferson Lake."

Aunt Rose's hands fisted on her hips. "Is this friend AJ Devlin?"

"Yes."

"Just because I'm glad he killed that louse Joseph Cullen doesn't mean I like him. Even with your father and brother's crimes sullying your good name, you're still too good for him."

"He's just a friend."

"Um hmm." Aunt Rose's tone suggested she didn't believe me.

"Maybe I can find out for sure if he killed Mr. Cullen." Like I'd come out and ask him, but Aunt Rose didn't know I wouldn't.

"You think he'd tell you?"

"I don't know." Probably not.

"Harrumph." Aunt Rose turned and went back to the kitchen.

I decided that meant the conversation was over.

SIX

I WENT TO the car and smiled when it started right up. "Thank you, AJ and Bull." I pulled onto the road and drove to the main road through Jefferson Grove. Near the edge of town, I took the right that headed up the mountains on the eastern side of the valley. The two-lane road was scenic and often packed during the fall when the leaves glowed orange, yellow and red. But today it was hot, and when the Brown Bomber started losing power and grunting like an old man, I wondered if maybe I was asking too much of it. I turned off the air-conditioning, which helped a little. But within minutes, sweat dripped between my breasts. My clothes clung to me, and not in a wet T-shirt contest sort of way, but like a gross uncomfortable way. But the Brown Bomber and I lumbered up the road.

"Come on, girl. You can do it." I patted the dashboard like my brother, Will, used to do with his BMW convertible, although his car didn't need the encouragement. I think he was just in love with it. Thinking of Will reminded me I was due for a visit with him and my father.

Near the summit, I took a right, heading along the ridge until reaching the main road to the lake. Like Jefferson Grove, Jefferson Lake sat in a valley, although smaller. There was a little welcome house at the entrance, but it wasn't manned. Anyone could come and go, making it a popular place for Jefferson Grove teens who wanted to get away.

AJ's home was on the other side of the lake. The area was less populated since the road wasn't paved in that section. There was a grouping of mailboxes where the paved road and mail service ended. I tried to remember if it had rained recently, which could make dirt roads a problem for the Brown Bomber. But the road looked dry and even fairly rut-free. There was a small wooden plaque with the lot number, but no sign of AJ's house. Knowing it was dangerous to show up unannounced… what if he was entertaining someone… I made my way down the gravel length of his drive. I came around a bend and a small wooden home came into view, sitting on the edge of the lake. The house needed help, which AJ must be working on if the amount of debris and wood piled in the yard was any indication. Even so, I sucked in a breath at the beauty of the location. It was a long way from Cooters Hollow.

Tears watered my eyes as pride in his accomplishment filled me. He'd set his mind to getting out and he had. Not many Hollow residents could say that. At least not without being in a body bag or handcuffs. I'd set goals, but nothing as lofty as his. Nothing that could so significantly change my life. I'd just spent six weeks groveling for a job that had me nearly working for a lecher bail bondsman and his witch wife.

All of a sudden, I felt foolish for feeling sorry for myself. I had so many opportunities growing up and, while my father's actions had resulted in my losing the life I knew, I still had more than AJ had growing up in the Hollow.

I parked the Brown Bomber, setting the brake and

crossing my fingers it would hold and the car wouldn't
roll down into the lake. As I approached the house, I
saw his door was open. The only thing keeping the bugs
out was the screened door. But that didn't keep the heat
and humidity out and was an indication AJ didn't have
air-conditioning. I couldn't stop the groan as I tugged
at the shirt plastered by perspiration to my skin.

I heard Radio Head playing in the background, loud
enough I wondered if he'd hear me. I knocked, waited,
sweated and knocked again.

"Hello?"

A clackity sound grew, coming closer and closer,
until I saw a beast charging for the door.

"Holy…" I stepped back, knowing the little alumi-
num screen door wouldn't keep the huge beast contained. But it stopped, its huge nose pressing against
the screen, making it bow outward. Slowly I backed
away, glancing toward the Brown Bomber to see how
far I had to go and praying the piddly screen door would
contain him.

The beast barked. It was a dog? I turned back just in
time to hear a click, and the screen door swung open.
A dog that could open doors. I only had a moment to
marvel at the feat, and then I realized he was lumbering
toward me again. A huge, charcoal gray dog that I could
probably ride. And could likely eat me in a single gulp.

"Nice doggy." I continued to back away, fighting the
urge to run. I'd heard running from animals was bad,
but it sure went against instinct. There was no way I
was outrunning this guy.

Oh God, Oh God. He was nearly upon me so I
ducked. I made myself as small as possible.

His nose poked at me.

"I don't taste good."

He didn't seem to believe me because a tongue the size of my arm lapped at me.

"Dutch. Sit."

I heard a thump and turned my head just enough to see the beast had sat next to me. Why hadn't the guy said, "Come?"

"Sophie?"

I craned my head a little more. "AJ?"

He laughed. I wanted to punch him for that, but his dog still looked hungry.

"Sophie, meet Dutch. Dutch, this is Sophie." AJ petted the dog. "Her name is short for Duchess. She won't hurt you."

I gave him my best dubious smirk, which I hoped covered up the shaking in my legs as I stood. Even sitting, Dutch could look me in the eyes. She waggled her head and then licked me again.

"Eww." I wiped my face.

"Don't you like dogs?"

"I like 'em fine when they're not chasing or tasting me." I looked Dutch straight in the eyes. "I'm not dinner."

AJ laughed.

"Are you sure she's a dog?"

"She's a Great Dane. Gorgeous, isn't she? Come on inside." AJ draped an arm around my shoulders and guided me toward the front door. I kept one eye on Dutch the whole way.

AJ's home was as hot inside as it was outside. Even with the ceiling and freestanding fans, the room was scorching. While he got me a cold glass of water, I sat in the fabric-covered chair, deciding the leather couch, while looking cool, would probably stick to my sweaty legs. Or I'd slide off. Dutch lay at the base of the chair, crowding my feet. My only option was to use her like an ottoman. All of a sudden, I wished I'd worn sneakers instead of flip-flops, to cover my exposed feet.

"Dutch likes you." AJ handed me a glass of water.

"Hmm." I eyed Dutch, making sure she wasn't thinking of feasting on my toes.

"Then again, she likes everyone."

I arched a brow at AJ. "Some guard dog."

With a grin, AJ sat on the couch. "Her size scares most people."

I couldn't argue with that.

AJ's smile turned sheepish. "I'm sorry about yesterday."

"To be honest, the way my life has been going, I'm lucky I wasn't arrested sooner." I sipped the water and savored the liquid as it cooled my insides.

His eyes narrowed. "You were arrested?"

I shook my head. "No. Just questioned."

He sat back, relief showing in his features.

"Were you?"

He shook his head. "But I expect it's only a matter of time."

"Well, if it makes you feel any better, my aunt Rose is willing to take up a collection to pay your legal expenses if you're arrested."

AJ's brows drew together and his lips quirked to the side. "Did Rose have a stroke? She's not known for… kindness."

"Shocked me too. But apparently she hates Joseph Cullen more than anything else."

"Really? Why?"

I remembered that AJ had been gone from the area for awhile too. "I don't know the details, but Aunt Rose said he bought up all my father's properties, raised rents, and evicted people."

"The police asked me about drugs they think he flies in."

"I heard that too."

AJ shook his head. "Once from the Hollow…"

"What do you mean?"

"There's a lot of drugs in the Hollow and since I grew up there, I must be involved."

"That's not the story the investigator was telling me. He suggested I orchestrated the murder to retaliate because apparently, Cullen outed my dad to the Feds. They think I hired you to kill him."

"I didn't kill him."

I was caught off guard by his statement. There was a vehemence behind it. As if it was important I believed him. "I didn't think you did."

An awkward silence filled the air. He stared at me like he was waiting for me to say something. Or maybe he was just wondering why I was there.

"I just wanted to make sure everything was alright."

"Well, the sheriff's investigators don't want me to go anywhere, which will make it hard to work, but I'm safe at the moment."

"It sounds like a lot of other people didn't like him." But I knew what put the focus on AJ wasn't motive, because besides repossessing his plane, there wasn't one. His problem was timing. Whoever killed Cullen did it not long after AJ left him. But there had to be someone else at the airport to know AJ and Cullen argued, because the investigator already knew that when he questioned me. Maybe that person was the killer.

"Did they ask you about a golf club?"

His brows furrowed. "They tried. I asked for a lawyer before we got too far into the interrogation. But that was weird. Who brings a golf club to kill someone?"

"I thought the same thing. Lani said he was hit and then choked with a club."

AJ was silent for a moment. "They must have the club. Otherwise, how would they know that?"

"They do. The investigator showed me a picture. It's the same brand my father owned." That was when I realized the club could actually exonerate us. "Since they have the club, they have to know you didn't do it. Your prints would have been on it, right?"

AJ shook his head. "I don't know. Maybe there were no prints."

That had to be the case. Otherwise, why would the cops still have their sights on him?

"Hopefully my lawyer will be able to keep me out of jail."

Ah, Becca. The old girlfriend. "I guess it's good you called her."

"Actually, I called Bull so he could come get you. I asked him to call her."

"Thank you for thinking of me."

His head tilted to the side. "Of course. I promised I'd get you home."

Sweat dripped down my spine. "Don't you have air-conditioning?"

"It's broken."

"It seems like that would be the first thing to fix."

He shook his head. "In March, when I bought it,

I didn't need air-conditioning. I was going to use the money from this repo to fix it. But now, I guess I'll just have to be hot."

He was hot. But that wasn't what he meant.

"Do repos pay a lot?"

"Yes."

I waited for him to say more, but he simply eyed me as he sipped from his water.

"Hello?" A feminine voice drifted through the doorway.

AJ looked and then stood. "Becca." He went to the door to let her in. I stayed where I was, mostly because Dutch was sleeping and I remembered hearing you were supposed to let sleeping dogs lie.

"God, it's too hot to leave the doors open, AJ." Becca stepped in, looking rich and sophisticated, in a navy striped, sleeveless dress that hugged ample curves with sleek, dark hair that wisped over her shoulders.

My short hair was sticking to my neck and forehead, but hers wasn't. How did she manage that?

"Oh. Hi." She stopped short when she saw me.

"Becca Thoroux this is Sophie Parker. Soph, this is my lawyer Becca."

"Hi." I waved. "I'd get up but—" I pointed to Dutch, who raised her head, glancing at Becca, sniffed and then put her head back down.

"Hello." Becca smiled, but her sharp eyes had a disapproving glare. I'd never met her before, so I wasn't sure why she apparently didn't like me. Was it because of AJ? Bull said they'd been an item once, so maybe she didn't like that he was spending time with another woman. Or maybe she'd heard about my notorious family. "We had an appointment."

"Yes. Sophie was with me yesterday, so she stopped in to make sure I was okay. You want some water?"

Becca tossed her hair back as she shook her head. "No." She reached into her bag and pulled out a bottle of expensive water I'd only seen when I lived in New York. Not that Jefferson Grove didn't have bottled water, but it didn't have much variety in brands and certainly not expensive ones.

AJ motioned for Becca to sit as he took a seat on the couch.

"We should meet alone."

I couldn't tell if she wanted to be alone for work or play or both.

"You probably want to talk to Sophie too. She was at the airport with me."

Becca glanced at me. This time suspicion laced her eyes. "Yes. At some point I will. But right now, I need to talk with you, alone."

I looked at Dutch and tentatively tapped. Her large head lifted and dark soulful eyes stared back.

"Gotta go, Dutch."

I didn't know if dogs shrugged, but it looked to me like Dutch did as she slowly heaved her massive body up and went to lay in front of a fan.

I stood. "Let me know if you need anything."

"Ah, just one thing," Becca said as I made my way to the door.

"Yeah?"

"Well… AJ is in a precarious situation. There's no evidence he committed this crime, but circumstances and appearances can hurt him."

My eyes narrowed at her emphasis on the word appearances. "Okay?"

"It's just with your family history, it wouldn't be good for him to be associated with—"

"Becca." AJ's sharp voice had both Becca and me flinching.

"I know it sounds bad." She turned her attention to me. "And I don't mean to be rude, but you have to know what I'm talking about."

"Yeah, I know." I was about to say "see ya around, AJ" then I remembered, I wasn't supposed to. Not sure what to say, I turned and hurried out the door. You'd think I'd be used to the embarrassment and humiliation by now. I was nearly to my car when I heard the screen door squeak open.

"Hey, Soph."

I stopped and took a breath to steel myself before turning.

"I'm sorry about that."

I waved his comment away, even though it hurt. "Don't worry. She's not the first person to think I'm not good to have around. At least she was nicer about it." I started toward my car again.

"Hey." AJ wrapped his fingers around my arm to stop me.

I looked at his fingers and then up into his crystal-line blue eyes.

"I like your kind."

My initial thought was how badly I wanted to lean into him for support. His words and kind eyes were so rare in my life now, I wanted to grab on to them like a life raft. The problem, of course, was that doing so would only make things worse. I didn't like it, but Becca was right. Sergeant Scowl had already suggested I was part of the murder too. It was best for both AJ and me to stay apart.

"I've gotta get to work." I withdrew my arm.

He nodded and helped me into my car. He looked like he might say something more, but instead, he shut my door. He stood with his hands on his hips. I couldn't read the expression on his face, and I thought about asking him about it. But then I remembered it wouldn't matter because I wasn't allowed to see him. I gave a little wave, started the Brown Bomber and slowly pulled away.

Since the ride was downhill, I was able to turn on the AC. It took several minutes for the air-conditioning to make any dent in my overheated and sweaty body, but by the time the Brown Bomber and I reached the outskirts of Jefferson Grove, my clothes weren't sticking to me anymore. But I was still uncomfortable.

During the drive, I started out annoyed at Becca warning me away from AJ. I finally had one more friendly face in my life, and now I couldn't see him. Then I reviewed my interview at the police station and realized her concern was probably justified. It wasn't just that I came from a family of criminals. It was that my father went to jail because of Joseph Cullen. Now Joseph was dead and I'd been in the vicinity when he was killed. Why hadn't the investigator pushed me on that more? Of course, it was still early in the investigation. I knew from the forensic shows I watched with Aunt Rose there was still a lot of investigating the sheriff's office would be doing. I wondered how long before they showed up at Aunt Rose's looking for me.

The question was answered as I opened the door to my aunt's house just as a dark SUV parked at the curb. Sergeant Scowl stepped out, along with another man, who looked familiar but I couldn't place. I debated whether or not to go in and pretend I didn't see him. But then I considered Aunt Rose wasn't going to like the cops coming to interrogate me. Then again, if anyone could intimidate a cop, it would be Aunt Rose. She'd been in Jefferson Grove all her life. She knew everyone and their history. It might be fun to see what embarrassing story she'd bring up about Sergeant Scowl.

"Sophie, if my electric bill goes up, you're paying for it. There's no need for us to cool the entire world."

"There's a sheriff's deputy coming up the walk."

"What?" Aunt Rose's chair squeaked, which meant she was getting up. Within seconds, she was at the door, squinting to see who was coming. "Is that you, Lawson?"

Sergeant Scowl rolled his shoulders. "Yes, ma'am, Ms. Rose."

"Good Lord, they made you a sheriff's deputy? After all you did?"

I turned my attention to him, curious as to his illegal antics.

"I was young then." He stepped up onto the front stoop. "This is Deputy Taylor. He's an investigator at the Jefferson County Sherriff's office."

I cocked my head to the side. "Ethan Taylor?"

Deputy Taylor smiled. "Yes, you remember."

I remembered an awkward, gawky, pimply classmate from high school. This Ethan Taylor was the opposite of that. He was the epitome of the ugly duckling turning into a beautiful, or handsome, swan. The frizzy dishwater-colored hair I remembered from high school was now short and styled. Gone were the too-big-for-his-face glasses, so now I could see just how chocolatey brown his eyes were. Ethan had been the only person I ever knew who had braces all four years of high school. Those were gone now too, giving him a friendly smile that made me feel safe and wishing he could be my interrogator, instead of Sergeant Scowl.

Before I could affirm that I remembered Ethan, Sergeant Scowl interrupted. "I've come to talk to Ms. Parker."

"I'm Ms. Parker." Aunt Rose stood at the door, with her hands on her hips.

"I meant Ms. Sophie Parker."

"Why? She's a good girl."

My head swung around so fast to look at Aunt Rose it was a miracle it didn't fly off my shoulders. I didn't remember her ever saying anything nice about me.

"It has to do with an incident at the airport yesterday."

"Joseph Cullen had it comin', if you ask me."

I winced because her comment could be construed as justifying my killing him. Or asking AJ to do it, which I guessed was going to be his approach.

"Even so, vigilantism can't be tolerated."

"Huh, look at you using that big word. I remember when you didn't have the good sense God gave a goose."

I bit my lip to keep from snickering. Deputy Taylor looked down and away, but I saw the upward curve of his lips.

"Aunt Rose, maybe we should invite them in. Or I could talk to him out here. I'll close the door." As fun as it was to see her pick at the investigator and his once lack of intelligence, I didn't need her insulting him if he thought I was a suspect.

"Well, come on in then. I suppose I should offer you some tea."

"That's alright, Ms. Rose. We won't be here long."

I glanced at the deputy before stepping inside. Why did he think he wouldn't be here long? Because he didn't have much to ask? Or because he was planning to arrest me and take me to jail? He and Deputy Taylor followed us into the little living area decorated with floral furniture and enough knickknacks to fill a curio store. At least she didn't cover the furniture with plastic like some of her card buddies did. I think that was because she never had children and as a result, no grandchildren to mess it up.

Aunt Rose sat in her chair, while I took one across from her. Deputy Taylor sat on the couch, while Sergeant Scowl remained standing.

"You sure you don't want tea?"

"No, ma'am, but thank you."

"So what's this all about?"

"I was hoping we could talk to Ms. Sophie alone?"

"Why? You gonna ask her on a date?" Aunt Rose turned her attention to me. "Could do worse. He's certainly better than AJ Devlin."

I avoided making a gagging sound, but it was hard.

The sergeant blushed, which made me want to gag more. "No, ma'am."

"You're not married. That wackadoodle wife of yours ran off, didn't she?"

Now I was starting to feel sorry for him, and I didn't want to feel sorry for him. "Why are you here, Sergeant Sc... Davis?"

He looked relieved when he turned his attention to

me. "I wanted to go over some of the statements you made yesterday."

"Alright."

"You said you ran into Mr. Devlin at the IGA and he invited you to go flying with him. That's why you were at the airport."

"That's right."

"When was the last time you talked to Mr. Devlin before yesterday?"

"The summer I graduated from high school."

Sergeant Davis frowned, his piercing dark eyes studying me as if he had some sort of lying radar. I wasn't lying. But still, I had to work to resist the urge to squirm under his dark gaze.

"That was the last time?"

"Yes. He left for the military and I went to college."

"What about visits home?"

"I came home a few times in college, but I never saw him. Until a few weeks ago, I hadn't been home in years."

"Why is that?"

You know why, you meanie. "Well, my father was having some legal issues and he thought it was better I stayed away."

"What do you know about your father's legal issues?"

I sighed. "Look, Sergeant Davis, let me make this easy. I had no idea what my father was doing or did until the FBI explained it to me in their interrogation of me."

"Did you know Mr. Cullen is the one that called the feds?"

"Not until you told me yesterday."

He stared at me. I shrugged, trying to act nonchalant about it all.

"Why are you asking about her daddy?" Aunt Rose leaned forward in her chair. "That's all said and done with. He's doing his time."

"He thinks Mr. Cullen's death could be some sort of revenge for turning Dad in."

"Pah!" Aunt Rose waved that idea away with a boney hand. "He's in jail, for one. And two, he's happy to steal your money, but he's not a murderer."

"Not him, Aunt Rose. Or at least not him directly."

"What do you mean, girl? Spit it out."

"He thinks either Dad, or maybe just me alone, wanted Mr. Cullen dead and had AJ kill him. Isn't that right, Sergeant Davis?"

"It's a theory."

"Well, you *don't* have the good sense God gave a goose after all if you believe that. Sophie and her family have some issues, but they're not killers. You'll just have to come up with another theory."

"There are no other theories." His hard, menacing gaze made my heart jump. For the first time, I thought I might be going to jail for something I didn't do. My stomach pitched and I willed myself not to be sick. I turned my attention to Deputy Taylor. His smile was apologetic, not reassuring.

"Well, let me help you out. How about that nasty no-good wife of his? Maggie Cullen. Or how about Ben Samuels? He's been telling everyone who'd listen how he'd like to string Cullen up by the balls."

"The evidence doesn't point to them. Your niece and AJ Devlin were the only ones at the airport at the time of Mr. Cullen's death."

"That's not true." The murderer was there, although, as I thought about it, I hadn't seen anyone else, except

Bull, but he never went in the office and was on the road before we took off in the plane. "There had to be other people, mechanics and whoever works there." And then I remembered. "What about the truck? Or the vehicle that pulled up just after we left?"

Both Sergeant Scowl and Taylor looked at me. "What truck?" they asked in unison.

"The one parked out behind the airport. You know, along that back road."

"What did it look like?"

Well, crap. I wasn't paying attention. "Just a regular truck. Black, I guess. The one that drove up as we flew over was dark too. A sedan. Or maybe an SUV, I couldn't tell from the sky."

"You guess? Are you sure you saw a truck?" Sergeant Scowl sure could be rude.

"Yes. But I didn't know there was going to be a murder, so I didn't take in every detail. I just know there was a truck parked behind Mr. Cullen's red Audi."

"How did you know he had a red Audi?"

Inwardly I winced, knowing I'd put my foot in it again. Outwardly, I blinked and tried to act calm. "Who else's would it be?"

Sergeant Scowl rolled his eyes, while Deputy Taylor hid his amusement behind a cough.

"Devlin told you, didn't he?"

He did, and I knew that would be bad for AJ. Why did he know it was Cullen's car?

"Car shmar." Aunt Rose waved a dismissive hand. "Why aren't you out looking for these other vehicles?"

"We would, if we had descriptions."

I frowned. Should I tell him to ask AJ or Bull? They might have been paying more attention than me. Or would my mentioning it get them in more trouble? Why didn't AJ mention it to them during his interview? Mostly likely because it hadn't been important enough to remember. Or he'd already asked for a lawyer by then.

"Can we take a look around?" Sergeant Scowl's eyes scanned the small living room.

"Here?" Aunt Rose asked.

He nodded.

"What for?"

"Just to look."

I couldn't decide if I was scared to death or annoyed. I knew I didn't kill Cullen, and I was getting irritated Sergeant Scowl kept asking me questions when clearly he didn't like or believe the answers. Still, who knew what they'd find that they'd construe into some sort of conspiracy?

"I'm not gonna let you go snooping through my house. Didn't your mama teach you any manners?"

Sergeant Scowl inhaled a deep breath. "I don't want to snoop into your business, Ms. Rose. I'm here on an official murder investigation."

"Sophie didn't kill no one."

"Maybe we should let him look."

"We've got a warrant." Deputy Taylor handed it to Aunt Rose.

Now I was scared. I couldn't stop the shake in my knees or my voice. "What are you looking for?" But then it came to me. The golf clubs.

"You can sit right there, Ms. Rose. It won't take but a few minutes." Sergeant Scowl ignored my questions.

The house wasn't that big, so it only took them a few minutes to walk through each room.

"Which is your room, Ms. Parker?"

Deciding he was talking to me, I pointed up the hall. "First room on the right."

Deputy Taylor frowned. "There isn't much in there."

"I don't have much. I told Deputy Davis that yesterday."

"Do you have a shed, Ms. Rose?"

"Just a small one. You can look, but close it up tight."

"Wait here, Taylor." Sergeant Scowl headed out the back door to the tiny shed barely big enough to hold the push mower the neighbor boy used to cut Rose's grass. He came back in a few minutes later.

"I told you, I don't have any golf clubs."

"What makes you think that's what we're looking for?" Deputy Taylor asked.

"Because Sergeant Scow… Davis asked me about them yesterday. And I heard that's how he was killed. Did you look in the trunk of Cullen's car? That's where he'd keep them if not at his house."

"We know how to do our job, Ms. Parker." Sergeant Scowl's voice lowered, a sure sign I was getting on his last nerve.

"Are you gonna arrest her?" Aunt Rose's voice cackled with annoyance.

"Not today."

"That's because you don't have evidence. I watch *CSI*." Aunt Rose waggled her finger at him. "I know my rights. I can ask you to go."

Sergeant Davis sighed. "Yes, ma'am." He nodded toward Deputy Taylor and then turned his cop eyes on me. "We'll talk again."

"Not without a lawyer you won't." Aunt Rose heaved herself out of her chair.

He shrugged and headed to the door.

"I never liked him." Aunt Rose walked to the door, looking out the side window as the detectives made their way to the car.

"I think he just wants to make me nervous." At least that was what I hoped. There was no evidence against me because I didn't do it. But people went to jail for stuff they didn't do all the time.

"He's a putz." Aunt Rose turned toward me. "If he does ask you out, Sophie, tell him no."

SEVEN

I WAS HAVING a heart attack. Either that or a panic attack. It was probably the latter. What else could be my response to the insinuation I was involved in murder?

I retired to my room, not wanting to give Aunt Rose time to hassle me about the investigators' visit. But alone, my brain ruminated on the fact Sergeant Scowl and Deputy Taylor seriously thought I was a murderer. Why else would they be searching my home and scrutinizing my statement? I'd been naively thinking I'd be okay since I didn't kill Mr. Cullen, nor did I have AJ kill him. Now I was beginning to see the truth wasn't going to set me free.

I was lucky Aunt Rose didn't put any weight on Sergeant Scowl's having me on his list of suspects. Once she did, I'd be homeless. Where would I go? Lani's? Her husband was a cop. I couldn't go there without causing them problems. Aggie and Gwen from my coupon group might be sympathetic, but they couldn't take me in without hurting their standing in the community. AJ wasn't allowed to see me. Where did Bull live?

The best solution was one that got me off the suspect list. For that, I needed advice and the only person I could think to contact was Lani. She worked for the sheriff's department so surely she could help me. I picked up my phone, hesitating before calling. Maybe it was wrong to ask her for information about my case.

Maybe she'd end up distancing herself from me because it was possible our friendship could hurt her job. It wasn't fair to put her in that situation.

On the other hand, my life was on the line. Well, not my life, but my freedom for sure. As bad as living with Aunt Rose could be, it was a million times better than prison. I visited my dad and Will at least once a month, and while my father was always able to make the best of his circumstances, I could see it was taking a toll on him. And he was in a cushy prison for twelve years, serving time for a white collar crime. Certainly, murderers had it worse. Virginia was a capital punishment state. A cold chill slid down my spine as that sunk in. Turned out my life *was* on the line. I called Lani's cell phone.

"Hey, girl. Got news about AJ?" Lani's cheerful tone suggested she didn't know the investigators had just been here.

"Hi, Lan. Are you busy?"

"Nah. They've got me organizing old files in the basement. What's up?"

"I guess that means you don't know my home was just searched."

"What!"

"I think they were looking for golf clubs to match the one at the scene of Cullen's murder."

"As if you'd be dumb enough to keep them after using one in a murder."

"I hope no one can hear you." I didn't need the cops thinking I was smart enough to get rid of evidence.

"Are you kidding? Down here it's just me and the cockroaches."

"I think I'm in trouble. Is there anything you know about this case you can help me with?"

There was a pause and I knew the answer was no. "You know I would, but that would get me in trouble. It might even be illegal."

"Any tips based on a rhetorical situation in which your friend is accused of murder?"

"Honey, get a lawyer."

I sagged against the couch, pinching the bridge of my nose with my thumb and forefinger as if that would stop the tension headache from spreading. "I can't afford a lawyer."

"Look, if they haven't arrested you, that means they don't have enough to bring you in. That's a good sign."

I let out a sigh. "It feels like it's just a matter of time."

"What about AJ?"

"I don't know. I saw him earlier today and he feels like I do."

"My advice is act normal. You didn't kill Mr. Cullen, so eventually they'll begin looking elsewhere."

I wanted to believe that, but I couldn't afford to put my life in the hands of a sheriff's investigator who thought I was guilty. I wondered what Ethan Taylor thought. "Do you remember Ethan Taylor?"

"Oh yeah. He's an investigator here now. Talk about filling out, eh? Did he visit you too?"

I nodded and then remembered Lani couldn't see me. "Yes. I thought he left town after high school."

"He did. He worked in vice in Richmond for awhile, but when his folks started to decline, he moved back. He's been here about a year. They've been hoping that, with his experience, he'll be able to put a stop to the increase in drugs in the area. In fact, he's the one who was investigating Mr. Cullen."

"If he's working the case, he'd have other suspects in the drug world, wouldn't he?"

"I'd think so, but Davis is the lead and he's got more seniority."

Just my luck.

"Hey, you working tonight or do you want to come over and binge watch *Once Upon a Time* with me?"

"I wish I could but I'm working."

"Too bad."

"Yeah, too bad." But a part of me wondered if maybe I should call in sick and spend time with Lani. It was possible my days as a free woman were numbered.

FOR THE FIRST time since being hired, I looked forward to going to work at the Booty Burgo. Or to be more accurate, I looked forward to the distraction working would allow. But as I sat in the Brown Bomber in the Booty Burgo parking lot, my heart continued to pound so fiercely it was a wonder it didn't pop out of my chest. Even worse was the sense I would start hyperventilating because I was unable to take a deep breath to calm it.

I'd handled the whole situation well at Aunt Rose's, but afterward, I felt like the world was crashing down around me. Even the drive to work hadn't stopped the panic from making my heart race. By the time I arrived, all the worry and fear had balled into my chest, threatening to crush me or maybe explode. Deciding that occupying my mind with activity was the best medicine, I forced myself to push my current fears aside and focus on being the best pirate wench I could be.

One good thing—probably the only good thing—

about the Booty Burgo was it was located on the northern most part of town, right off the main highway into the Blue Ridge mountains. At least half of the patrons were tourists, enjoying the mountain scenery and the outdoor activities. The other half were Jefferson Grove and surrounding township residents who wanted to get away from the prying eyes of small town living. Sort of like Vegas—what happened at the Booty Burgo, stayed at the Booty Burgo. Not that much happened, but if it did, it didn't get back to town. Usually. Some waitresses who didn't get the tips they thought they deserved might let slip about clandestine meetings between a man and a woman who wasn't his wife.

I inhaled as deep as I could and readied to exit the car when there was a knock on my window. My heart jumped into my throat and stuttered to a stop. Deputy Taylor stared at me. My fingers shook as I opened my door. By now, the car was sauna-like and since I had to work, it didn't make sense to simply roll down the window.

He stepped back, pulling the door open for me. "I'm sorry. I didn't mean to startle you."

On jelly legs, I stepped out of the car. "Are you arresting me?"

His head jerked back in surprise. Then he laughed. "No, Sophie. I'm sorry."

I didn't think it was funny, but since he said he wasn't about to cuff me in my wench outfit in front of the Booty Burgo, I let it go. "You have more questions for me?"

He shook his head, his eyes soft and apologetic. "No. I'm off duty." His head tilted down and he shifted side

to side on his feet. Finally, he lifted his head. "I just…
well…wanted to check on you."

Huh?

"I know it has to be hard living back here after all
that happened with your family."

"Uh huh." Why did he care?

"You were always nice to me in school, Sophie. I
just… I thought you could use a friendly face." He
shifted again.

Ethan and I shared several classes through high
school, mostly honors and a few AP courses. We weren't
friends, but we were friendly. We chatted on occasion
in class and sometimes compared notes. I never teased
him or avoided him like many other students had, but
neither did I go out of my way to be his friend. I never
sat with him at lunch nor invited him over to study or
to my social functions.

"Thank you."

He looked toward the Booty Burgo and then back
at me.

Before he could ask, I said, "It's the only place
around here willing to hire me."

He nodded. "I don't want to keep you from work.
Maybe we could get some coffee sometime."

I liked that idea. I needed all the friends I could get,
except… "Is that allowed? I mean, I think Sergeant
Scow… Davis thinks I'm guilty."

Ethan shrugged. "We just can't discuss the case."

I wasn't sure what else there would be to talk about
because, except for my job and couponing, being involved in a murder investigation was about all that was
going on in my life. Still, it was sweet of him to check
on me. "You don't worry being seen with me will hurt

your reputation? I mean, now you're an investigator and you…well, you've changed." I didn't know how to say he'd gone from ugly duckling to handsome swan without offending him.

"It's true people don't avoid me anymore, but deep down, I'm still a nerd."

He didn't look like a nerd.

"Your circumstances have changed, but inside you're still smart, nice Sophie. I'd rather be your friend than theirs."

I bit my lip to keep from bawling. It was amazing what a few nice words could do to the emotions. "Thank you, Ethan. That's really sweet."

"So, coffee sometime?"

I nodded.

"I'll call you. It might be a few days, but I'll call."

I watched as he got in his car and drove away. I was grateful he went out of his way to find me and offer his friendship. I couldn't imagine Sergeant Scowl would approve. Surely there had to be rules about befriending murder suspects. My stomach did a slow roll as I wondered if maybe Ethan's intentions weren't all friendly. Maybe he was trying to befriend me as part of the investigation. Was that legal? To make friends with someone simply to investigate them? Of course it was. That was what undercover work involved. Now the tears threatening to ruin my cheap mascara were of disappointment.

"Stop your blubbering." I used the words Aunt Rose would. And she was right. Getting sad wouldn't change anything. I blew out a breath. "This too shall pass." That was what my father told me. It would be nice if it passed quicker and into something better, because I felt like I was in a freefall into the pit of despair.

I stepped into the cool air and dark ambiance of the restaurant. The coolest thing about the Booty Burgo was that the bar looked like a pirate ship. The rest of the place looked like a Caribbean hurricane had hit, with Jolly Roger flags, gold coins and jewels, old rum bottles and barrels and swords strewn willy-nilly on the walls. But, of course, most of the people who came to the Booty Burgo were too distracted by the wenches to notice a poor decorating job.

What was really odd to me was how ridiculous our uniforms were, yet nobody laughed. The wenches wore white off-the-shoulder blouses, held up by a red with black striped corset and a short black skirt and black boots. The few men who worked there wore red and black striped pants, black boots and a pirate shirt that looked just like the one from the *Seinfeld* show. Only two people didn't wear a uniform: Kyle Dingle, the manager, because he was too important to demean himself, and Spike, the head bartender, because Kyle was too afraid to make him.

I passed the bar and headed to the back room, where the manager's office was located and logged in my start time. I took a deep breath and headed out to the floor to find out what section of the restaurant I'd be working tonight.

"Hey, Parker."

I turned toward Kyle, who was waving me toward the bar. Kyle was twenty-three, with a scrawny build and the face of a twelve year old. He overcompensated by acting like he was master of the universe. He was the epitome of a big fish in a small pond. He liked to lord his power over all the waitresses, but especially me because I wouldn't respond to his attempts to make me feel small. Usually his comments involved asking how I was smart enough to go to college, but too dumb to get my orders right. For the record, I only got my order wrong once, on the first day I worked there.

"Kyle."

"You're a college gal. Do you know how to mix drinks?"

"Absolutely," I lied.

"Good. You're with Spike tonight."

"Really?" I glanced at the bartender, a little thrill of excitement that I wouldn't be serving wench burgers running through me.

"Come on over, Parker." Spike winked and I think he knew I didn't know the first thing about mixing drinks. In some ways, Spike was like Bull, but instead of sporting a scary biker look, he exuded scary pirate, which might also be the reason Kyle didn't make him dress up. He didn't have to. He had a shaved head, a gold hoop earring and a dark, well-groomed beard with a dastardly moustache.

I stepped behind the counter and immediately looked for a cocktail recipe book.

"You're a virgin, aren't you?"

I gaped, too shocked to be offended.

He smirked. "A cocktail virgin."

I glanced over my shoulder to make sure Kyle wasn't lurking about. He was hassling Tina, a new waitress, over her uniform. "I can make rum and coke."

"I'll mix tonight. You serve beer, bottle and tap, and the wine and shots."

"Okay. Where is Rhonda or Jace?" I asked of the other bartenders.

"They ran off."

"Together?" Rhonda was old enough to be my mother, I thought. It was hard to tell because a life spent in the sun or a tanning bed made it difficult to judge her age. While her skin was orange leather, her hair was bleached white straw, except for the black streak along her part. Jace, on the other hand, wasn't much older than Kyle.

"That was my response. But, Jace will go wherever there's free sex and drugs, and Rhonda offered that in spades. They've got a little love nest up in the Hollow."

I laughed, and yet, it was sad. I really had to find a way out or I might end up forty-something years old running off with some kid.

"You play your cards right, maybe you can be a regular bartender."

That perked me up. "I wonder if I could ditch the wench uniform."

"I don't know." Spike's gaze raked up and down my body. "Could help with tips."

At least I wasn't having to dance. "Will you teach me to mix?"

"Yep, if you help me use that college degree you have in fairy tales to pick good stories for my little girl."

Spike had a daughter?

"Don't look surprised, Parker. A virile guy like me, it was bound to happen."

"I didn't know you were married or with someone."

"Nah. Her mom and I are quits, but I'm trying to be a good dad."

I'd always liked Spike, but now I liked him more. "I know lots of great kid stories."

"It's a deal."

Spike gave me a tour of the bar, showing me the

draft versus tap beer, rail versus call booze, and house wines, and gave me a quick tutorial on how to serve drinks, including which glasses to use for which drinks and how full to fill them. Fortunately, there were only two men at the bar and the waitress' orders were for beer, so I was able to practice before it got busy. But as 6:30 approached, business at the Booty Burgo picked up. I did my best, but I still had too much head on my beer and no idea what the difference was between an ale and a stout when asked by a young man celebrating his twenty-first birthday.

"You're twenty-one. Does it really matter?"

He grinned. "Gimme an ale."

I chose one that Spike had said was from a micro-brewery in Charlottesville and served it to him.

"Sophie?"

Oh geez. Sitting next to the birthday boy was Randy Danner, Vivie's husband. Although I'd seen him from afar, mostly sitting at the bar of the Booty Burgo, since returning to Jefferson Grove, I hadn't actually talked to him. "Hey, Randy."

"It's Randal."

"What?"

"I go by Randal now. It's more professional sounding. More grown-up." Even as he said it, his eyes drifted to my cleavage, enhanced by the corset of my wench waitress uniform.

"Uh huh. My eyes are up here, *Randy*."

He was still a perverted douche, apparently.

"I come here all the time and haven't seen you."

"I'm usually waitressing."

"I guess a college degree isn't worth what it used to be."

I rolled my eyes. "What can I get you?"

"How about a slippery nipple. Or sex on the beach." He grinned at his own cleverness.

"How about a cock in a vise?"

Birthday boy nearly did a spit take, so I handed him a napkin.

Randy winced and sat back. "Sam Adams."

"Coming right up." I blew out a breath and once again wondered how much longer I'd have to put up with the jokes and condescension. Maybe not long if I went to jail.

How come my life was getting worse? It didn't seem possible I could fall any lower. Still, as much as I hated the Vivies and Randys of the world, I was certain jail wouldn't be better. What I needed to do was figure out who killed Joseph Cullen so I could get AJ and me off the hook. But what did I know about sleuthing? Only what I saw on ID TV with Aunt Rose. I could be nosey and ask questions, but didn't crimes get solved by science? I stopped mid-popping the beer top off. Did the investigators have AJ's DNA from the scene of the crime? I shook my head and finished popping the top. If they had hard evidence, AJ would have been arrested.

I returned to Randy and handed him the beer and realized I could question him. Vivie, after all, had had an affair with Joseph Cullen. But I couldn't just blurt out a question like that. Could I?

"I heard you were with AJ Devlin when he killed Cullen." Randy took a swig of his beer.

Thank you for the opening, Randy. "I was with him when he repossessed Cullen's plane. But he didn't kill him."

"How do you know?"

Good question. "I just do. Lots of other people wanted him dead."

"You got that right." Randy pointed at me with his bottle.

"Do you know who could have killed him?"

"His wife, for one. Some of his business partners, maybe."

"I heard he slept with married women."

His eyes narrowed as they studied me. "So I've heard."

"That would make a husband mad, I'd think. I mean, if Vivie cheated on you—"

"If?" He let out a loud guffaw.

So he did know.

"I can't keep up with Vivie's sexcapades and I don't care to."

"You don't mind her sleeping with other people?"

He shook his head. "You've met Vivie, right? When she's with others, she's not with me and that suits me fine."

I looked at him. Really studied him to figure out how the high school football star lothario I dated for a week in high school could become an overweight married man that couldn't care less that his wife was cheating. "Why not get divorced if you're so miserable?"

He laughed derisively. "We can't afford it. With a mortgage, three kids doing eighty-seven different activities and Vivie's constant online shopping, we can barely stay afloat."

"So the couponing doesn't help?" Why was I bothering if I wasn't going to save any money?

"It helps save money, but she just spends it on manicures or whatever else she buys."

"Wouldn't your parents help out if you divorced?" Vivie and Randy both grew up in affluent families like mine.

"They're broke too. Bad investments." His brows lifted and he quirked his lips to the side, and I knew he meant my dad had stolen their money.

"I'm sorry."

He surprised me by shrugging. "I told them not to do it."

"You knew my dad was stealing money?"

"No, but I didn't feel right about his investment plans. Plus, you shouldn't ever combine money and friendship. I told mine and Vivie's parents that, but they didn't listen. They were sure their old friend Monty Parker was going to make them rich."

"They should've listened to you."

"What do I know? I'm just an accountant."

"You're here to work, not gossip, Parker." Spike snapped a cleaning towel at me.

"Sorry. I've gotta get to work."

Randy nodded and went back to his beer.

Turned out I was pretty good at bartending. Or maybe I just enjoyed it more than waitressing. Whatever the reason, the time went by quicker and more enjoyably. I was a couple hours into my shift when Spike pulled me aside.

"Parker, you know that guy down there?"

I looked to where Spike pointed toward the other end of the bar. I was expecting Randy, but instead, AJ nodded a hello to me.

"Yes."

"He wants to talk with you."

"Okay." I started toward AJ, but Spike stopped me.

"He wants to talk outside. You okay with that?"

I looked at Spike, who wore his protective face. "Yes. He's a friend."

"Take ten then."

"Okay. Thanks." I rounded the bar and headed to AJ.

He stood and followed me outside. "I thought you were a waitress."

"Tonight, I'm a bartender. If I'm lucky, I won't have to waitress again."

I followed him to his truck parked on the far side of the parking lot near the woods. It would have been creepy with the long shadows cast by the trees in the neon lights of the Booty Burgo sign, except I trusted AJ. He put the tailgate down. "Want to sit?"

All of a sudden, there was a scuffle against the metal of the bed and a huge figure loomed over me. I stepped back as AJ's dog rushed to the edge of the bed.

"Down, Dutch."

Dutch's butt plopped down, her tail thwapping on the bed of the truck. Her head bobbled in a way that looked happy, but maybe she was thinking, "Supper!"

AJ gave her head a scratch and gently pushed. "Lay down, Dutch."

She backed up a foot or so and then lay, taking up nearly the entire truck bed.

I eyed AJ warily.

He shrugged. "I couldn't leave her home alone. She likes you."

"Who watches her when you're gone?"

"Mrs. Kaczynski. She's an old widow who lives next door. She loves Dutch about as much as I do, so we share custody. Come on. Dutch is harmless. I'll help you up."

I needed the help because the tailgate was high enough I couldn't get on it without looking like a four year old climbing into a chair. AJ put his hands on my waist and lifted me up. Once I was settled, AJ hopped up to sit next to me. Dutch slipped her head between us, resting it on her paws.

AJ petted her head. "You're not going to get in trouble taking a break are you?"

"No." At least I didn't think so. Kyle might hassle me. He acted like he was the boss of the world, instead of just the Booty Burgo. I decided he was putting on airs because, despite the Ralph Lauren shirts with the huge Polo emblem to make himself look rich, the rumor was he lived with his mother in a trailer in one of the hollows.

"I just wanted to apologize for earlier. What Becca said about you staying away."

"It's okay. Perception is everything."

"You got that right." He knew it better than anyone. He'd been living it his entire life, being judged because he'd been born and raised in the Hollow.

"I just hope I haven't made it worse for you."

AJ shook his head. "I'm the one that would make it worse for you."

"I don't know about that. You wouldn't have a motive for killing Cullen without me."

"What?" AJ turned to look at me. "I don't have a motive. How would you give me one?"

"It's just like your lawyer said. I hired you to kill him in revenge for his turning in my dad to the feds."

His eyes narrowed. "No one believes that."

"Detectives Davis and Taylor questioned me about

it earlier. In fact, they searched the house looking for golf clubs. Did they search your place too?"

AJ turned away and swore. After a moment, he looked at me. "Yeah. I'm sorry, Sophie. This is my fault."

"No, it's not. It's whoever killed Cullen's fault. And bad luck."

He let out a breath. "I just wanted to check on you. Make sure you were alright. This wasn't at all how I hoped we'd connect again."

I remembered how Bull had said it wasn't a coincidence AJ showed up at the store. Although, how did he know I'd be there?

"I didn't know you knew I was back."

"I'd heard about it, but I don't go to Jefferson Grove if I don't have to."

"I don't blame you."

"But Patch got stuck on a repo in Chicago and Gordo asked if I'd get the one here. Since I was going to be in town, I thought I'd check on you."

"How'd you know where to find me?"

"I knew you were at your aunt's, but I wasn't about to go there."

I laughed. "Coward."

"I'm smart." He grinned. "I followed you to the bail bond place and then from there to the store."

"Just to check on me?" My heart felt full, not romantic gooey full, but someone-cares-about-me full. It was a reminder how alone I often felt.

He looked at me. "You seem surprised."

"I guess not. You always looked out for me in high school. You're like my guardian angel."

He snorted. "Some guardian angel. I've gotten you in trouble with the law."

"Hopefully the sheriff's department will look at all the other people who wanted Cullen dead too. From what I've learned so far, there were a lot of them."

AJ nodded. "But none were there minutes before he was killed."

"One was." And I was determined to find out who it was so I could clear both AJ's and my name.

AJ inhaled a breath and looked toward the sky. "It's not quite like when we sat in your backyard watching the stars."

"You remember that?"

He turned his head toward me, his brows drawn together in puzzlement. "Yes. You think I'd forget?"

I shrugged and watched my feet as they swung off the back of his truck. "I didn't think it was something that would stand out."

"Why not?"

I'd been pretty sure I was the only one who remembered every second of every minute I'd spent with AJ because I'd had a big crush on him. Even then, I knew it was one-sided. His interest in me was just as a friend. Especially after my brother had left for college. AJ was around to fill that protective big-brother role. "I just thought you were being nice."

"Nice is bad?"

I huffed out a breath. "No. What I mean is, I thought you were just spending time with me because you were trying to be nice, not because you really wanted to."

"Boy, I wasted a lot of time then."

I finally gained the nerve to look at him. His expression was a combination of annoyance and bafflement. I must have looked like the proverbial deer with my eyes caught in the headlights because I could only stare. What could I say to that? I opted to take the conversation elsewhere.

"At least you succeeded in your goals. You used to talk about all your plans to be a pilot and now you are."

His head seesawed side to side. "I guess. I didn't think I'd be back here."

"At least you're still flying. Still pursuing your goals." I felt my eyes burn with the threat of tears. How'd I get here? "Look at me. A college grad working as a wench waitress. I wouldn't blame them if they revoked my degree."

His gaze turned soft and sympathetic. "What do you want to do?"

I laughed derisively. "That's the problem. I never had any real plans, except go to college. I never really thought about what I'd do career wise. How stupid is that?"

"Hey, Soph." His arm wrapped around me and pulled me to his side, squishing Dutch, who pulled her head out from between us. "I'm sure you never thought your dad's money would run out."

I looked at him. "That's still pretty pathetic. How could I think I'd just live off him forever?"

AJ wiped a tear that I hadn't realized was there until his thumb brushed over my cheek. "I don't think you thought that. You worked some, right?"

I nodded.

"It's just, when you had money, it wasn't as pressing that you find a job. You could be choosy and only do the things that interested you. Now things are different, and you have to adjust. And I know you will. You're not only smart, but you're feisty and strong. You're learning to take care of yourself later than most, but you're doing it with grace and wit."

"I'm still not very good at it."

"Well, it can't be easy in this town."

I nodded. "I feel like they lord my poverty over me."

His expression turned concerned. "Do you have any friends?"

"Only Lani."

"What about your coupon group?"

"Vivie is in the group. And she hasn't changed."

AJ snorted.

"Her sister, Tracy, is okay. She was in your grade."

AJ nodded. "I remember her."

"There is Gwen, who is a few years older than me. I didn't know her before, but she's nice enough." Except that she had eyes on AJ. "And Aggie Parnell."

"As in fourth grade teacher Ms. Parnell?"

I nodded. "She's been really nice to me."

He smiled. "So, you're not all alone?"

"No, but it feels like it sometimes."

"I know you, Sophie. You'll rise above all this."

I laughed, cheered up a little by his pep talk. "If this flying thing doesn't work out, you can become a shrink."

"Yeah, well, I'm not flying now."

"We're a pretty pathetic pair."

He laughed. "Cheer me up. Tell me a story, Sophie."

"Really?" During our late night star gazing sessions when I was in high school, he often asked me to tell him a story. I'd thought it was sweet and sometimes read more into it than was there. After I'd told him every mythological love story from Cupid and Psyche to Pyramus and Thisbe, and he still hadn't gotten a clue, or he did but wasn't interested, I'd realized he was just being nice to indulge my interest.

"What sort of story do you want to hear?"

"I guess it needs to be short since you've got to get back to work. Choose one with a happy ending."

I scanned my brain through my vast storage of stories and told him the one about the Japanese woman in the wooden helmet.

"That sounds like you." He interrupted when I got to the part where the woman in the story loses her father and mother.

"Except her parents died."

"Yours are still gone. Leaving you alone, just like her."

I shrugged. "Do you want me to finish?"

He nodded, and so I told him how she found work with a man who had a sickly wife. When their son saw the beauty she was hiding under the helmet, he knew he had to marry her, but his family forbade it.

"You'd think she was from the Hollow." AJ shook his head.

"Yes, well, he wins in the end, and once they're married, the helmet bursts and shatters into jewels. They have a big party and live happily ever after." I sighed. There was nothing so lovely as a romantic fairy tale.

"That wench outfit is kind of like your helmet," AJ said when I finished.

I snorted. "It's the opposite of the helmet. It was meant to cover her beauty." I felt heat rush to my cheeks as I realized I suggested the wench outfit made me beautiful.

"It does. It takes away from your natural…cuteness."

Cute? Was there anything worse than being called cute by a man I'd spent most of my post-pubescent life lusting after? Still, I'd rather be cute than whatever adjective best described me in this getup. "Doesn't matter. I'm sure there's no one in the Booty Burgo who is going to save me from my predicament. And if there is, I'm not sure I'd want him."

"Good point. I noticed Randy Danner ogling you again."

"Ffftttt. I can handle him."

"Then why did you have me come save you at Jefferson Lake?"

"Because I kneed him in the jewels and he couldn't drive."

"Ouch." AJ winced and shifted away from me. "Remind me to never take advantage of you."

Like that would ever happen.

"But if you do need someone to run interference with him, let me know."

I waved his comment away. "He's slow and soft now. I'm sure I could take him."

"I'd like to see that." He laughed and tugged on one of my curls.

I worked up a smile, but my happiness was bittersweet. I was glad AJ was there, but our lives were such a mess.

"Chin up, buttercup. Things can only get better from here."

He was right, of course. After all, things couldn't get much worse.

EIGHT

MY INITIAL EMOTION upon waking the next morning
was relief. No more waitressing! Spike had vouched
for me so Kyle assigned me bartending duties for the
time being. Spike sent me home with a recipe book and
told me to study up on Long Island Iced Tea and martinis, dry and dirty. Even losing the battle to get rid of
the wench uniform couldn't totally dampen my spirits
at having a new job.

But then I remembered I was being investigated for
murder. My spirits plummeted. I flopped back in bed,
throwing my arm over my face. Why couldn't I catch
a break? My only recourse was to try and save myself,
and AJ, while I was at it.

I rolled from bed and grabbed my notebook. I didn't
know the first thing about investigating a crime. I wondered what the library might have on it. Maybe I could
read an Agatha Christie novel. No. I should probably
pick something more modern. A mystery was really a
puzzle, right? I picked up my pen, opened my notebook
and wrote down the pieces I already had.

*Joseph Cullen was murdered within minutes of our
leaving the airport.*

*He was killed with a golf club. Where did it come
from? Why was it there? Where were the rest of the
clubs? The truck? The third car?*

AJ and I were picked up in Richmond and questioned about the murder forty to fifty minutes after leaving.

I stopped writing and cocked my head to the side, deep in thought. That wasn't a lot of time. Not for someone to kill Cullen, someone else to discover the body and call 9-1-1, have the sheriff's deputies arrive, someone tell them AJ was there and call Richmond police in time to have them at the airport to pick us up. That had to mean the murderer was already at the airport while we were there. He had to kill Cullen immediately after AJ left him, and someone had to find Cullen right after that to call the sheriff's department.

I shook my head. It all seemed so tight. No wonder the investigation was focused on AJ. Not only was he there and the only one who fit the timeline, but also my being there gave him a motive.

I sighed. There was another explanation. *Maybe AJ did it.* I shushed the little voice in my head. No way did AJ kill Cullen. *Ten years is a long time apart from someone. People change.* Shut up! There had to be another person there. But even so, how was he found so fast and the sheriff's office called so quickly? Unless, the killer called 9-1-1.

Yeah. Maybe the killer witnessed AJ and Cullen fighting and saw his chance to pin it on him. So he killed Cullen as soon as AJ left and called the cops to report the murder. He could even report the argument between Cullen and AJ. He would have known AJ flew off with Cullen's plane. It could also explain why the investigators weren't interested in Bull. He was there, but only AJ had been identified. This idea wasn't far-fetched. I bet criminals reported their crimes a lot to put the suspicion off of them and onto someone else.

But who else was there? I wracked my brain to re-member if I'd seen anyone around the hangar or the office. But all I could remember was Bull, AJ and Mr. Cullen. I looked at my piddly list of clues and shook my head. Undaunted, I made a list of suspects. Vivie had an affair with Cullen. Randy said he didn't care about it, but I found that hard to believe. Maybe he didn't like her around, but it didn't seem possible a man would be okay with his wife sleeping with another man.

Aunt Rose, Aggie and Randy volunteered Cullen's wife, Maggie, as a suspect. Plus Aunt Rose mentioned a disgruntled renter. What was his name? Sam. No… Ben. Ben Samuels, that was it. I wrote their names on my list. Then there was the drug angle. Was Cullen just smuggling drugs in for someone else or was he a dealer too? Who was involved with him?

I sat with my few clues and list of suspects. Then I remembered Bull said AJ wasn't even supposed to do the repo. Some guy named Patch was. Was it just a lucky break that had him unable to do the repo or was AJ set up by him too?

With my notes, I felt a bit more organized but no closer to knowing what to do. I was scheduled to talk to my dad on Friday, so I could ask him, but I was certain my father didn't have any part in the murder. He just wasn't the type. Plus, if he was going to kill Cullen, he'd have been smarter to do it before Cullen testified against him. But maybe my father knew something about Cul-len that could put me on the right path. He'd always been a big help when I was stuck on a problem. "Go to the beginning, Sophie, and work your way through."

That was it. I needed to go to the scene of the crime… literally.

I PARKED THE Brown Bomber in front of what I took to be the main building of the small airport. It wasn't a terminal, but neither was it a hangar. It was a drab tan building with double glass doors for the entrance and windows along the front with green bushes underneath, as if that would improve the aesthetics. I sat for a moment, unsure of my next step. AJ had followed Cullen into a doorway connected to a hangar. If there were clues, that would be where I should look. The problem was, I didn't know what to look for. Any clues that existed were probably picked up by the investigators. So, my best bet was to talk to someone who'd been there yesterday.

I exited the car, not bothering to lock it. What was there to steal? I was sure I could leave the keys in it and it wouldn't get stolen. Not wanting to test that theory, though, I dropped my keys in my purse.

I walked through the double doors and was met with the blast of arctic air from the air-conditioning.

"It's hot out there today." A sixty-something-looking woman with bright orange hair stacked like a nest on top of her head fanned herself with a brochure from behind a counter.

"Yes, well, thank goodness you have air-conditioning." I wished I'd brought a sweater. It was freezing.

"It helps some. What can I do ya for?"

I stood, frozen like the proverbial deer. What should I say? "I wanted to ask about the murder yesterday."

Orange hair lady stopped mid-fanning to gawk at me. "Why?"

"Insurance." Is that what was involved after all deaths?

Her eyes narrowed. "The airport isn't liable."

"Oh no." I waved her comment away and added a little laugh, hoping my one drama class in high school taught me enough skill to act my way through this situation. "I'm sorry. Life insurance."

The woman tilted her head. "He had life insurance?"

Didn't everyone? "Well, sure. To take care of his family."

The woman laughed. "I don't think he cared about that." Her brows drew together, and she leaned forward. "You thinking his wife killed him?"

"Do you?"

The woman leaned back and shrugged.

"So you didn't see anything yesterday?" I held my breath, waiting for her to say, "Of course, I saw you and your friends kill Mr. Cullen."

"No. Not much happens around here."

That seemed like such a strange statement, considering a murder had just happened, but I didn't mention that. "Do you have surveillance cameras?"

"Sure. The cops took the tapes, but I doubt they'll get anything from them."

"Why?"

"Well, for one, they're only outside and two, they're crappy quality."

"Do they monitor the back of the airport?"

One drawn-on brow rose. "Yes. Why?"

"I'm told cars park back there sometimes. In fact, I believe Mr. Cullen's car was there."

"You sure know a lot."

"It's my job." I just hoped she didn't ask me for coverage rates. "Do you know of anyone who wanted Mr. Cullen dead, besides his wife?"

The woman started fanning herself again. "Who

didn't? He was a lying cheat. Do you know he hadn't paid his hangar fees for nearly six months? I'm not at all surprised his plane was repossessed."

"Really?"

"I hadn't seen him in forever. I figured he was avoiding us because, you can bet, if I saw him, I was getting my rent. But he's been MIA for awhile. That's why I told the bank guy to come get the plane."

Or he was sneaking in through the back. Why else would his car be parked on that back road?

"The bank or the repo company?"

"The repo man. George something."

"Gordo?"

"Yeah, something like that."

Gordo originally was going to send Patch to do the repo, but he couldn't go, so AJ went instead. I wondered if the sheriff's investigators had interviewed Gordo and Bull. If AJ wasn't originally supposed to do the repo, he wouldn't have been here, which should have cleared me and AJ of conspiracy to kill Cullen. "I wonder why Mr. Cullen was here?"

"I didn't even know he was until the cops came screeching in. Maybe he was getting ready to run. Rumor is he smuggled drugs. Through my airport!" The woman's face pinched into indignation.

"You think he was going to run because the sheriff was getting ready to arrest him for drugs?"

The woman shrugged. "That or for being an all-around jerk. I hadn't expected he'd be murdered, even if he deserved it."

So far, I hadn't learned anything new, except he hadn't been seen around the airport for awhile. The victim and the main suspect were both here by accident.

"Would it be okay if I looked at the crime scene?"

"I don't have a problem, but the sheriff might. It's still taped off."

I nodded. "Is it okay if I just walk around?"

"Knock yourself out."

I exited the building and was immediately poleaxed by the wall of heat and humidity. It was one of the challenges of summer; staying at the perfect temperature. It was too hot outside and often too cold inside.

I walked toward the hangar I'd seen AJ and Mr. Cullen walk into. Yellow crime scene tape crisscrossed over the outside office door. I peeked into the window, but it was grimy with dirt, blurring everything in the room. I continued along the building to the large opening of the hangar. Looking around, I didn't see anyone and made my way inside. To the right was another door I determined went to the office as well, as it too was covered with crime tape, except for the couple of strands hanging down. It was hotter in the hangar and I wondered if it had melted the stickiness of the tape.

I reached out to open the door but then remembered about fingerprints. I didn't need the investigators finding evidence of my being there. Scanning the area, I saw a toolbox with a rag laying on it. I picked up the oily rag and used it to turn the knob. Ducking under the yellow tape, I entered the room. It had a desk, a couple of wooden chairs, a couch, a file cabinet and a bookshelf. A few papers were strewn on the floor, but there wasn't any indication a murder had taken place. Didn't they outline the body with tape anymore? I really needed to go to the library and get some books on investigating murder.

Sitting on the couch was a folded blanket and pillow. What I didn't see were golf clubs. Or any other clues, for that matter. The investigators would have taken anything interesting, so I knew I was wasting my time. Still, I tried to imagine what had happened. Did Cullen know his attacker? Could a vagrant have wandered in and killed him? I couldn't imagine why a vagrant would have a golf club, except maybe for protection, but where would he have gotten it? Especially a rare expensive club. Cullen had money. He'd bought up my father's holdings, which meant it was possible he'd bought my father's clubs. But why would his clubs be in an airport hangar office? Had Cullen and the killer quarreled and the attack happened in the heat of the moment? That couldn't explain a golf club either. Unless the attacker was a golfer and kept his clubs in the car. In that case, he'd have brought the club with him to purposefully kill Cullen or he'd have gone to his car, retrieved the club from the bag in his trunk and returned to kill him. But wouldn't I have seen someone leaving this office and heading to the parking lot while I was waiting in the plane?

Movement sounded from outside the door and my heart shot to my throat. Was the killer back? My gaze darted around the room for a place to hide. Under the desk offered the only protection, although it wasn't much. Deciding it was better than nothing, I dropped to the floor and scooted under, making myself as small as possible. It was the first time in a long time I celebrated the fact I was petite.

"You know we'll get into all sorts of trouble being here," a man's voiced echoed in the room.

"I've got to look, Cal. The sheriff's investigators are hard set on pinning this murder on me. I'm not going to sit by and let 'em." I recognized AJ's voice and let out a sigh of relief, but not enough to let him know I was there. Knowing AJ saw himself as my protector, I was sure he'd kept some of what he knew or thought about the murder from me. But maybe he'd tell this Cal guy.

"There ain't nothing here, AJ."

Peeking toward the voices, I saw what I took to be Cal's work boots hovering by the door. A pair of sneakers walked to the center of the room. It was AJ, and the fact I could see him clearly meant he could see me as well. I scooted back. As I resettled, I felt something hard under my knee. It was painfully uncomfortable, but I didn't dare deal with it.

"Where are the clubs?" AJ turned, scanning the room.

"Huh?"

"The clubs. Cullen was killed with a golf club. Where are the clubs? Is there a closet or—" AJ stopped as his gaze reached the desk. Or more accurately, under the desk. On me, to be precise.

"Sophie!" AJ's wide-eyed surprise morphed into disapproval. "What are you doing here?"

"Same thing you are." I crawled out from under the desk.

"How do you know what I'm doing?" He placed his hands on his hips, glaring at me, not unlike my mother used to do. I considered telling him that, except he looked perturbed and I didn't want to make it worse.

"You're not supposed to be here either. But like me, you're looking for clues to clear your name."

He shook his head.

"AJ, we shouldn't be here." Cal, an older man with a white tuft of hair, glanced out the door and back at AJ.

He wore a mechanic's jumpsuit making me wonder if he worked there. Maybe he'd seen someone.

"Go ahead, Cal. If we get caught, I won't let anyone know you helped."

Cal nodded, the old skin under his chin wobbling like a turkey. "Close the door when you go." Cal ducked under the tape and exited the room.

"Who's that?"

"My uncle."

That didn't really tell me who he was. In Cooters Hollow, there were lots of people called relatives, who weren't actually blood kin. Or maybe they were. The families of the Hollow had been there for centuries, while very few new folks ever moved into the area. Odds were, by now, everyone *was* related to everyone. But since I wasn't there for a genealogical history of AJ's family, I let it go.

"Did he see anything?"

"No. You shouldn't be here."

"Neither should you and yet, here we are."

He scowled. I stared at him, daring him to do all the things I imagined he was thinking, like dragging me out kicking and screaming.

"A man was murdered here yesterday."

My stomach dropped and I scanned the room for evidence of murder, like a puddle of blood. "I know."

"Murderers don't take kindly to people getting in their business."

"I don't want to get into their business." That didn't make sense because clearly, I was doing things that could be construed as poking my nose where it didn't belong. "I'm not here to find out who killed Mr. Cullen. I want to prove it wasn't you or me."

AJ blew out a breath. "I'm not sure the murderer would care."

I shrugged.

"What have you found out?"

It took me a moment to realize AJ was letting this bone go. "Well, I know no one knew Mr. Cullen was here. The lady in the office said she hadn't seen him in a long time. She told Gordo it was clear to repo the plane because he wasn't coming around anymore. Bull said Gordo originally wanted someone else to take the plane, so you shouldn't have been here. That alone should clear us."

AJ shrugged.

"You don't think so?"

He scanned the room. "The investigators can interpret things all sorts of ways. In the end, maybe we saw our opportunity and took it."

"But you didn't think he'd be there."

"But he was. The investigators could think we set it up so he'd show."

My hope sank. "The lady in the office thinks he was going to make a run for it."

"For what?"

I shook my head. "I don't know. From law enforcement, I guess. She thinks, like everyone else, he was smuggling drugs."

AJ bit his lip. "We should go."

"What? Why? We haven't found anything."

"And we probably won't. But the cops aren't the only people Cullen might want to run from."

It took me a moment. "The drug dealers?"

AJ nodded. "Maybe something went wrong in the partnership."

"He was losing his plane and he hadn't paid his hangar fees in months. Maybe his partners didn't like he wouldn't be able to smuggle for them."

"You *did* find out a lot."

"But not proof that it wasn't us. What happened when you were in here with him?"

AJ shook his head. "He was angry I was taking his plane."

"I saw that outside, but when you two walked back here, he seemed... I don't know...deflated...resigned maybe."

"I thought he was resigned too. I asked him for the books, and he handed them over without a word."

"What books?"

"The records for the plane. I don't get full payment for the repo without them, so I was relieved he didn't fight me on it."

"Did he say anything? Did he seem afraid?"

AJ shook his head. "I asked him if there were drugs on the plane, because that could cause problems. That's what I thought all the cops were about. That or he'd reported the plane stolen."

"What did he say about the drugs?"

"Nothing." He shook his head.

I frowned as I realized what that meant. "You took me on a joy ride on a plane that might have had drugs on it."

He rolled his eyes. "That's the least of our problems."

"Now it is. Then it was the possibility of drugs."

"Bull searched the plane—"

"Not the inside."

"If the plane had had drugs, Cullen wouldn't have relinquished the plane so easily."

"Easily? From what I saw, he was ready to fight you." I planted my hands on my hips and glared at AJ. How could he be so nonchalant about this?

"That was just anger at losing the plane. He knew his time had run out."

I stared at AJ for a long moment. "Is that how it always is when you take a plane?"

AJ gave me a cocky grin. "Are you worried about me?"

"Should I be?"

He shook his head. "Usually the plane is ready and waiting for me to take it. It's only a few cases where there is a problem."

"You were anticipating a problem this time, weren't you? That's why you prowled around the airport."

"Cullen wasn't responding to the bank or to Gordo's calls. Usually that's a sign of resistance. Sometimes they hide the plane or run off with it. We usually find it in the end, but it becomes a chase, and often I have to sneak in to get it."

His job was interesting, but now wasn't the time to learn more. "Do you think he was in trouble with the drug dealers?"

AJ shrugged. "Maybe, but I can't imagine a drug dealer using a golf club to kill."

"That's what I can't wrap my head around. Who brings a golf club to a murder?" I scanned the room again, wondering if there was a spot we were missing that was housing the bag of clubs.

"It doesn't seem likely it was a planned murder, so odds are it was handy." AJ walked around the room, but his expression suggested he thought, as I did, that the investigators would have taken anything important.

"Why would a club be handy? Unless it was Cullen's club but, even then, most people keep their clubs in the car."

Since I was there, I scanned the area around the desk. I might not find clues to who murdered Cullen, but maybe I'd learn something about the man. I used the rag to open drawers and look around. There were pens, papers and a can of chew. But I didn't see anything that revealed why he was killed.

Folders, papers and other items littered his desk and were strewn on the floor. I scanned them and was about to give up when I noticed a small round disk sitting under the desk. It was the item my knee got stuck on when I was hiding. I squatted down to get a closer look.

"What is it?" AJ squatted and looked at me under the desk from the other side.

"Do you have a pen or something?"

"Here." He stood and picked one up from the desk. Squatting back down, he handed it to me.

"AJ, now your prints are on it."

He laughed. "I'll take it with me."

Frowning, I took the pen and poked at the disk. It was about the size of a penny, silver with dimples and had a gold strip across the diameter with the letters JAC.

"What is it?"

I lifted my head to look at him under the desk. "It's a golf ball marker."

"A what?"

"A golf ball marker. You know, you put it on the putting green to mark where your ball is. This one is nice. JAC must be his initials."

AJ's brows furrowed as he stood and moved toward the couch. I stood as well, wondering what he was thinking.

He poked at the blanket and pillow. "Do you suppose he was living here?"

"The office lady said she hadn't seen him."

"If he owed on the rent, he wouldn't want to be seen, but what if he parked somewhere else and came in from the back?"

"Is that possible?"

"This is a small county airport. The security isn't top notch. That's how I'd have gotten the plane if it hadn't been out already."

"He has a home and wife. Why would he be here?"

"Maybe he was hiding. Or maybe the lady in the office is right and he was getting ready to run and he had his clubs with him."

That made sense, but I knew it was all conjecture. "The only problem with that is where are the rest of the clubs? He wouldn't bring just one club with him."

"The investigators have the club so they probably took the bag too."

I shook my head. "Then why did they ask me about my clubs and search our homes for them?"

He didn't say anything and I figured he was just as confused as I was about the situation. Finally, he moved back to me, putting his hand on my shoulder. "You should go."

"Me?" I frowned up at him. "A minute ago you said we."

"We then. But you and I aren't supposed to be seen together, remember? If we're caught, it will make things worse."

Oh yeah.

"You go first."

"What are you going to do?"

He took the pen from my hand and shoved it in his back pocket. "I'll look around and then leave when I know you're gone. Go straight home, though. Okay?"

I nodded, even though I still planned to stop at the library on my way home. I pulled out my phone from my pocket and took a picture of the golf marker. I wasn't brave enough to take it, but I wanted to have a record of it, just in case. "Will you tell me if you find out anything?"

He paused. "Yeah, okay. You working tonight?"

I nodded and grinned. "I'm adding Long Island Iced Teas and martinis to my drink serving repertoire."

He laughed. "Only you could find a silver lining working at the Booty Burgo."

NINE

I'D TOLD AJ I'd head straight home, but I stopped by the library to research how crimes were solved. How much trouble could I get into at the library? I used the computer to do Internet research on how to solve a crime. The basic steps were to create a timeline, follow leads, gather evidence, take notes and persevere. I knew the timeline was what was hurting AJ and me the most. I had no idea about leads or evidence. Was the golf ball marker evidence? Wouldn't the investigators have taken it? At least I'd already determined I needed to keep notes and I knew I could be tenacious when properly motivated. The risk of the death penalty was pretty motivating.

Feeling like there had to be more I could learn, I checked the stacks for books. Most of the nonfiction books about detectives were for children and didn't explain much about the process police used in solving crimes. There was one writing book on how to pen a mystery that discussed how the sleuth needed to talk to all possible suspects to determine motives and unlock the clues.

I pulled my list of suspects out to study what I had. Although I was no Sherlock Holmes, it made more sense that whoever killed Mr. Cullen knew him and was fairly close to him. Close enough to want to kill him with the nearest golf club. In my mind, that made his wife, Maggie Cullen, a top suspect. Aunt Rose and Aggie both put her at the top of their list, too.

Second, if he was smuggling drugs, he was mingling with a dangerous group of people. I decided I needed to talk to Maggie Cullen. Not that she'd tell me if she killed him, but she might let something slip that would give her away if she had, or she might have information on whether or not her husband was really bringing drugs into the area. I found a phone book in the library and looked up Maggie Cullen's address, writing it down next to her name on my suspect list.

I put my list in my purse and checked out the mystery writing book and a cozy mystery written by Agatha Christie. Before leaving the library, I made a stop near the magazines to check out the community coupon box. The library left the coupon and sales inserts from the newspapers they received in the box. The public could take any coupons or inserts they wanted and were encouraged to leave any they had that they didn't want in the box. I had a few I could contribute, except they were at home in my binder. I always felt bad taking coupons without leaving a few behind, but rifling through the box, I saw shampoo and pain reliever coupons I couldn't pass up. With my new coupons stuffed into my wallet and books tucked under my arm, I got ready to head out.

"Sophie Parker."

My heart jumped and I stiffened. The few times I'd visited the library since returning to Jefferson Grove, I worked to avoid the woman attached to that voice because I couldn't bear to know if her opinion of me had changed. Had she lost money to my father? Would she shun me either way?

I mustered a smile and turned toward the librarian, who had nurtured my love of fairy tales and introduced me to folklore and mythology.

"Mrs. Wayland."

She was older, her once-slim body now a little plump, and her face held a few more wrinkles. Reading glasses on her head held back brown hair with a few gray streaks. But her hazel eyes were still kind, even as they stared at me in a mixture of concern and annoyance.

"Why haven't you come to see me?"

I swallowed the worry and guilt. "I don't get out too much anymore."

"Not even to see old friends?"

Now the guilt swallowed me. She'd always been good to me. For a few summers, when I was a teenager, she hired me to help with children's programming. I bit my lower lip. "I'm sorry. I just… I wasn't sure you'd…"

"You think I'd hold your parents misdeeds against you?" Disappointment shone in her eyes.

I looked down, unable to face my mistake. "Not everyone is happy to see me."

"Who's not happy to see you?"

"Ah…well… Mrs. Coker…"

Mrs. Wayland rolled her eyes. "Madge Coker is an old bitty. Why would you be seeing her anyway?"

"A job. No one wants to hire me."

"No one?" Her tone was the same disbelief my mother used when she thought I was exaggerating my plight in life.

"Mr. Hampton laughed at me."

"He's a jerk."

"Mr. Bryson said his clients would be uncomfortable with me. I guess they're afraid I'll take their money"

She huffed out a sympathetic breath. "I suppose you can't blame people for worrying about that sort of thing in a banking job. But what about your old friends? Aren't they nice to you?"

"Lani is. Most are gone now. Others just avoid me." I didn't bother to mention Vivie, because she'd never been my friend. In fact, thinking about it, Vivie was one of the few people who treated me the same now as she had in high school.

"So, not everyone is against you." Her tone chastised me.

I wanted to defend myself, but I couldn't. Sure, my life in Jefferson Grove was significantly different, and I was struggling with the change. But I had *some* friends. Lani was always there for me. The ladies of the coupon group were friendly, except for Vivie, of course. Still, people looked at me sideways when I was in town. "I don't like the whispering and side glances."

"That's what you get in a small town."

I nodded.

"But that doesn't mean they don't like you or won't like you. I imagine most of them are intrigued. Nothing happens in a small town, so when it does, people are curious." She smiled in a way that suggested she was trying to cheer me up.

"I'd rather go about my business without them staring at me."

"Oh pah." Mrs. Wayland waved her hand. "It's just small-town gossip, Sophie. Did that private college education make you forget your roots? We like to talk, but we're also friendly and forgiving folk. Who do you think helped your aunt until you got back to town? We did. So, a few people aren't quite comfortable enough to let you near their business finances, most people here go day to day and don't think one iota about you or your family anymore. You're a child of Jefferson Grove, and you can't let a little gossip keep you from living life here again."

I inhaled a breath as I took in her words. She was right. Only the Mrs. Cokers of the town were outright mean. Truth be told, I had friends, some of who I hadn't had growing up in Jefferson Grove, like Gwen. The whispering was uncomfortable, but I couldn't control what people thought about me. What I could do was control how I reacted to them. "I'm sorry I didn't stop by sooner."

Mrs. Wayland nodded, and her gaze drifted to my books. One brow arched. "Don't like fairy tales anymore?"

"I love them. I'm expanding my reading."

She tapped the mystery writing book. "You're not planning to write the mystery of Mr. Cullen's murder, are you?" So she knew about my being at the airport when Mr. Cullen was killed.

"No." That wasn't a lie. I wasn't planning on writing a murder mystery.

"You know, if you don't want people gossiping, you shouldn't give them reasons to talk."

I shrugged. What could I say? It wasn't like I set out to get embroiled in murder. I checked my watch since there was still a lot to do before I had to go to work.

"Am I keeping you?"

"I have a few errands before work."

She frowned. "Is it true you're working at the Booty Burgo?"

I nodded.

"You're too smart for that."

"Tell that to the people who wouldn't hire me."

She studied me for a moment. "We have a job here. It's not full-time. In fact, it's only a few hours a week, but it's right up your alley. Helping with children's programming this summer just like you did during high school."

My heart leapt at the idea. "I didn't see it in my job search."

"We only just posted it."

I hadn't checked jobs that morning. "Do you have an application?"

"It's on the website."

I looked toward the computer area and saw there was a free PC. "I'll go apply now."

"Good. I can't promise anything, Sophie."

"I know. Thank you, Mrs. Wayland."

"Don't be a stranger."

I smiled and accepted her hug. Then I headed to the computer station, pulled up the job and started the application. It was only ten hours a week, so I'd still have to work at the Booty Burgo, but at least it would involve one of my favorite things—books. I completed the form and hit submit then headed to the exit, waving at Mrs. Wayland as I left.

Once in the Brown Bomber, I steered the car toward the affluent Monticello Heights neighborhood to continue my sleuthing. Normally, this was the type of adventure I'd have asked Lani to go on with me. In high school we often ventured out on some escapade, like when we decided to hitchhike to an amusement park in Richmond. Neither of us knew how to drive at the time, and none of our family or friends would drive us. We got there and had a blast but hadn't thought about getting home. It was only under the dark of night we realized our mistake. Fortunately, AJ came to our rescue.

But now that we were all grown up, Lani had a job that prevented her from helping me, which was unfortunate because she'd have a better chance of getting into the gated community of Monticello Heights. The only way to get in was to have a residence pass or to be on the guest list. Assuming I could get in, I needed a reason, beyond investigating murder, to see Mrs. Cullen. That was easier to solve. I stopped at a florist. Before going in, I opened my sales code app to see if there was a coupon or discount code I could use to save on flowers. There were several, but they required ordering online. I bought the nicest arrangement I could afford and tried not to think about the smirks and pitying looks I'd get from my group for paying full price. My plan was to give the flowers to Mrs. Cullen, along with my condolences. Before I could do that, I had to get through the gate.

I scanned my brain for who I still knew at Monticello Heights that might let me in, but the only people I could think of were angry investors of my father's, and Vivie Danner. I couldn't imagine any of them, especially Vivie, helping me. The only other option was to pretend I was there to meet a Realtor to see a house. Potential home buyers and real estate professionals were always let in.

I made another quick stop at the gas station to pick up a real estate magazine from one of the bins outside the minimart. I scanned the back of the booklet and saw a brick colonial for sale in Monticello Heights. Grabbing a pen from my purse, I circled it and then set the magazine in the front seat so the gate attendant would see it.

I drove up to the guest entrance of the neighborhood and rolled down my window. "I'm here to meet Debbie Sue Martin about a home on Monroe." I picked up the magazine and showed the attendant the home I'd circled with Debbie Sue's name.

The guard looked at me and then at the Brown Bomber. One fuzzy gray brow rose when he returned his gaze to me. I hadn't considered my car might blow my cover. Monticello Heights was filled with Audis, BMWs and Mercedes. It might have a few Volvos too, but probably not thirty-year-old poop brown ones.

"I'm on a scouting trip for my boss, Mercedes Beemer. They just sold their summer home in the Hamptons and want to buy a home here." I smiled, hoping he'd buy my lie.

"No one called you in."

"What?" I looked at my watch. "I'm supposed to meet her in ten minutes." Should I be worried about how quickly the lies came to me and how easily they rolled off my tongue?

"No real estate agent has come through today, either."

My quest was coming to an end. A car pulled alongside me at the resident gate. A bar code on the side of the car activated the bar, which rose to let the car through. I looked over as the sleek red Mercedes drove through. Vivie. She looked at me with furrowed brows as she drove through. I sent her a meek smile and turned back to the guard.

"My boss is going to be unhappy if I can't preview this home. Is there something you can do to help me?"

"She'll have to take it up with the real estate agent."

"Come on. Help a girl out." I gave him the Betty Boop pout.

He rolled his eyes. "I can't let you in without an invite. You'll need to pull through the gate and make a U-turn to leave."

The phone in the guard house rang. He held up his hand, telling me to wait. Maybe he thought that was the call I needed to get in. Of course, it wouldn't be, so I prepared myself to turn around and leave.

After a few moments, he returned, handing me a guest pass. "Mrs. Danner said you're a guest of hers."

His expression was dubious. I tried to keep mine from looking shocked. "We're old friends. She's coming on the tour with me."

The guard poked a button and the gate lifted. I drove through, heading toward Vivie's house, instead of Mrs. Cullen's. I'd been to Vivie's before for a coupon group, which had been the only reason she'd let me in her house. So I was surprised and leery at why she called the gate to let me in.

I parked on the street and made my way up the sloping walk toward the colonial style home, complete with white columns.

Vivie opened the door before I could knock. "You're not actually buying a home here, are you?"

I wondered if Vivie's tone was because she didn't want me as a neighbor or shock I could afford a home there. "No."

"Then why are you here?"

"Why did you let me in the gate?"

Vivie pursed her lips and stared at me as if she was trying to decide how to proceed. Finally, she stepped back to let me in. The house reminded me of a model home; clean and professionally decorated. There were no signs of children, which was strange since I knew she had three of them.

"Where are the kids?"

"Camp Mema."

"Camp Mema?"

"My mom takes them a couple days a week during the summer so I can have some time alone."

I followed her back toward the family room. Before I could fully enter the space, she whirled on me. "Are you sleeping with Randy?"

I stopped short and reared back. "What? No!" My no came out sounding like "ew," which was what I'd been thinking.

Vivie's narrow hazel eyes glared at me as if she was trying to decide if I was telling the truth. "It wouldn't be the first time."

"Actually, it would. In high school, you had broken up with him to go out with Todd Napier when I went out with Randy. And I never let him touch me."

"Friends don't go out with other friend's exes."

"We were friends?" That wasn't how I remembered it. "What does it matter now? That was over ten years ago. And I only went out with him for a week." It had been the longest week of my life, until my dad was arrested. Or this week.

"He's seeing somebody." She turned and walked the rest of the way into the family room and motioned me to sit. "Do you want sweet tea?"

I shook my head as I sat. "No. Thank you. What

makes you think he's seeing someone?" I wondered why she cared. After all, she'd cheated on Randy with Mr. Cullen.

"Because he spends all his time at work and the Booty Burgo. I don't care if he's part owner. He has a staff to take care of the place. He doesn't need to be there unless he's boinking one of the wenches." She sat across from me.

"Randy is part owner of the Booty Burgo?" My stomach clenched. I hadn't done a good job hiding my opinion of him. I wondered why he hadn't fired me.

Vivie huffed. "Yes. Who's he seeing there?"

"Wasn't Joseph Cullen part owner too?"

"God, Sophie. How'd you ever get into college? You're totally missing the point of this discussion."

Actually, I just wanted the discussion to go a different way, but to appease her I said, "I don't know who or if he's seeing anyone."

"You work there. You must see him."

"He sits at the bar and drinks. That's all I've ever seen." I wondered if I should mention the flirting and leering.

"Are you telling me the truth?"

"I have no reason to lie, Vivie."

"You'd lie if he was seeing you."

I rolled my eyes. "I have zero interest in Randy. Less than zero."

"What does that mean?" Vivie's back straightened and her voice was defensive.

"It means it's not me and won't ever be me."

She sat back and huffed out a breath. "There's someone."

"If it bothers you, you should ask him."

"It doesn't bother me." She waved my suggestion away.

"Then why are you grilling me on it?"

"Because it looks bad if he is. You know this town, Sophie. What people think is everything."

She had a point.

"I will *not* tolerate people thinking I can't keep my man happy."

I thought about telling her that she wasn't keeping her man happy, at least according to her man.

"I mean, look at me. Men still find me attractive."

"Like Joseph Cullen?" I pounced on my opportunity to ask her about their affair and what she knew about him.

She slanted me a look that suggested she didn't like my asking. "Yes. Among others."

I wanted to ask why it didn't matter that the town knew about her cheating but somehow it would be bad if Randy cheated. But that would take us off the topic I needed to know about. At the same time, I needed to tread lightly. "Was he good to you?"

Her head cocked to the side, as if she hadn't expected that question. "He was alright."

"What do you think happened? Who killed him?"

She shrugged. "The list is as long as my arm."

"But you knew him. Surely he told you something that indicated if he was having trouble with anyone."

"God, Sophie, you sound like the cops. When did you last see him? What did you talk about? Blah, blah, blah."

So she'd been interviewed by the cops.

"I just slept with him a few times and, to be honest, it wasn't that great. But we rarely talked about anything."

"Why?"

"Because all he cared about was getting off…"

I shook my head and tried not to groan. "No. Why did you spend time with a man who didn't talk and wasn't great in bed?"

"I don't know." She shrugged.

"Seems risky to sleep with your husband's partner. It would be risky for him too."

"Like Randy would care." There was a hint of disappointment in her voice. Had she wanted Randy to care?

"You don't think Randy had a problem with Mr. Cullen sleeping with you?"

Randy told me he didn't care that she was having an affair, but he could be lying or he might not have liked his partner being the one she was cheating with.

"Randy doesn't care about anything I do, except spending too much money."

"Do you know anything about their business relationship?"

"Why would I know that boring stuff?"

"Maybe he said something. They were partners. Randy is an accountant. Maybe they had a dispute over money."

She frowned. "Well… Randy was his accountant for his other business ventures, but he's not for the Booty Burgo. Randy was a bit put out about that because he didn't feel he was getting all the information in his partner financial reports."

"Why wouldn't Randy be the accountant for the Booty Burgo?"

She shook her head. "I don't know."

"Is there another partner?"

"I don't know. I try to stay out of all that. I mean, who cares as long as there's money in the bank?"

Somebody cared. They cared so much they killed Mr. Cullen.

Vivie's brows pulled together. "One time when Joey and I were getting a hotel in Charlottesville, a man approached him. I think Joey called him Fletch. He was really affected by that meeting."

"Really? How?"

"He couldn't perform...you know..."

I pushed away the vision of Vivie and Joseph Cullen with a wilting willy. "Did he say anything to you about it?"

"I already told you, we didn't talk much."

Clearly, she didn't know anything, so it was about time for me to go. But I thought I'd ask one more question. "Do you think he was smuggling drugs?"

"I wouldn't put it past him. I think he'd do anything for a buck."

I'd learned a few things from my visit with Vivie, but nothing that helped clear my or AJ's name. Was it like that for the investigators too? They talked to a lot of people but hadn't seemed to have gotten anywhere either. I thought it was because they were hyper-focused on us, but maybe it was because the information they were getting wasn't helpful.

I thanked Vivie for inviting me and promised to keep an eye on Randy and headed out to see Mrs. Cullen. Her home was a large brick Tudor-style house sitting at the end of a cul-de-sac. In high school, I'd babysat the kids that had lived in the home. I wondered what had happened to the family. I hoped my father hadn't taken their money, causing them to have to downsize.

I walked up the brick path, carrying my little flower arrangement, and knocked on the door. A tall, lean woman with her hair pulled back tight in a long pony-tail, wearing skinny jeans and a white tank top, opened the door. She placed her hand on her hip and stared at me with a blank expression but didn't say anything.

"Hi."

One expertly coifed brow rose.

"I'm Sophie Parker. My father was a partner of your husband's. I heard what happened and wanted to stop by to offer my condolences."

"Why?" Her expression bordered on bored.

"Ah…well…"

"You never met my husband, did you?"

"No, but…"

"Because if you had, you'd be bringing me champagne, not condolences."

Wow. "Okay."

"He was a world class jerk."

"I've heard that. Sometimes being related to someone like that can be hard in this town, so I wanted to stop by in case others didn't."

"What would you know?" She scoffed.

"My father is Monty Parker."

Maggie Cullen just stared for a moment and then her brows lifted. "My husband put him in jail."

"I heard."

Her eyes narrowed. "And you still want to offer me condolences?"

"I don't blame your husband. My father broke the law. In a small town like this, people like to talk about other people's hardships."

"Like I care." But she stood back and motioned me to come in.

I followed her up the long hallway. Her home was

similar to Vivie's in that it was clean and looked like a museum. The difference was that it was completely white. The walls, the furniture, the carpet, the tile…all white. Even the picture frames were white with black and white photos. She motioned me toward a white leather couch. I checked my clothes to make sure there was nothing on them that might dirty the spot where I sat. My eye caught a white vase that looked eerily like a Qianlong period pale jade vase my mother once had.

"So, how did you know my husband?" She set the flowers I brought on a side table and sat in a chair across from me.

"I didn't know him. I only saw him once."

She frowned. "Then why are you here?"

"I know how Jefferson Grove can be and since I heard some unkind—"

She snorted. "That's an understatement." Then her eyes narrowed. "What do they say about me?"

I vacillated between being vague, outright lying, and telling the truth. "It's not flattering either."

She threw her head back and laughed. "I think I like you, Sophie Parker. None of that fake southern hospitality for you."

"I know it can be hard, so if there's something I can do for you…"

She shook her head. "All I need is to get out of this godforsaken town. I should have never let Joe drag me down here. All I've had is misery. Look at these." She held her hands out toward me and waggled her fingers. The nails were colored in a blood-red polish. "I haven't had a decent manicure since we moved here. The nail salon here is filled with beauty school dropouts."

"That would be hard." So far she hadn't been the

mean snake I'd heard about, but she was clearly not the nicest woman in the world either.

She sat back in a huff.

I couldn't figure out how to segue into my questions, so I decided to just go for it. "Mrs. Cullen, did your husband play golf?"

"Joe loved three things." She held up one finger. "Joe." She added two more fingers. "Money and golf. In that order."

"Would you know why he had his golf clubs with him at the airport?"

The corner of her mouth and a brow quirked up in question. "Why would I know? I imagine he played wherever he flew off to."

"Was he planning to fly off somewhere when he was murdered?"

"You sound like the cops." Her tone turned suspicious. "Even they were asking about his clubs. Searched the house even."

I smiled and tried to look relaxed. "I'm sorry. Just an armchair detective. We haven't had a murder in Jefferson Grove since Mrs. McGill poisoned her husband's shoofly pie when I was in kindergarten."

"I don't know anything about Joe's business or mistresses or any of it. I do know he made a lot of enemies in this town. You could add me to the list." She thought for a moment. "Shoofly pie, huh? I wish I'd thought of it."

"You wanted your husband dead?" I asked tentatively.

"Me and everyone else. And I thought about it. A lot. I even once considered beating him to death with his golf club."

I wondered if she'd told the investigators that. "Why didn't you?"

"Because, as much as I hated him, I liked having money. That, and he spent a fortune on those clubs. He said they were a steal when he bought them off a business partner who was going to jail."

That had to mean he'd bought my father's clubs. I glanced back at the vase. Had they bought my mother's vase as well? I wanted to ask what all the Cullens had bought of my family's when my father liquidated his assets, but that wasn't the pressing issue of the moment.

Mrs. Cullen bit her lower lip and tilted her head to the side. "Although, recently, he was losing money hand over fist, so his days were numbered."

I couldn't stop my brows from lifting straight up into my hairline. Had she been plotting his death?

"Divorce, honey. I wouldn't have really killed him." She had a sinister little smile that made me doubt her.

Before I could answer, there was a knock on her door.

"My goodness. Another neighbor feeling sorry for me?" She stood and made her way to the front door.

I was finding it hard to believe the investigators weren't taking a closer look at her. She admitted to wanting him dead and even thinking of ways to off him.

I heard talking as she made her way back to the living area.

"Join us, won't you?"

A tall, lean fortyish man reeking of money in an expensive charcoal tailored suit, with perfectly plucked eyebrows over dark, ominous eyes, stepped into the room. He exuded power and he gave me the willies. "I was hoping we could speak alone."

"You'll have to wait in line then. Ms. Parker was here first." Mrs. Cullen returned to her seat.

The man looked at me with an expectation that I would leave. He emanated with the kind of power that probably had most people jumping at his every whim.

Instead, finding my inner Mrs. Cullen, I stood and extended my hand. "I'm Sophie Parker."

He studied me as he shook my hand. "Parker?"

I was about to confirm I was the daughter of the local Ponzi crook, but he said, "You were at the airport when Joe was killed."

I pulled my hand back and chanced a glance at Mrs. Cullen to gauge her reaction.

"You were with Joe?" She appeared more intrigued than bothered.

"I was with the man who repossessed the plane." I stepped back from the man but didn't sit. There was a chance I'd need to run. My bravery went only so far.

"The one the police think killed him?" The man stayed where he was, his dark eyes plastering me to my spot.

"They don't know who killed him."

"Well, how could they?" Mrs. Cullen sat back in her chair. "The list is too long."

"You don't seem very broken up about it." The man turned slightly to Mrs. Cullen.

"I'm not. I wish I'd known it was coming so I could have bought life insurance and planned a party."

I winced. She *was* a cold, cold woman. And yet, without life insurance, she didn't have much of a motive.

"Your husband was supposed to meet me the day he died."

My misgivings about this new visitor faded as I realized he might have information that could help me.

"I don't know anything about it."

"Did you work with him?" I chanced a question.

"More like we were partners." The man slid his hands in his pockets and widened his stance, as if he was relaxing. But his face was hard and fierce.

Partners? Was he another Booty Burgo owner?

"In what business?" Mrs. Cullen asked.

The man shrugged. "Import."

"Uh oh," ran like a mantra through my mind. Import. As in drugs? My heartbeat sped up a notch.

"He was going to give me important information about some issues in the business. You wouldn't happen to know where he kept it?"

"As I was telling Sophie, I don't know anything about Joe's business."

The man's dark gaze turned to me. "What's your interest in all this?"

Gulp. "Just curious." My voice squeaked like a mouse.

"Did you see anything?"

I shook my head. "If he was going to meet you, he probably had your information with him." Maybe that was why there were papers strewn about Cullen's office at the airport. His killer was looking for it. What was on it that was worth killing him for?

"She's right." Mrs. Cullen studied her fingernails. "I suppose the sheriff has it now. It wasn't something… illegal was it?"

The man's eyes narrowed. "Why would you say that?"

Mrs. Cullen waved a hand. "Just a joke. Mr. Fletcher,

you need to lighten up." She smiled and even cooed a little bit, and I wondered if Mrs. Cullen was looking for a new, rich husband.

He didn't seem amused or enticed. His jaw tensed. "The information is important. And in the wrong hands…well, let's just say the information is sensitive."

Fletcher? I wondered if that could be the Fletch person Vivie had mentioned seeing with Mr. Cullen. According to her, this Fletch person had unnerved Cullen. The Mr. Fletcher standing in front of me was unnerving.

"I can't help you."

He managed a smile through clenched teeth. "Well, if you find anything, please let me know."

Mrs. Cullen stood. "Do you have a card?"

He reached into his breast pocket, pushing aside the coat enough that I saw a gun holstered at his side.

Hoping I didn't pee my pants on this nice white carpet, I scooted my way around Mr. Fletcher. "You two clearly need to talk alone. It was lovely to see you, Mrs. Cullen. I'll show myself out." I don't think I was running by the time I exited the front door, but it was close.

TEN

I HEADED HOME, my mind whirling with the information I'd learned and trying to sort out what it all could mean. Aunt Rose wasn't home, and I remembered Thursday was her bridge group at the senior center. Even so, I stole away to my room and opened my notebook to record my thoughts.

Joseph Cullen had scheduled a meeting with Mr. Fletcher on the day he died but hadn't made it. What sort of "import" business was Mr. Fletcher in? Could it be Cullen was importing the drugs and Mr. Fletcher was a dealer? Were they partners?

Of course, it was possible my imagination was running away with me. Maybe Mr. Fletcher imported white rugs and Cullen planned to buy one for his wife.

Then there was Maggie Cullen. I could see why Aunt Rose and Aggie suspected her. She clearly hated her husband and wished him dead. But did she kill him? I smacked my forehead as I realized I hadn't asked her where'd she'd been at the time of her husband's death. The first step in the "how to solve a mystery" instructions was getting the timeline, and I'd messed up by not learning where she was. For that matter, I didn't ask Vivie either. Clearly, I wasn't cut out to be a sleuth.

I tossed my book aside and pulled out my coupon binder to add my new coupons. I checked my watch. I still had a couple of hours before I had to be at work. I decided to study the booze book Spike gave me, make a list of great stories for his daughter and take a catnap.

Hours later, I walked into the Booty Burgo in my wench uniform. Avoiding Kyle, I clocked in and headed straight to the bar.

"How's it shaking, Parker?" Spike was pouring a shot of tequila for a customer at the bar.

"I'm alright. I've been studying. Oh, and I made a list of books your daughter might like. They're mostly Hans Christian Andersen." I handed him the slip of paper.

"*The Ugly Duckling* guy?"

I nodded. "And *The Little Mermaid*, *Thumbelina*, the *Emperor's New Clothes* and *The Snow Queen*. That's what the movie *Frozen* was based on."

"Huh. Okay, thanks."

I frowned. "They're good stories."

"I believe you." He slipped the paper in his pocket.

I sighed. Not everyone enjoyed the magic and mystique of fairy tales.

"Parker!"

I jumped at Kyle's voice.

"Yeah."

He held up two fingers, wagging them in a "come here" motion.

"You're in trouble now," Spike said in a low tone.

I smirked at him but dutifully went to Kyle, while I thought of satisfying ways to bring him down a peg or two. "Problem?"

"What's this I hear about you being part of a murder?"

I worked to keep my face placid. "No."

"You weren't at the airport yesterday?"

"Oh that."

He rolled his eyes.

"I was there with a friend, but we'd left before that man was killed."

"You were with AJ Devlin. The sheriff thinks he did it."

"He didn't, though."

He put his hands on his hips and glared at me. "How do you know?"

"I just do."

"So, you don't really know." He eased back slightly.

"Like I told you, it wasn't him. We left."

"That's not what's going around town."

"Oh come on, Kyle. You can't believe everything you hear around town. I surely don't believe the things they say about you." Inwardly, I winced, knowing his next words would be "You're fired."

His nostrils flared. "I don't need people thinking I've hired a crook *and* a murderer."

I clasped my hands behind my back to keep from punching him in the throat. Then I plastered on my most innocent looking Betty Boopish smile. "Well, good, because I'm neither. I just want to work."

"Then get to it." He turned and stalked toward Kim.

I made a face at his back and then headed back to the bar.

A couple hours into my shift, AJ and Bull took seats at the bar.

"Hey, guys." I put a napkin in front of each of them. "What'll you have?"

"I thought you were a waitress." Bull plucked a few peanuts from the bowl.

"Tonight, I'm a bartender."

"She can make martinis." AJ winked at me. The only

problem was, no one ordered martinis, so I couldn't be sure I could make one. I suspected Spike was humoring me, because most people at the bar ordered beer, wine, shots or mixed drinks, like bourbon and soda.

"I'll have a beer. Whatever is dark on tap," Bull said.

"Make it two."

I grabbed a glass and begin to fill it. They sat close enough to the tap I could still talk to them. "Did you learn anything today?" I asked AJ.

He shook his head. "No, but Bull here has some info for us."

"Really?" I set a beer in front of Bull and picked up a second glass.

"It's about Cullen smuggling drugs." Bull took a sip and wiped the foam that stuck to his moustache with his napkin.

"What about it?" I filled AJ's glass and set it in front of him.

"Some friends of mine have suggested he was helping a big-time dealer in the northern and eastern parts of Virginia expand west."

"I've heard there are more drugs around here, but wouldn't we notice drug dealers hanging around?" I pulled out a can of peanuts and refilled the bowl to give me an excuse to talk to them.

"Not if he recruits the local dealers. They already have buyers. This way they get more inventory and, even paying the boss a cut, they end up making more." Bull finished off his beer.

"Does this boss have a name?"

"Everyone calls him Fletch."

I nearly dropped my peanut can.

"Soph?" AJ reached over and took the can.

"I think I met him today."

"What?"

I nodded. "I went and saw Mrs. Cullen and a partner of Mr. Cullen's showed up. I think that was him."

"How'd you even get in the gate?"

Pulling my wits together, I put the can away and checked to see where Spike was. I didn't want him yelling at me for chatting with AJ and Bull. Spike was serving a group of regulars, including Randy Danner, at the end of the bar.

"Vivie let me in."

"I thought she didn't like you," AJ said.

"She did it to accuse me of sleeping with Randy." I said Randy's name softly to avoid him hearing me over the din of voices.

AJ scowled at Randy.

"Then I went to see Mrs. Cullen, who, by the way, admitted to wanting to kill her husband with his clubs. While I was there, a man named Mr. Fletcher stopped by."

"How come the police ain't looking at her?" Bull pushed his glass toward me and nodded for me to refill it.

"I don't know. Maybe she has an alibi. Anyway, she acted like she'd never met Mr. Fletcher."

"Why was he there?" AJ asked.

I refilled Bull's glass and handed it to him. "He said he was supposed to meet with Cullen on the day he died. Cullen was going to give him something but never showed. He showed up at Mrs. Cullen's home wanting whatever Cullen was planning on giving him."

"What was it?" Bull wiped his mouth with the back

of his hand. I handed him a new napkin and he gave me a sheepish smile.

"I don't know. But maybe that was why Cullen was killed."

AJ's brows drew together in thought. "Why would he kill him before getting what he needed?"

I shrugged. "Maybe someone killed him because they didn't want Cullen to give whatever it was to Mr. Fletcher."

AJ inhaled deeply. "Either way, Soph, you should stay out of it. Fletcher isn't someone you want watching you."

"Got that right." Bull's head bobbed up and down.

"He did give me the creeps." I shivered as I remembered his dark, deadly eyes. "What I don't get is that if there is a drug connection, why aren't the investigators looking into it more? Ethan was—"

"Ethan?"

"Deputy Taylor. He's helping Sergeant Davis on Cullen's murder. He was a drug cop in Richmond and is supposed to be looking into the drugs in the area."

"You're calling the investigator who wants to put us in jail by his first name." One of AJ's dark ginger brows arched up.

I stared at AJ a moment, unsure as to why he seemed bothered. "I went to high school with him. It doesn't matter." I waved AJ's question away. "The point is, it doesn't seem like the investigators are looking into the drug angle."

"Either way, it's usually best to stay out of the way of criminals and the police." Bull spoke in a way that suggested he'd had experience trying to do both. "Especially the criminals. Murder is a dangerous business."

"So is capital punishment."

AJ reached out and took my hand. "I won't let that happen to you, Soph."

"Parker!" Spike's deep voice cut through the crowded bar.

I flinched. "Gotta go."

"Wait." AJ gripped my hand. "Do you have a break coming?"

I checked my watch. "In twenty minutes or so."

"I'll wait outside for you."

"Why not wait here?"

"Can't leave Dutch alone too long."

"I'm headin' down the road, Miss Sophie. Don't forget what I said, though. Stay out of trouble. But if you find trouble, you give ole Bull here a call. All right?"

I smiled. "All right."

"I'll be outside." AJ tossed money for his beer on the bar as he stood and then followed Bull out the door.

I'd had time enough to serve two tourists a glass of wine when Kyle interrupted. "Parker." He nodded for me to follow him. Sighing, I complied.

"Was that AJ Devlin you were talking to?"

"I served him and his friend beer."

He shook his head. "He's a murderer."

"No, he's not."

"You don't know that. You need to stay away from him. Away from all of it, if you want to keep your job."

"All of what?"

"Anything to do with Mr. Cullen's murder. He was an owner of this place. It's bad enough you were there when he was killed. It's disrespectful of you to spend time with the man the sheriff's investigators think killed him. Don't see him. Don't be asking questions."

My heart jumped in my chest.

"That's right, Parker. I know you've been asking Danner questions. Knock it off."

Knowing there was no way to win this argument and still keep my job, I nodded. "Of course."

"Hey, Soph, I need a beer."

I turned toward the voice. Speak of the devil. Randy Danner was waving his empty beer bottle toward me.

"Don't forget, Parker."

"I won't." I returned to the bar and got Randy a new beer.

"Douche," Randy muttered. "The only reason I don't fire him is because he's good at managing this place."

Had Randy just saved me from Kyle? I wanted to ask him to put in a good word for me, but the last thing I wanted was to feel indebted to Randy. There was no telling how he'd want me to pay him back.

"Did you tell him I was asking you questions about Mr. Cullen?"

"I don't think so." Randy's face scrunched up as if he was scanning his brain. "Maybe. I don't know."

I rolled my eyes. "He thinks I was."

"Well, you were. Tell me, Sophie, do you think I killed him?" His smirk suggested he was joking, but I took his question at face value.

"I don't know. If this place is doing well, getting rid of him means less of the profits you have to share."

"I suppose. Lucky for me I've got an alibi." He waggled his brows suggestively, and I knew then that Vivie was probably right in assuming he was having an affair.

I considered telling him Vivie was on to him but didn't want to agitate him. I didn't need him *and* Kyle gunning for my job. Still, if he was willing to admit to having a female friend as an alibi, he wasn't keeping it a secret.

"Did you tell the investigators?"

He pressed his fingers over his lips. "Shhh. They promised they wouldn't tell unless it was important to the case. But it's not."

Randy was quickly moving from tipsy to drunk, which meant Spike and I needed to stop serving him.

"I've gotta get back to work, Randy. Let me close out your tab."

He frowned. "I'm not done."

"You are here." Spike's deep voice came from behind me.

Randy pouted as he nearly fell off the stool to get his wallet. He placed his credit card on the bar.

"Here. Have some peanuts. And I'll get you some water." I placed the bowl of peanuts in front of him.

"That'll kill the buzz, and I need it before going home. Vivie is waiting to chew me out about one thing or another."

"Killing the buzz is the point, Randy. You'll just have to face her like a big boy." I wondered if Vivie had already figured out Randy's mystery mistress. I didn't like Vivie, but I couldn't blame her for wanting to let Randy have it.

I never understood cheating. At least not with married people. So many said "it just happened" or "it was an accident." But in my mind, there are plenty of opportunities to catch oneself before cheating, such as during the kissing or the unclothing. It wasn't like you fell and ended up naked and entwined. But that was Randy and Vivie's problem. I had my own troubles to worry about.

I got Randy situated and served a few more customers when I remembered AJ was waiting in the parking lot. "Can I have a break, Spike?"

He checked his watch. "Ten minutes, Parker."

I checked for Kyle, but he wasn't around. Hoping he was in his office, I made my way outside.

At first, I didn't see AJ. As I approached his truck, I noticed the back was down and one of his legs was dangling out of the end. I frowned as a worry niggled up my spine. But as I got closer, I heard exaggerated snoring. When I got close enough to see, AJ was reclined in the back of the truck, his head resting on Dutch's belly. Dutch raised her head, her dark eyes peering at me through the shadowed darkness.

"Huh, well, I wouldn't want to wake him, Dutch. Tell him I was here." I stood at the end of the truck with my hands fisted on my hips.

"Took you long enough." AJ sat up and scooted off the end of the truck bed.

"Yeah, well, I got an earful from Kyle about talking with the likes of you."

AJ stopped. "What do you mean?"

"You're a person of interest in a murder. I was there. It's all very bad for the Booty Burgo's image." I pursed my lips in disdain. "Fortunately, Randy saved me from the tongue lashing."

"Danner." This time it was AJ's face showing disgust.

"I know."

AJ helped me onto the back of the truck bed. "You sure you should be out here talking to me?"

"I'm sure I shouldn't, but here I am. I figure if I get fired, I can go dance in Richmond."

Dutch maneuvered her large body to rest her head on my thighs.

"Sophie." AJ gave me that disapproving big-brother glare. "You can probably find a better job in Charlottesville. For the life of me, I can't figure out why you're here in the first place."

I shrugged. "Someone has to watch out for Aunt Rose. Plus, I was...still am...too broke to go anywhere else." I blew out a breath, not wanting to rehash the mess my life was in again, so I changed the subject. "I think the investigators talked to Randy."

"Makes sense. He had the Booty Burgo to gain." AJ hoisted himself up to sit on the other side of her.

"He said he has an alibi. He was with another woman." I patted Dutch's head.

"That makes sense too. You don't believe him?"

I seesawed my head side to side. "I believe he's a cheater, but it's strange how he suggested he was able to get the investigators to keep his alibi a secret."

"Did he ask you to keep it a secret?"

"Sort of. But why trust me?"

"Because you work for him. He has to know you need this job."

"Maybe."

"Or, perhaps he was letting you know he's available."

"Ew, gross." But AJ was probably right.

"Bull is right, though, Sophie. You should stay out of investigating this murder."

"Me? What about you?"

"I haven't had a run-in with a notorious drug lord. Plus, I have a lawyer who's able to give me information."

"Like what?"

"Why I haven't been arrested, for one."

I shuddered at the thought. "They don't have evidence."

"They have evidence, but nothing that links to me. The only bad thing for me is being there minutes before his death and having argued with him."

"And I give you a motive."

"That's pretty weak, though."

I turned to look at AJ. "So what evidence do they have that doesn't fit you?"

"The club has two sets of prints, Cullen's and someone not in the system."

"Are you in the system?"

He nodded. "Yes, but not for getting arrested."

I furrowed my brow. "So, shouldn't that clear you?" And by extension, me?

"Apparently there was an attempt to clean off the club, so there is the possibility it was still me. I just cleaned off my prints."

"What else?"

"The clubs. The investigators think like we do that the murderer took Cullen's clubs."

"That's why they searched our houses. Mrs. Cullen's house too. But if you'd taken the clubs, they would have been stashed around the airport or on the plane. You didn't have time to dispose of them."

"Right. They checked out Bull's place too."

"Oh no, they think Bull is in on it now too?"

AJ shook his head. "I don't think so. The airport cams show him leaving before we took off, and traffic cams have him in Jefferson Grove a few minutes later. He wouldn't have had time to go back to kill Cullen."

"But you're still on the hook."

"Yes, but at least they can't arrest us. Becca is earning her fee for sure."

"Becca." I hadn't realized the jealous tone I'd used until one of AJ's brows arched at me.

"You have a problem with Becca?"

I couldn't tell him my teenage hormones didn't like her, so I opted to go with a different answer. "I like that she's keeping you out of jail. But I didn't like that she said we couldn't be friends. Although, you're the one breaking that rule."

He smiled as he rested his hand on mine. "What can I say? I'm a rebel."

"It's that Scots Irish blood."

"And here I thought it was the red hair."

I laughed. "It's all part of the same." I wanted to stay with AJ and Dutch all night, but I was pushing it to meet with him at all. If I was late, I'd be on Spike's bad side and I couldn't afford that. "I've gotta get back to work."

AJ nodded and jumped down from the truck. He set his hands on my waist but didn't move. "I mean it, Sophie. You need to stay out of this. It's dangerous and I don't need your help."

"Because you have Becca."

He tilted his head to the side and studied me. I worked to make my face placid so he couldn't see my irrational jealousy.

"Yes."

I swallowed the lump and chastised my heart for retaining its silly feelings for AJ. I nodded, but mostly because I wanted to get back to work. Not because I was agreeing to stop sleuthing. Not that I had any grand investigative plans.

AJ helped me down from the bed of his truck and walked with me to the Booty Burgo door.

"Sophie." AJ's fingers wrapped around my wrist and slid down to my hand.

I looked at our joined hands and then up to his face.

"Stay out of trouble."

I smirked, saluting him with my free hand. "Aye-aye, sir."

ELEVEN

MOST PEOPLE LIKE FRIDAYS. Last day of the work week. What makes it awesome for them is going out and living it up. Many end up at the Booty Burgo, which is what makes my Fridays and Saturdays stressful. This weekend would be especially tough because I hadn't yet bartended during the busiest nights. On the other hand, once people had a drink or two in them, they might not care if I served their drink in the wrong glass.

The third Friday of the month was also the day my father called me from prison, so I usually stuck around the house. Aunt Rose was off at the senior center playing Bunko. My father used to say Aunt Rose could have made a living shooting craps. She had a way with dice. Fortunately, she stuck with Bunko and Yahtzee.

There was nothing to do with my coupons, unless I wanted to resort them. This was another area that vexed me. It seemed obvious how to sort coupons, until you actually had to do it. In my group, Aggie and Tracy sorted by category, such as dairy and bread. The problem was that this method wasn't always easy to use in practice. Milk and ice cream were both dairy but were located in different parts of the store. Aggie decided to sort ice cream into "frozen," while Tracy sorted it into "dessert," but this method still wasn't foolproof. For example, there were a variety of frozen foods from fruits and veggies, bagels, juice, ravioli and complete dinners. But many of those were also found canned or fresh. There was the same problem with "dessert;" the ice cream was frozen but cookies were in another aisle, while candy was in still another and both were separate from baking.

Lani and Gwen sorted by store layout. I liked the store layout idea, except not every store was laid out the same and sometimes they moved things around. Vivie's system involved a spreadsheet only she could understand. Deciding I didn't want to bother my brain with coupons, I pulled up the job search app on my phone to see if anything new had been posted. Jefferson Grove was small enough that it took only a few seconds to scan the current openings. Except for the library position I applied for yesterday, there weren't any new postings. I sat back on my couch/bed, scanning my brain for other ideas. AJ was right. If I didn't come up with a new plan, I could be a wench waitress living in Aunt Rose's house forever. Or at least until she died. The problem was, Parker women tended to live a long time. Aunt Rose's mother, my great-great-grandmother lived to 104. If Aunt Rose lived that long, I'd be here for another twenty years or so. I'd be nearly 50 before I got out again. I had to come up with another solution.

Maybe I should research all those work-at-home offers that popped up when I searched for jobs. Not the get-rich-fast ones, but I'd heard people really do work at home. Maybe one of those places needed someone with a knowledge of folklore. Or perhaps a gaming company needed lore created like I did for my college friends.

I did a quick job search on "work at home folklore" and "gaming folklore writer," but there were zero results. "Folklore writer" resulted in a substitute Celtic

Studies position at a California university. I blew out a breath, as regret for not going to graduate school made my belly clench.

Done with job search disappointment, I pulled out my mystery books and notes to see what, if anything, I could give to Sergeant Scowl and Ethan to get them off AJ's and my back. AJ told me to stay out of it, but I figured talking with the cops wasn't the same as talking to a drug dealer.

As I went through what I'd learned, I realized I didn't have much more than when I started, except that Randy said he had an alibi. I wondered if that was true. Not just that he had an alibi, but that he told the investigators, who agreed to keep it hush-hush. It was so odd for him to tell me about it that I couldn't quite bring myself to believe it was true. Was he bragging? Was it because he was inebriated? Was AJ right that Randy was feeling me out to see if I wanted to be his next notch? Gag!

When my phone rang, I picked it up, expecting to accept the charges from my father.

"Hey, Sophie. It's Ethan."

"Hi, Ethan."

"How are you?"

"Fine." I know I sounded curt, but until I knew if this was a social or a professional call, I had to keep my guard up. Then, remembering my manners, I asked, "How are you?"

"Good. I'm off tomorrow and thought we could have that coffee we talked about."

Social call. This should have made me feel better, but my belly had alternate sinking and fluttery feelings. I didn't completely trust that he was being kind because he wanted to be nice to me. He could be playing me as part of his investigation. On the other hand, it couldn't hurt to have another friend in the sheriff's department.

"What time? I have to work in the evening."

"How about eleven? Before the lunch rush?"

"Sounds good. Where?"

"Jefferson Java Joint?"

"Okay. I'll be there."

"You holding up alright?"

"Could be better, but I could be worse." I heard radio sounds in the background.

"That's a call. I've gotta run. I'll see you tomorrow."

"I'll be there." I clicked off and sat on the couch, wondering if I should have said no. I couldn't wrap my brain around why he'd sought me out. I wanted to believe he was being nice, but I didn't trust myself to know people's intentions. Was he asking me out as part of a plan to find out what I knew about the murder? I didn't know any more than what I'd already told the investigators, but clearly, they didn't believe me. Ultimately, I said yes because I figured I could ask him about Mrs. Cullen and Fletcher. And maybe Randy too.

I putzed around my room a little more and then, because I knew it would be a busy night, I took a nap until I heard Aunt Rose come home. I checked in with her, but she was in a snit over Carl Jackson cheating in Bunko, so I left her to fume. It wasn't until I was dressing for work that I realized I hadn't heard from my dad. It wasn't the first time he'd missed a call in the time he'd been in prison, but it was rare enough that I worried a little bit whether he was okay. Unfortunately, I couldn't call him without a bunch of hassle. I checked my e-mail to see if I had a message alert, the closest thing to e-mailing my father had available to him, but there was no message. I didn't have time to hunt him down before work, and chances were he was fine. He'd probably forgot. He said it was harder to track his days and weeks anymore.

So, I headed off to work. And just to get me in the mood, I played "Hi Ho, Hi Ho," in the car on the way.

I NOT ONLY survived a busy Friday night bartending at the Booty Burgo, but I walked away with enough tips that I could justify paying for printing coupons at the library. I made a ton of mistakes, and I hated to admit the wench outfit probably helped until the beer buzz settled in and the customers didn't care anymore if I messed up their order. Even better, Kyle was out for the night, leaving Spike to manage the place. So, all in all, it was a good night, and I went to bed feeling tired but not down and out, as usual.

The next morning, I woke to Aunt Rose arguing on the phone with a friend about Carl Jackson taking her money. I pulled the pillow over my head and tried to go back to sleep, but it was no use. I went through my usual morning routine and joined Aunt Rose in the kitchen. She made eye contact with me but was too involved on the phone to do much else. I was okay with that. I didn't want to tell her I was meeting Ethan because I couldn't be sure of her response.

Instead, I went back to my room and used my phone to research the coupons I wanted to print on my next trip to the library. Then I got ready for my coffee date with Ethan.

Jefferson Grove had two main streets. The one actually called Main Street had two lanes running one-way northward. The other, Market Street, had two lanes running southbound. It never made sense to me because it created a hassle getting to downtown shops. If I was coming in from the north to a shop on Main Street, I had to drive practically to the end of Market Street then cross over on First Avenue to head back up Main Street. There was a lot of backtracking involved in getting around downtown. But finally, I found a parking spot on the left-hand side of the street. A crosswalk bisected Main Street, although there were no stop signs or lights. Only a warning sign to drivers to watch for pedestrians. As a result, crossing the street always had the potential to be fatal.

I trotted across to Jefferson Java Joint, the local coffee spot, to meet Ethan. I'd never been there or to any of the new shops lining the streets of downtown. It was easier to hide than to endure the stares and whispers. As I made my way near the entrance, I saw Ethan through the window. He stood and waved to let me know where he was. I scanned the rest of the café as I opened the door, wondering who might be there.

"Hi, Sophie. What can I get you?" He held out my chair.

"A regular coffee is fine."

"No milk or froth?" He smiled, and it was hard to remember I was supposed to question his intentions. He wasn't only handsome, but his face, especially his brown eyes, appeared kind. Friendly.

"Maybe a little cream. And sugar."

"I'll be right back."

I sat, my back to the café, looking out the window. At one time, my father had owned much of the commercial real estate in Jefferson Grove, including the building I was now sitting in. According to Aunt Rose, Mr. Cullen had snatched up many of the properties when my father went to jail. She said he raised rents and forced many businesses out, which was probably why, as I scanned the buildings across the street, I didn't see the old hardware store that had also sold ice cream. That space was empty, except for a big "Rent Me" sign in the window. Next to it had been the music store, but that was gone, replaced with a nationwide chain pharmacy. In fact, none of the stores I'd known growing up in Jefferson Grove were still in business.

"Hey, aren't you the lady who was with the repo guy?"

My back stiffened as I looked at the woman who stepped up to my table. Actually, she wasn't quite a woman. I pegged her to be in high school. "Yes." I tried to smile, but it probably looked like a grimace.

"I watch that show. The airplane repo one. What a wild ride that must have been."

I studied the young girl. "It was an adventure all right."

"Did the guy kill Mr. Cullen?" A young man appeared next to the girl.

"No."

Both their expressions fell. "Too bad. Cullen was bad news."

"Hey, Kelly and Matt." Another young man called from across the café.

The girl, presumably Kelly, waved. "We're meeting friends."

"Have fun."

"Tell that repo guy we're rooting for him."

I wasn't sure what that meant. Did they think he killed Cullen but hoped he got away with it? Or did they mean they hoped he could go on more repo adventures. I supposed it didn't matter, so I said, "I'll let him know."

As they walked off, Mrs. Wayland's words came back to me, reminding me it was possible people were talking about me because they were curious, not necessarily because they didn't like me.

"Coffee with a little cream. I grabbed a couple of sugar packets in all colors. I wasn't sure what you might like." Ethan set a large white coffee mug in front of me, along with several colorful packets.

"White is fine." I might be the last woman in the world who used regular sugar. I ripped open a sugar packet and poured it into my coffee.

Ethan sat across from me. "Who were they?"

"Some local kids saying hi."

He frowned. "They weren't hassling you, were they?"

"No. I think they were more curious than anything."

"Good."

We stared at each other in awkward silence.

"So, you're an investigator now."

He laughed, as if he knew I was trying to break the ice. "Yes. After high school I did a couple of years of community college and then went to the criminal justice academy."

"Why not a four-year college? You were really smart in school."

"I guess you wouldn't look at a gawky geek like me and think cop, huh."

Guilt rose. "I didn't mean that. I just…most kids want out of Jefferson Grove. You could have done that."

"I did. I worked as a cop in Richmond, for a time. But my parents are getting on and a job opened up here."

I'd forgotten his parents had been older when they had him. "Do you like being a detective?"

"Sure. I haven't actually done much homicide, though. I was vice. In fact, that's why I was able to get this job. In the last year or so, a lot of drugs have been coming into the area."

"So, why are you on this case?" Of course, I had an idea why. If he was investigating Cullen for drugs, and now Cullen was murdered, it made sense he'd be involved. But I was curious what he'd tell me.

He studied me. "We're not going to talk about the case."

"So, you *were* investigating Cullen."

He had an amused smile. "No comment."

I rolled my eyes. I thought about pushing the matter but it could backfire and he'd end up questioning me. So I decided to move the topic of conversation elsewhere. "Are you glad to be back?"

He glanced out the window. Then he turned back. "People are nicer to me now."

"You say that like it's a bad thing." I blew on my coffee and took a sip. It was strong, just how I liked it. I hadn't had a great cup of coffee since being back in Jefferson Grove, until now.

"I'm the same person I was in high school. Only my packaging has changed."

"Nobody is the same as they were in high school." Except Vivie. "Maybe they're nicer because they're mature and don't worry about whether you're a nerd or not."

He shook his head. "I don't trust it."

Speaking of trust. "Why did you ask me out for coffee?"

He cocked his head to the side, as if he hadn't been expecting that question. "I told you. I thought you could use a friend. Since you were always nice to me, I wanted to return the favor."

I looked out the window again.

"Why?"

When I turned back, I studied him, but I still couldn't determine his sincerity. His eyes were narrow in question, but his features appeared concerned.

"I'm in the middle of a murder investigation and you're one of the cops investigating it. I can't imagine it's okay for you to socialize with me."

He sat back, his fingers turning the cup between his hands. "You think I'm tricking you?"

"I don't know."

He looked insulted. "We agreed we wouldn't talk about the case, so how could I be tricking you?"

I shrugged. "I could let my guard down, let something slip."

"Like what?"

"See." I pointed my finger at him. "Like that. I didn't have anything to do with what happened to Cullen. But you'll turn what I say around."

He studied me for a long moment. "I'm not working, Sophie. I'm not trying to get you to reveal anything to use against you."

I huffed out a breath. "I've been in town for nearly two months and haven't seen or heard from you until you showed up at my aunt's house asking questions that suggested you think I'm part of Cullen's murder. You had to know I was back in town, so you can't pretend the other day was the first you knew of my return."

He looked down. When he looked up, he took a deep

breath. "I knew. And I wanted to call you. But I'm still that awkward guy inside. I didn't know how to approach you."

For the first time since seeing him again, I could see the unsure, slightly off boy I knew in high school. But I couldn't let him sway me. "I can't afford to be naive, Ethan."

He nodded. "I understand that." He sat silent for a minute. "If you can't trust me now, we can wait until this is over."

My brows knitted. "You want to see me that bad?" Once it was out of my mouth, I realized how dumb that sounded. Embarrassed heat rose to my cheeks.

But he laughed. "Yes."

"My life has gotten very complicated."

He nodded and put his hand over mine. "I know. And I'm sorry. But from where I sit, you're tough. You'll get through."

I looked to where his hand covered mine and was surprised by the comfort it brought.

I ENDED MY coffee date with Ethan the same way it started, unsure if I could trust him but wanting to because I needed friends and allies. I didn't kill Joseph Cullen, so I shouldn't be worried anything I said would be used against me, and yet, I was mixed up in murder simply because I was in the wrong place at the wrong time. The truth didn't seem to matter much at this point. Perception, proximity, and timing were working against me.

"Can I walk you to your car?" Ethan stood next to me on the sidewalk outside the coffee café.

"It's just across the street." I nodded toward the Brown Bomber.

Ethan looked to where I'd indicated. "That's quite a car."

I laughed. "That's a nice way to put it. But it runs and has air-conditioning."

"Those are the two most important features to have on a car. And a good radio."

"I don't drive very much, so I don't use the radio very often. Only when I visit my dad."

He nodded. "Do you see him much?"

"About once a month."

"It's nice of you to stand by him."

I sighed. "I don't condone what he did. In fact, I'm disappointed in him that he did it. But he's still my dad and I love him."

Ethan smiled. "You overlook the faults of people. I think that's why I like you."

"Thank you." His compliment felt a little weird. I didn't feel I overlooked faults. I noticed Vivie's and Randy's all the time. I didn't think I overlooked my dad's either. I just had a hard time reconciling the wonderful man who raised me with the one who stole millions of dollars from people who trusted him. "Well, I'll see ya around, I guess."

"See ya."

As good-byes went, it was awkward, but I gave him a small smile and then took the few steps to the crosswalk to head to my car. Like my parents taught me as a kid, I looked for cars before stepping into the street. I glanced back to see if Ethan was still there, but he'd turned and was walking up the street. With a shrug, I stepped off the sidewalk. I'd made it about halfway across the two lanes when I realized there was a car barreling straight at me. Like a dope who couldn't walk and chew gum at the same time, I stopped and looked at the dark sedan as it picked up speed and crossed the right lane into the left, where I was standing.

"Holy—" I worked to get my legs moving again, but it was as if they were glued to the spot.

"Hey, watch out!"

"Sophie!"

I was tackled, knocked to the ground, rolling until we hit the tires of a parked car. There was scrambling and pulling until I thought my arm would come out of its socket. I was dragged to the curb as the car sped by, taking the right mirror of the parked car with it as it passed.

"Oh my God, are you alright?" A chorus of voices gathered around.

I stood stunned, my breath catching in my chest. Before I could get my bearings, Ethan took off running. Without Ethan, my legs gave way, and I plopped down in a heap on the sidewalk. I turned my head to watch Ethan, wondering how his legs could work after all that. He sprinted around the corner and out of sight. Was he chasing a car on foot?

I took a shuddering breath, and that's when the pain surfaced. The bruises and scrapes burned and throbbed. And then came the shakes. I could have been killed.

"Are you alright?"

"I'm calling nine-one-one."

I looked up to a group of people, their faces with various expressions of surprise, concern and wonder. I nodded.

"Just a few scrapes." I looked at my walking shorts,

now soiled with whatever crud was in the road. A few buttons were missing on my shirt, so I pulled it closed to keep myself modest.

"Look at your shoulder."

I glanced down and realized my sleeve was torn, hanging halfway down my arm. In its place was a large, red, angry-looking road rash sore, with bits of asphalt pebbles embedded in my skin. Weird thing about scrapes. They often don't hurt until you realize they're there. Once I saw it, it began to burn and throb like it was on fire. I squeezed my eyes shut and inhaled deeply, hoping for strength enough to keep from disintegrating into a puddle of weepy nerves.

"That guy was gunning for you."

I looked toward the voice. He was a young man, maybe even still in high school, like the kids I'd just met.

"He probably wasn't paying attention." I focused on steadying my breath.

"It looked like he was trying to run you down to me," a woman said.

"Why would anyone want to run me down?" Mostly, I was thinking out loud, trying to distract myself from the pain and panic. Would the car make the loop around Market Street and head back up Main Street to make another attempt at running me down?

"You must have ticked off someone good," the young man said. "Hey, aren't you that lady whose dad and brother ripped everyone off."

There was an audible "oh" from the group as the young man's revelation registered with the small gathering.

"Poor girl. Her family is in jail or run off, and she's

left to take care of crazy old Rose Parker." An older woman shook her head with a tsk tsk as she looked down at me. "And now someone is trying to kill her."

I knew people would be angry at my father and might project that anger on me, but I couldn't imagine anyone wanting to kill me over my father's and brother's actions. I'd been good. Keeping my nose down. Avoiding confrontations. Who'd want to kill me?

Unless it was related to Joseph Cullen. I'd been too panicked to make out the driver of the car. I couldn't even say if it was a man or a woman. I couldn't imagine Maggie Cullen coming after me. I had no doubt Fletcher wouldn't hesitate to kill anyone, and yet, driving like a maniac down a street filled with witnesses didn't seem like his style either. Maybe he'd sent a henchman.

"Sophie." Ethan trotted back up the street and squatted in front of me. "You alright?"

"I'll live."

Just then a county sheriff's car came speeding up, screeching to a halt near us.

"Why don't I take you to the hospital? You might have hit your head."

I had hit my head. The bump throbbed like it had to be the size of a bowling ball. I reached up to touch it. Not a bowling ball, more like a golf ball. But it still took second behind the inferno burning on my shoulder. "I just need ice and a quiet place to sit."

A sheriff's deputy pushed through the small crowd. "Sophie?" Dwayne Lafferty, Lani's husband, squatted down to eye level with me.

"Oh, hi, Dwayne."

"What's going on?" Dwayne looked to Ethan.

"Someone tried to run Sophie down. I pursued the

car, but he got away. I did get a plate number." Ethan showed him a piece of paper but didn't hand it over to Dwayne.

"Okay, show's over." Dwayne stood and began shooing away the bystanders. "Let me get you some water, Sophie, and then I can take the report."

By the time I was done, the pain from my injuries had turned into a dull throb. Even the scrape on my shoulder had calmed to a slow burn. Ethan persisted in wanting me to go to the hospital, but I got in the Brown Bomber and drove home. The house was quiet, thank goodness, so I got a glass of water and a few pain relievers. I checked that all the doors and windows were locked, in case someone was still after me. I took a cool shower, which enraged my shoulder burn, but I forced myself to endure it to avoid infection or having my skin close over the asphalt pebbles. I heaved my physically and emotionally bedraggled body to my room and lay down. There were several hours before I had to be at work, which was probably how long it would take for me to get my bearings back. Why would someone want to kill me? Was it related to Mr. Cullen? It had to be, but why? My brain was too addled to get my thoughts in order, so I closed my eyes and let darkness take me away.

My phone startled me awake. Looking at the time, I'd been out for nearly two hours. I groaned as my body protested when I sat up. "Hello?"

"Sophie, oh my God, Sophie, are you alright?" Lani's worried voice came through the line.

"A little shaken, but fine. How'd you know what happened?"

"Dwayne told me. Plus, Taylor and Davis are working on it. What happened?"

I flopped back on the bed and then winced as my shoulder reminded me I was missing a layer of skin. "I don't know. I really don't."

"Are you sure you're okay? I can take the rest of the day off and come over."

"No. I'm good. I have to work tonight anyway."

"Are you sure you should? I mean, someone is trying to kill you."

Thanks for the reminder. "I'll be okay. I just need to rest a little bit."

"Maybe it was Vivie. The other day she was going on and on that you were doing naughty things with Randy."

"Now I do feel sick."

Lani laughed. "Yeah, Randy isn't what he used to be."

"Yeah, he is. He just looks different on the outside."

"Get some rest. Call me when you have time. You can come over and we'll make wine coolers."

"Did I tell you I'm bartending now? Maybe I can make you a martini."

"Well, we do have some catching up to do. I'll call you later."

I hung up with Lani, dropping my phone on the bed and turning over to get more sleep when my phone rang again.

"Yeah?"

"Sophie? It's Ethan. How are you feeling?"

"Okay, I guess." Why wouldn't the world let me sleep?

"We have something on your case. Can you come down to the station?"

"That fast?" I perked up at the idea my would-be killer had been found.

"Yes. Can you come down? Or if you like, I can pick you up."

"No, I can come. Do you know how long it will take? I've got to work tonight." I checked my watch to see what time it was.

"An hour, maybe."

I'd be cutting it close to get to work, which meant I'd need to wear my Booty Burgo uniform to the sheriff's office. Well, that wasn't gonna happen. "Let me get cleaned up and I'll be down."

My uniform wouldn't hide the scrape, so I decided to risk Kyle's wrath, and maybe my job, by wearing a white T-shirt instead. It was scooped neck and form-fitting, suitable for a place like the Booty Burgo, and, more importantly, better suited than an off-the-shoulder top that would expose my scrape and a corset for visiting the sheriff's office. I put a bandage on my wound, which did little to reduce the pain of a bra strap, but I was willing to endure it to avoid my uniform top.

An hour later, I walked into the Jefferson Grove sheriff's office. Located downtown, it was housed in the site that a hundred years earlier had been the Jefferson Grove High School. After WWII, the population of the town grew and by the 1950s, a new school was needed.

"Sophie." Ethan put his hands on my shoulders, making me wince at the pressure on my wound. "Oh, sorry." He withdrew his hands, but he studied me.

"So, what did you find out?"

"Come with me."

He led me to his desk and pulled out a chair for me to sit.

"Ms. Parker." Sergeant Scowl joined us.

"We traced the plate." Ethan sat next to me.

"Okay." There was something strange in the way he said it and looked at me. As if I wouldn't like what he was about to tell me. Or wouldn't believe it. Had Aunt Rose tried to run me down?

"The car is registered to Liza Devlin."

"Liza Devlin." I scanned my brain to remember who that was. Clearly, she was related to AJ, but most of the residents of the Hollow were related to AJ in one way or another.

"AJ Devlin's mother."

I glanced at Sergeant Scowl. "I don't know her. I'm not sure I've ever met her. Why would she want to kill me?"

"It wasn't her." Ethan's voice was gentle, especially compared to the gruffness of Sergeant Scowl.

I turned my attention back to Ethan. "But you just said—"

"She was in a pottery class offered by the retirement community she lives in."

"Okay." I wished they would just spit out whatever they were taking their sweet time to tell me.

"This is video footage of the residential community building and the garage where the car is kept."

"Video? You do work fast."

"Yes, well, Deputy Taylor seems to have a vested interest in this case and drove directly to Charlottesville to get the tapes." Sergeant Scowl's voice suggested he didn't like Ethan's "vested interest" in the case, which had to mean he knew Ethan was being a friend to me.

Ethan poked a button on his computer. A grainy video played, showing what looked like a woman walking into the community center lobby. There were a few stills of her walking along the residential area hallways. "That's the hall Ms. Devlin lives on."

The video changed, and the woman was walking into the parking garage. "We don't have her getting into Ms. Devlin's car, but we do have a shot of her in the car from the street cam right outside the garage."

A part of me was amazed at how quickly they'd gathered this evidence. But another part of me was wondering what it all meant.

"Do you recognize her?" Sergeant Scowl's gruff voice cut in.

"Can I watch it again?"

Ethan replayed the video. I studied the woman. The video was black and white, so I couldn't see colors. But I could tell the hair was light, and in a short style worn by older women. She wore a long, trench-like coat, pulled tight around a plump middle. The coat was odd, considering it wasn't raining and it was over ninety outside. As the woman approached the staff counter in the residential facility, I could tell she was taller than usual. The next scene she was making her way up the corridor. Something about the way she walked was strange. Not just in the gait, but in style.

"Are you sure that's a woman?" I turned to look at Ethan.

"Why would you ask that?" His tone suggested they questioned this person's gender as well.

"She doesn't walk like a woman."

"Not all women flaunt their stuff," Sergeant Scowl said.

I sent him a piercing glare. "It's not that. It's…" I watched the woman a little bit more. "She walks flat-footed, not heel to toe. And…well… I wonder if that's a disguise because it's too hot for a trench coat."

"We agree." Ethan turned the video off. "In fact—"

"We believe it's AJ Devlin."

My head swung around to Sergeant Scowl. "What?"

"Who else would have access to his mother's car?" Ethan's voice was soft and sympathetic. He knew I wouldn't like what they were saying.

I returned my attention to him. "AJ? He wouldn't try to kill me."

Ethan glanced at Sergeant Scowl and then back at me. "You place him at the scene of a murder."

I shook my head, unable to wrap my brain around what they were saying. "No. That's wrong."

"I'm afraid it's not. We've got him in an interrogation room right now. I'd like to interview him more, so I need you to tell me what you saw today, what AJ may have said to you before. Have you seen him since the murder?"

The room was spinning. I put my hand on the desk to hold on so I didn't get tossed from my chair.

"Let me get you some water." Ethan patted my hand and stood.

"What is your relationship with AJ?" Apparently, Sergeant Scowl didn't care that my world was tilting off its axis.

"A friend. He wouldn't do this."

"What kind of friend?"

In some ways, I was grateful for Sergeant Scowl's gruff demeanor. It got my dander up, which pushed aside the unsettled feelings. "A friend friend. He's like a big brother to me. He wouldn't hurt me."

Ethan returned with a coffee cup filled with water. I

took a sip, letting the cool liquid soothe my constricted throat. What if they were right? No, they couldn't be right.

"What does the lady at the front counter say?"

"She confirmed our suspicion that this is a man."

"And she let him in?"

"Apparently she thought it was amusing the lengths Liza would go to for conjugal visits."

Eww. I shook my head. "Then it couldn't be AJ. Wouldn't the lady at the counter know him?"

"Have you talked to AJ since the murder?" Ethan ignored my question.

I nodded. "Just briefly." I turned my attention to Sergeant Scowl. "He apologized for putting me in this situation."

"Why were you in that situation?" Sergeant Scowl wasn't moved by my plea.

"I told you before. I ran into him and was having a bad day. So, he invited me to go along on his repo of the plane. If he intended to kill Mr. Cullen, he wouldn't have invited me. He wasn't even supposed to be there."

Ethan frowned. "How do you know?"

"Another man was supposed to do the repo."

"We don't think this was a premeditated murder. We think Mr. Devlin and Mr. Cullen got into an altercation and Mr. Devlin killed him. Your statement supports that. You saw them argue." Ethan rested a hip on the edge of his desk.

I closed my eyes, hating that my statement was putting a noose around AJ's neck.

"Your statement hurts him. It could put him in jail for life. Maybe even under the needle."

I really wanted to punch Sergeant Scowl.

I shook my head and worked up the strength to appear confident. "Mr. Cullen tried to hit AJ, but AJ backed away. He wasn't being aggressive."

"So maybe it was self-defense. But it doesn't change the fact AJ killed Mr. Cullen." Sergeant Scowl was like a dog with a bone. But it couldn't be true.

"And because you can place him at the scene, at the time of the death, and you can attest to their arguing, you can put him away. That's a strong motive for murder." He crossed his arms across the barrel of a chest like an exclamation point to his statement.

My stomach rolled in my belly. It couldn't be true. And yet, what they were saying made sense. I looked at the still shot of the person in the video. Grasping at straws I said, "AJ isn't fat."

"We think that's a pillow." Sergeant Scowl had an answer for everything.

"Sophie." Ethan's voice, calm and gentle, drew my attention. "Even with all this, we can't arrest AJ."

The fact that my nerves spiked suggested I was beginning to believe them. I was afraid of AJ.

"The car was wiped down. Not even Liza Devlin's prints are in it."

"Even if AJ's prints were in the car, a lawyer would say, as her son, he'd have access to it," Sergeant Scowl added.

"And this video is too grainy to know who it is." Ethan put his hand on mine that was now gripping the desk. "What we're saying is, you may still be in danger."

"Okay." So what then?

"You need to watch yourself," Sergeant Scowl said. "Stay home and keep the doors locked. Stay around people when you're out."

"I was around people when I was crossing the street."
Sergeant Scowl shrugged.

"What we're saying is you need to be diligent about
your safety." Ethan nodded and, by osmosis, I nodded
back. "We're not done with this case, but unless he
confesses today, we don't have anything to hold him."

I looked into Ethan's dark brown eyes. "Is it possible
it was someone else?"

His eyes shone with pity. "Who else wants you
dead?"

I shook my head. "No one."

"Let us see what we can get. I'll be in touch." Ethan
stood. "Let me walk you to your car." His eyes scanned
my short black skirt and snug T-shirt. "Are you working tonight?"

I nodded.

"Is there someone who can escort you to your car
after work?"

"Spike."

"Okay. When you drive, lock your doors. Ask Spike
to stay and not leave until you do."

I nodded and turned to leave.

Ethan walked next to me. "It'll be okay, Sophie."

But I knew he couldn't be sure of that.

TWELVE

THE TWENTY-MINUTE DRIVE to the Booty Burgo gave me time to think. And the more I thought about what I'd just learned, the more guilt I had for doubting AJ. Yes, everything Sergeant Scowl and Ethan said was true. I did see AJ argue with Mr. Cullen. I was a witness that put him at the scene near to the time of the crime. But if AJ wanted me dead, there were so many other times he could have killed me. At his house or here in the Booty Burgo parking lot would have been much better places than on a busy street in Jefferson Grove. But what really had me rethinking Ethan and Sergeant Scowl's logic was the golf club.

I parked my car and sat for a moment as I ran through all the information that proved AJ couldn't have killed Cullen. First was the fact he wasn't even supposed to be there. Some guy named Patch was. Second, if the killer took the golf clubs, AJ would have had to have brought them on the plane, which he didn't. And if he had, the police confiscated the plane right when we landed, so AJ didn't have time to dispose of them, which meant the police would have found the clubs on the plane. This was all stuff AJ told me that Becca had explained. Surely the investigators realized it too.

I imagined Sergeant Scowl would have some response, such as AJ hid them and went back later to get them, which I supposed could be true, except where could he have hidden them at the airport that the sheriff's investigators wouldn't have found them?

I was so deep in thought that I didn't notice anyone approaching my car until he rapped on the window. I jumped and opened the car door. "Ethan?"

He gave me a sheepish smile. "I just had to make sure you got here alright."

I stepped out of the car, a little annoyed. "I don't need a bodyguard."

"Someone tried to kill you today."

"Yes, but it wasn't AJ." I closed the car door, waiting for Ethan's response.

He cocked his head and put his hands on his hips. "How do you know?"

I knew telling him AJ would never hurt me wasn't going to convince him. So, I went with the facts. "For one, the golf club."

His brows drew together. "What about it?"

"AJ didn't have one."

"It was a crime of opportunity. It was in Cullen's office already."

"A wedge?" I shook my head incredulously. "A putter, maybe. But no one keeps just a wedge in their office."

"How do you know?"

"Because I used to play golf. My dad and a bunch of his friends played golf."

Ethan shifted back and forth on his feet. "Maybe he pulled it from the bag."

"So, where's the bag? I don't have it, as you know. AJ doesn't have it. It wasn't with us on the plane when the cops searched it. My guess was it wasn't in Cullen's car."

Ethan turned his head toward the lush green slopes of the Blue Ridge, but I was certain he wasn't admiring the scenery.

On a roll, I continued on. "Why would someone take the bag but leave the club? And why would the bag be in Cullen's office in the first place?"

Ethan shook his head. "Where should it be?"

"If he was playing a lot, most likely he'd keep them in the trunk of his car. They were nice clubs, so maybe he was afraid they'd be stolen, but still, why bring them into his office? Unless he was leaving and taking them with him. Or maybe staying there."

"You mean like living in his office?"

I nodded. AJ and I had pondered that question and it made sense. Maybe he was hiding and getting ready to run. But from who?

"He did a lot of business in Florida. There are a lot of golf courses in Florida." Ethan offered another explanation.

"And drugs."

Ethan nodded. "But we have no evidence he brought drugs back with him."

"But you have your suspicions. You were investigating him."

"You say that he wouldn't have just a wedge club with him. That he'd have the entire bag, but why would the murderer take the bag and leave the murder weapon?"

I shrugged. "You're the detective." I tried to be nonchalant about it, but I was wondering the same thing. "Maybe there was something in the bag. Bags have lots of pockets to store things. A golf buddy of my dad's used to sell moonshine from his golf bag on the course."

"Moonshine?" Ethan's brows rose in skepticism.

"Honest to God." I lifted my right hand in salute. "He could fit several of those thin pint bottles into his bag. He sold out every time he played."

Ethan shook his head. "The point is, someone tried to kill you today. And only AJ had a motive and access to his mother's car."

"That we know of." I didn't like the idea that someone I didn't know was gunning for me over something I didn't know about, but it was the only thing that made sense.

"Remember when you told me you couldn't afford to be naive?"

I nodded.

"Are you sure you're not being naive about AJ? What's your relationship with him anyway?"

I sighed. "He's just a friend. He looks out for me, like a big brother."

"I just don't think you can so easily dismiss him," Ethan said.

"And I don't think you can focus on him to the exclusion of other possibilities. If you're so worried about my safety, then you need to consider someone else was in that car." The burn of my annoyance rose.

"How would someone else get AJ's mother's car?"

"I don't know. Perhaps you can investigate it." I know I was being snarky, but I was sore, physically and emotionally.

Ethan rolled his eyes.

I had a ton of questions about the drug investigation and Mr. Fletcher, but I was irritated at Ethan's dismissal of my ideas and about to be late to wench duty. "I've got to get to work." I stepped around him and started toward the front door of the Booty Burgo.

"Remember to have someone escort you to your car when you leave."

"Yeah, yeah."

I walked into work and headed straight to log in, hoping Kyle didn't see me and send me home to change. Or fire me. Making a quick scan of the room, I saw him over by the doors to outside seating, wagging a finger at Kim. I was starting to feel sorry for her.

I punched in my time and scurried to the bar.

"Hey, Parker." Spike took in my T-shirt. "Is that Kyle approved?"

"Probably not. But I was in an accident and my shoulder looks like hamburger. That's not something people in a restaurant want to see."

"That was you? I heard about someone nearly getting run down."

"That was me."

"Parker? What are you wearing?" Kyle's voice rang through the restaurant.

I closed my eyes and prayed for strength. I plastered on a smile and turned to Kyle just as he reached me. "I didn't think you'd want people seeing this huge scrape on my shoulder." I pulled my shirt collar aside and lifted the edge of the bandage so he could see.

"Gross. That was from nearly getting run down today?"

"Yep. And it hurts, a lot. But I'm here, Kyle." After all, I could have called in sick.

"I need to talk to you." He nodded toward the back. My stomach sank. He was going to fire me. I glanced back at Spike, who shrugged, then followed Kyle to the office.

"Look, I'm sorry about not wearing—"

"It's not that." He motioned me all the way in the office and then shut the door. He looked at me with his stern manager scowl, which wasn't easy since he had a boyish face. "All this attention on you with Mr. Cullen's murder, and AJ Devlin, and then today, nearly being run down…well, it's not good for business."

I frowned. "I haven't noticed a drop." Although I was working the bar now. Maybe there were less customers in the restaurant and I didn't notice.

"People are talking. They're uncomfortable with a possible murderer serving their food." He pulled out a coin from his pocket and began playing with it between his fingers.

"It's a pirate bar."

He stared at me.

"Pirates are murderers. I'm a novelty." I smiled, but he didn't seem amused.

I sighed. "I didn't ask for this, Kyle."

"Rumor is you're poking your nose around the investigation. That doesn't help."

I wondered how he knew that. Was Randy narcing on me again?

"I didn't have anything to do with Mr. Cullen's murder. I want to clear my name."

"If you want to work here, you have to keep a low profile. Let the sheriffs' people find the murderer. You just look pretty and serve drinks."

At least he wasn't firing me. Yet. I nodded.

"Now, get to work."

I hurried out of his office before he changed his mind.

Spike looked up as I came around the bar. "We

should create a drink after you. The Sophie Splat." He winked at me.

I smirked. "I'm sure that would be a big seller." But then it had me thinking. "Can you make up drinks?"

"You mean can *we* or can it be done in general?"

"Both."

"We don't have much need for fancy drinks here."

He was right. It wasn't like *Sex and the City*. I doubted the Booty Burgo ever received an order for a Cosmopolitan.

"But yeah, you can mix and match to create your own drinks. Mixology. There's a whole science to it. You have something in mind?"

"Nah. I was just curious."

"Maybe some time when it's slow you can experiment. Or come in early, before the lunch crowd."

"Really?" I don't know why, but that cheered me up.

"But right now, you need to find out what Kim and Missy need for their tables."

Saturday nights at the Booty Burgo were as busy as Friday nights. I felt overwhelmed at times keeping up on the drink orders, especially now I'd graduated to mixing drinks. Even so, it was better than waitressing.

"Do you know you look like Betty Boop?" Walt Cuthbert grinned at me from his wrinkled pug-like face. He had to be nearing the century mark.

"She's too young to know who that is," Walt's buddy, Paulie, who was just as old and wrinkled, said.

I set their glasses of beer on the bar. "Boop-oop-a-doop."

"Hey." Walt's face lit up. "You do know."

I winked and left the two men to their beers and

reminiscing about the old days, which in their case was just after WWII.

"Sophie."

I turned and saw Randy Danner and another man, who looked familiar, but I couldn't place, take a seat at the bar. I quickly glanced at Spike, hoping he'd be able to serve them. Randy was as regular at the bar as Walt and Paulie, but not as charming. But since Randy was part owner, I was forced to be nice, which wasn't easy. Unfortunately, Spike was busy mixing a martini.

I blew out a breath and stepped to the two men.

"Good evening, gentlemen."

"Sophie, you remember Bobby Cunningham, don't you?"

Not really, but I nodded.

"I was on the football team with your brother."

Oh yeah. He used to hang out with my brother's other teammates at the house sometimes.

"He's in town visiting family so I thought I'd take him out for a drink." Randy patted Bobby on the shoulder.

"So, what can I get you?"

The two men ordered beers, but before I could turn to get their drinks, Bobby said, "I thought you got out of town. Why are you bartending in a dumpy restaurant?"

"Hey." Randy glared at Bobby in offense.

"Long story," I replied.

Randy leaned over and said something to Bobby. Bobby's gaze flicked to me and awareness came into his eyes. Yep, that was me. The daughter of the Ponzi king. I got their drinks and was eager to move on to the next customer, but Randy wasn't having any of it.

"Heard about what happened downtown today. You look pretty good for nearly being run over."

"Thanks." I tried to turn again. I was just reprimanded because customers were discussing my woes. I didn't need Kyle coming out and noticing Randy and Bobby talking to me about my near hit-and-run.

"Do the cops think it's related to the murder you witnessed?"

"Murder?" Bobby stopped mid-drink to stare at me.

"I guess so."

"So they think Devlin tried to kill you?" Randy had it out for AJ, just as Sergeant Scowl and Ethan did. I supposed everyone in town wouldn't have difficulty thinking AJ was a murderer, considering the circumstances. But I imagined Randy had a personal grudge since AJ had come to my rescue when Randy got too frisky one night at the lake when we were in high school. I thought I'd done a pretty good job fending Randy off with a knee to the groin, but AJ had felt compelled to add insult to injury and punched Randy. Twice.

"Which one?" Bobby asked.

"They're looking into that, but I don't believe it was AJ." I scanned the restaurant to make sure Kyle wasn't lurking. Maybe Randy was setting me up to get fired. Although, as part owner, he could do it himself, couldn't he?

"AJ Devlin?" Bobby sipped his drink. "I thought he got out of Jefferson Grove too."

"Not far enough." Randy sported a smug smile I wanted to slap off his face.

"So, who's dead?"

"Cullen."

Bobby whistled. "Huh. I guess he had it coming."

I forgot my other customers and stepped closer to the bar near Bobby. Apparently, he knew about Cullen and I wanted to know it too. I chanced a glance at Kyle, who was busy wagging a finger at Kim again. If he hassled me, I could say Randy brought it up. Which was true. And Randy was now the sole owner of Booty Burgo, unless Mrs. Cullen got her husband's half. He'd keep me on…wouldn't he?

"Bobby's parents had to close their business because of Cullen," Randy explained to me.

"Personally, I wasn't heartbroken. My dad wanted me to take over, but I like living in civilization and had no plans to return to Jefferson Grove. Still, the business had been in my family for three generations. My dad left and then the store next to him…the one owned by the Samuels family also closed. A couple others went out of business as well within six months of us."

"I guess he hurt a lot of people." I felt some guilt. If my father hadn't run his scam, Mr. Cullen wouldn't have taken over as landlord to the buildings and put these families out of business.

"Yeah, but only AJ was there when he was killed."

I knew Randy was poking at me. My teenage crush hadn't been a secret, and, like his mean, old wife, he was enjoying bugging me about it.

"She's right though. I bet half the town isn't sorry he's gone. If AJ did it, they should give him a medal."

I wanted to offer Bobby a drink on the house. His thinking was basically the same as Aunt Rose's.

"He wasn't well liked, that's for sure. Even his wife thought he was awful and she's no peach. Maybe she did it."

Maggie might be a nag of a wife, and she certainly

wanted her husband dead, but there wasn't any evidence pointing to her. Was there?

"It wasn't her." Gwen sidled up to the bar next to Bobby. "Can I have a white wine, Sophie?"

"Chardonnay or Pinot Grigio?"

"Pinot."

"How do you know it wasn't her?" Randy glanced at Gwen but apparently wasn't interested and turned back to his beer.

I quickly grabbed the bottle of wine so I could hear Gwen's answer.

"She was getting her nails done. At least that's what Susie Minor said when she was doing my nails."

I poured the wine and placed the glass in front of Gwen.

"She's hoping Mrs. Cullen will move away. Susie says she's a terrible customer. Always complaining and rarely tipping."

"So, not the wife. That leaves AJ."

I took Randy's beer bottle before he was finished.

"Hey." He grabbed it back. "I'm not done."

"Did you ever notice anything funny about Cullen's books?" Bobby asked Randy.

That had my attention.

Randy shook his head. "All I saw was legitimate dealings. But I wouldn't be surprised if he had a second set of books somewhere."

I wanted to ask why Randy was doing Cullen's books but he didn't do the books for the Booty Burgo, since he was part owner. I wasn't sure how to ask without appearing nosy.

"Maybe he was killed for that," Bobby offered.

"Rumor is he smuggled drugs on his plane." I wiped

down the counter, hoping Spike didn't notice I wasn't working.

"No kidding?" Bobby said.

"I think his little empire was circling the drain and he was doing anything and everything to save his fortune." Randy made a circling motion with his finger.

I studied Randy. "He was going broke?"

Randy nodded. "Yep."

Well, of course he was. He hadn't paid his hangar fees and his plane was repoed. Except, he was part owner of the Booty Burgo. As far as I could tell, it did good business. But again, I wasn't sure how to ask about their partnership.

"His only business venture that was making money was this place, although, over the last few months, profits are down a little bit, but still, pretty good. It wasn't enough for a high and mighty guy like him, though. And his wife spent more than even my wife does. He couldn't afford to live like that and desperate times call for desperate solutions," Randy said.

"You think he was smuggling to make money?" Bobby asked.

"I think anything is possible. That man would sell his mother to save his fortune."

"Parker!" Spike's voice cut through the din of voices.

"Gotta go." I hurried to the next customer but Spike stopped me.

"You've got a phone call. Make it quick." He nodded toward the phone on a shelf at the back of the bar.

"Hello?" Who the heck would be calling me at work?

"Sophie?"

"Aggie?"

"Sophie Parker, you need to call your aunt Rose right

now. That woman is worried sick about some news that you were run over today. Was that you?"

"Well, I wasn't run over, but I was nearly hit."

"Call your aunt. She thinks you're dead."

The phone clicked off. I glanced over my shoulder at Spike, who was serving margaritas to a couple of young women I didn't recognize. I dialed Rose's number.

"Who is it?" Aunt Rose's cranky voice answered the phone.

"Aunt Rose? It's Sophie. I heard you were looking for me."

"Sophie? Is that you? You better be in the hospital because you haven't been in touch with me all day and I've got the church phone line ringing off the hook wanting to know about your funeral."

"I'm fine. I'm at work."

"Then what's all this about you being killed by a Mack truck on Main street today."

I shook my head at the ridiculousness of the grapevine. "A car almost hit me, but I'm fine."

"Why didn't you tell me? You need to tell me things. How will I be able to look your father in the eye, assuming he gets out of jail before I die, if you're killed on my watch. Huh? Tell me that."

"I'm sorry." A sharp thwap snapped on my butt, making me jump. Spike dragged his hand across his neck in the universal sign to cut off the phone. "You were out today so I didn't have a chance to call you. I've got to get back to work, but I'll tell you all about it tomorrow."

"If I'm alive then. You scared twenty years off my life. You know what that makes me now, Sophie? A hundred and six."

"I'm sorry."

Spike depressed the switch, cutting the line.

I closed my eyes, imagining the wrath I'd get for hanging up on Aunt Rose.

"Get to work." Spike pointed to the end of the bar where Gwen, with an empty glass of wine, was leaning intimately close to Bobby, who was hailing me for more drinks. I guess he was her next frog. Randy was turned away from them, his phone pressed closely to his ear.

I served Gwen another glass of wine and Bobby a beer just in time to hear Randy say, "No, dawlin', they don't know anything." He cast a glance at me as I reached for his now-empty beer bottle. He lifted a finger to indicate he wanted another one then turned back to his call. "Sure, honey, I'll be there later."

"That your alibi?" I set Randy's beer in front of him.

He winked and saluted me with his beer. "Think I'm getting lucky tonight."

I wanted to slap him. Or gag. I spent the rest of the evening serving drinks and pondering Joseph Cullen's murder. With so many others who truly despised the guy, why were the investigators so focused on AJ? Granted, the timing and the argument between the two men didn't look good, but the airport was a public place. Anyone could have been lurking about and killed him, like whoever was in the two cars parked behind Cullen's Audi.

What was most disconcerting, though, was that whoever it was thought I knew something, otherwise why try to run me over? So, what did I know?

THIRTEEN

IN MANY SMALL towns in the south, life significantly slowed down on Sundays. People went to church and had supper with the family, and that was about it. It was the same in Jefferson Grove, where everything was closed on Sunday, except for the Booty Burgo.

My family was one of the few in town that weren't regular church goers, but Aunt Rose was and insisted I join her. So, Sunday morning I spent with Aunt Rose and her buddies at church, then I planned to go with her to a potluck held at Tilly Watson's house. But I got a call from Lani saying she'd hit the mother lode of coupons and she was willing to share.

"Dwayne was patrolling behind the IGA and he found stacks, and I mean stacks, of bundled coupon inserts. I couldn't possibly use them all."

"Who else is coming?"

"Well, I had to invite the others. But there's plenty to go around. And it's just clipping. No exchanging."

"Vivie too?"

There was a pause on the phone. "I had to invite her and Tracy. They're in the group."

I understood that. I'd never ask Lani not to invite them, but I could decide not to go.

"But she and Tracy can't come. There's some shindig at her mom's house. So, you're safe."

Well, in that case. "I'll see you in a few." I changed out of my church clothes and grabbed my binder.

"You're leaving me again?" Aunt Rose sounded exasperated as she put the finishing touches on her potluck dish.

"I'll be back. And I'm okay." I couldn't assess if she was really concerned or just overzealous in her commitment to watch over me.

She put the lid on her casserole and turned to me. "How do you know some maniac isn't out there waiting to take you out?" I couldn't be sure, but I wasn't going to say that.

"I'll be fine. Go enjoy your potluck. I know they love your corn casserole."

"Well, of course they do."

"I have to work tonight, so if I don't see you, after your potluck, that's where I've gone."

Her eyes squinted. "You act right, Sophie Parker. That place is filled with sin."

"Yes, ma'am."

Fifteen minutes later, I parked in the lot in front of Lani and Dwayne's townhouse. The community was built in the 1970s and offered affordable housing for first-time home buyers like Lani and her husband. Their unit was on the end, which meant it had more windows and only one shared wall, which was important when Dwayne worked nights and slept days.

"Hey, girl." Lani opened the door holding an inch-high stack of coupon inserts. "Happy birthday." She thrust them at me. "And there's more where that came from."

"He did hit the mother lode." I took the coupons as I stepped into her tidy little home. "Is Dwayne here?"

"He's at his mom's house. He's painting her kitchen. So, we can have a coupon party. Gwen's already here." Lani did a little dance.

I followed her back to her kitchen, where several large stacks of coupon inserts sat on her table. Each stack contained hundreds of the same type of insert. Even in my limited experience with coupons, I understood that this was good. Not just because having lots of coupons meant lots of savings, but also, having a bunch of the same coupon made it easy to stock up. My one great purchase so far was a doubled fifty cents off toothpaste on sale for $1.50. That meant I got it for fifty cents. It would have been nice to have five of those coupons so I could have stocked up and had enough toothpaste to last the year.

"Hello?" Aggie's voice rang through the home. I turned and saw her peeking through the doorway.

"Come on in, Aggie," Lani called from the kitchen.

Aggie joined us, her eyes growing round at the sight of all the coupons. "Great day! Look at that. I don't think I've ever seen so many coupons. All these were just sitting out for Dwayne to pluck up?"

"Can you believe it?" Gwen looked up from the insert she was thumbing through. "Who knew we should be dumpster diving for coupons?"

"Pretty great, huh?" Lani grinned.

"They were in the dumpster?" I hung my purse on the chair and set my binder on the table.

"No. They were in bundled stacks next to the dumpster. Dwayne saw them when he drove through the back side of the IGA." Lani grabbed a mug from her cupboard. "Want coffee, ladies?"

"Yes, thanks." I eyed the bundles of coupons. "You

don't suppose they were supposed to be used by a pa-perboy?"

"Well, if they were, he shouldn't have put them by the dumpsters." Gwen had a glow on her face that made me think of Christmas morning. Or maybe she got lucky with Bobby.

I should have been more excited than I was. But the weight of being a murder suspect, and possibly becoming a victim, hung heavy over me. That, and my body ached from nearly being run over yesterday.

"How you feeling, Sophie?" Lani handed me a mug of hot brew and I sat at the table.

"I've been better, but I've been worse."

"Yeah, what was that I heard about you getting hit by a truck?" Gwen took her coffee from Lani.

I laughed. "It was a car and it didn't actually hit me. Ethan knocked me out of the way before it could run me down."

"Ethan?" One of Gwen's brows twerked upward.

"Ethan Taylor."

"You may not know him, Gwen. He was in Sophie's and my class. He moved back about a year ago. He's a cop." Lani handed Aggie coffee and joined us at the table.

"He's a cop on your case and you call him Ethan?" Gwen had this strange and annoying habit of thinking every man-woman interaction had some undercurrent of romance. Or maybe just lust.

"It's not like that."

"What's it like?" Aggie's narrow eyes studied me. She wasn't thinking the same thing Gwen was, was she?

I shrugged, hoping they'd get the hint there was nothing romantic between Ethan and me. At least not from my end. What Ethan wanted was still a mystery. I wanted to think he wanted to be friends. Maybe there'd been a little current of attraction during coffee. But I couldn't get past my fear it was just a ploy to incriminate AJ and/or me. "He's working with Sergeant Sco—Davis on the Cullen murder."

"He was interrogating you over coffee?" Lani's lips quirked up slightly, suggesting she wasn't buying my explanation either.

I blew out a breath. "I was nice to him in high school and so he's trying to be nice to me now."

"Remember what I told you the other night, Sophie," Aggie warned. "You can't let some man come in and fix your life."

I shook my head. "He's not fixing it and it's not like that."

"Why not? He's cute." Lani waggled her brows. "A lot different from high school."

"What was he like in high school?" Gwen sipped her coffee.

"Nerd," Lani said. "Nice, but really geeky."

"Well, if he's a cop and cute, and if someone is out to get you, it couldn't hurt to have him around," Gwen said.

"Is someone out to get you?" Aggie leaned forward, concern etching her brow.

"The sheriff's investigators think it was the same person who killed Mr. Cullen."

"They think it was AJ," Lani blurted. "I know you like him, but maybe you should stay away from him."

I frowned. "It wasn't AJ. And I *am* staying away because Kyle and AJ's lawyer have told me to stay away. Apparently, I'm bad news all around."

"What?" Lani had the good graces to look indignant. "How is that even possible?"

I held up one finger. "First, my father and brother are in prison. Two, Mr. Cullen put my father in prison. Three, I was there around the murder, linking us all together."

"So?" Gwen asked.

"So, us hanging out looks like a conspiracy to kill Mr. Cullen."

"You didn't kill him." Lani reached over and patted my hand.

"AJ didn't either."

"Are you sure?" Aggie's concerned gaze held mine. "Sometimes feelings can mess up good sense."

I sat back. Annoyance flared hotter than probably appropriate, but I was tired of having to defend myself and AJ. "He didn't do it."

"How do you know?"

I glared at Gwen. "Because of the golf bag."

All three of them stared at me in blank confusion. "What does a golf bag have to do with it?" Gwen finally asked.

"He was killed with a wedge club that was probably owned by my father."

"Oh?" Aggie's face pinched into a "that's not good" expression.

"But a golfer doesn't keep a wedge in his office. He'd keep a putter." I explained my theory about the club being taken from a bag and that the killer had probably taken the rest of the clubs with him.

"Why take the bag and leave the murder weapon?" Lani asked.

I shook my head. "Panic? Or maybe he knew the clubs belonged to my dad once, and he was setting him up."

"But you weren't supposed to be there," Aggie argued.

"No, but it wouldn't have mattered. If they'd been able to link the club to my dad, they'd have talked to me either way."

"Why would Mr. Cullen have your dad's club?"

I could almost see the wheels in Gwen's head turning. "My father sold a bunch of his stuff when things started going bad for him."

"So you and AJ would be in the hot seat either way," Lani said.

"I would. But AJ wasn't supposed to be there. The only reason he's on the hook is because of the timing."

"And what about AJ's mom's car?"

So Lani knew the car that nearly hit me was AJ's mom's.

"What about it?" The talk of murder seemed to have completely distracted Gwen and the others from the goldmine of coupons stacked on the table. I wanted to start clipping, but I knew they wouldn't let this bone go.

"Ethan traced the car to Liza Devlin, AJ's mother. She lives in an assisted living facility in Charlottesville."

"Oh, that's not good." Gwen grimaced.

"And another reason to stay away from the Devlins." Aggie's comment surprised me because she was one of a few people who didn't hold the Devlins in such disdain.

I inhaled a breath, working to calm my agitated nerves. "Can we just check out these coupons?"

Lani's eyes softened. "Sure, honey."

In silence, we opened our binders, pulled out our scissors, and scanned the coupons.

After several blissfully quiet moments, Gwen couldn't seem to let the topic go. "If the guy who ran you down is the same guy who killed Mr. Cullen, and they used Liza Devlin's car, it seems like that would make it easier to pinpoint who the killer is."

Lani sent her a pointed glare from across the table.

"The obvious is AJ, but if it's not him, it has to be someone who, like him, has ties to both places—that facility and Jefferson Grove, right?"

She was right.

"Can anyone just walk into those places?" Gwen asked me.

That was a good question.

"She has a point." Lani nodded.

I couldn't be sure if Lani really believed that or if she was trying to appease me. I went with the former. "The person on the surveillance tape was wearing a disguise. Why would AJ try to hide who he was and then take his mother's car? That makes no sense. It had to be someone who knew Liza had a car and had access to her keys." Why hadn't I thought of that sooner? Why hadn't Ethan or Sergeant Scowl?

"AJ or not, you need to watch your back, child." Aggie waved her scissors at me. "Now. I want all condensed soup coupons."

Clipping coupons kept me distracted from my problems, and thankfully, Gwen stopped bringing the conversation back to the murder. After filling my binder with great coupons, including several for a pain reliever I was sure I'd need for weeks if the soreness in my body was any indication, I headed out to my job at

the Booty Burgo. Although I had to endure Kyle's reminder to keep my nose clean, Randy was a no-show,
so, all in all, it was a good shift.

FOURTEEN

I WAS GLAD when Monday morning finally came around and I had two days off. Usually I used the time for job interviews, but since I didn't have any lined up, nor had I heard back from Mrs. Wayland about the library job, I decided to head to Cooters Hollow.

So far, in my little investigation, I'd learned some interesting things, but nothing that helped clear AJ and me. Gwen had a point about the tie between the residential facility that Liza Devlin lived in and Jefferson Grove, unless, that was what the killer wanted us to think.

The murderer couldn't have purposefully set us up because there was no way he'd have known AJ and I would be at the airport that day. Unless, of course, AJ's boss, Gordo, or Bull was the murderer. I put that option aside for the moment. While the murderer didn't know we'd be there, he, or she, could use the fact that we were to his advantage. He'd have been better off to leave the clubs because, in my mind, that was what cleared us. It also meant it was possible there was something about the clubs or the bag that required the killer to take it.

The killer had to know AJ and I were suspects, but since the investigators couldn't arrest us, perhaps he worried that the focus would turn on him. What better way to put the focus back on AJ than to steal his mother's car and try to run me down? If the person was from

Jefferson Grove, they'd know, or would be able to easily find out, about Liza Devlin and be able to concoct this crazy plan. If I was right, that meant the motive and murderer were still anyone's guess.

The more I thought about Mr. Cullen and the list of people who wanted him dead, the more I focused on the drug angle. People were murdered for many reasons, but it seemed a more likely scenario that a drug smuggler would be killed in a drug war. Sure, a lot of people hated Mr. Cullen, but most people didn't murder people they hated. Although I was no expert on the illegal drug industry, what little I knew suggested they had the highest per capita rate of murders.

I didn't know the first thing about drugs, so I needed to find out about them from someone who did. That was when I thought about Rhonda and Jace. According to Spike, they were living in a hazy drug-infused bliss in a trailer up in Cooters Hollow.

Life in the hollows of the Blue Ridge was different than other places. Television and movies often depicted mountain folk as dumb and inbred, with missing teeth. But while they were poor and few had more than a high school education, the people of the hollows had strong traditions and close family connections. They were also leery and suspicious of outsiders, so I wasn't sure how my visit would go. Should I call AJ? Since I hadn't heard from him, I decided he was either holding fast to the no-contact rule or he was mad about being accused of trying to run me down. I considered calling him, but he was so protective, he'd probably try to talk me out of my investigation. So, the Brown Bomber and I made our way up into Cooters Hollow alone.

The trees were thick, blocking much of the midday

sun. I pulled into the driveway of the address I'd gotten from Spike for Rhonda's trailer. The home was nearly swallowed up by the growth of the woods, suggesting it had been there for years. The siding could use a good wash to remove the moss and mold, but the rest of the area around it was tidy. There weren't any discarded tires or other junk filling the yard as the cliché of trailer living in the mountains would suggest.

Hoping I wasn't waking her (did drug users sleep late?), I knocked on the door. After a minute of nothing, I knocked again. I was about to give up and leave when the door cracked open.

"Yeah?" Jace stared at me with squinty, bloodshot eyes. He didn't have a shirt on and I was afraid to look down in case he'd forgotten his pants too.

"Jace."

"Yeah?" He stretched with one hand and yawned.

"I'm Sophie Parker. I worked with you at the Booty Burgo."

"Yeah. Right." He nodded, but he didn't appear to remember me.

"Is Rhonda here?"

"Nah. She's out." He scraped a hand over his face. He clearly knew a thing or two about drugs.

"Maybe you can help me. I need some information about drugs."

"Drugs?" He perked up. "Well, you've come to the right place. Except, Rhonda is the one you need to talk to. But I've got a little something I can share with you until she gets back." He opened the door and stepped back to let me in. The stench of old cigarettes and stale booze hit me, nearly making me gag.

"Actually, I don't want to try any. I just have questions."

"Why? You a cop?"

I shook my head. "No. I work at the Booty Burgo. Remember?"

"If they need drugs, you need to talk to Rhonda. Kyle knows that."

"Kyle does drugs?" I didn't know why that surprised me. Probably because Kyle reminded me of a grumpy old man in a twenty-two-year-old body.

"Just a little weed to settle the nerves, you know. It's all good."

"I didn't know."

"Yeah. He used to be a real stoner, like me." Jace grinned like a loon. He had all his teeth, but I was sure they hadn't been brushed in awhile. "But he's working his way out of the Hollow, you know. Got himself an important job. Says he's gonna be a big businessman someday."

"No kidding?" That I could see. Kyle struck me as the sort who'd scrap and scratch his way to riches. What I couldn't see was how managing the Booty Burgo would help him in his quest. I supposed he had to start somewhere. It now made more sense why he was so worried about my reputation hurting the Booty Burgo. It would be a bad reflection on him for having hired me.

"So, what can I do you for?" Jace picked up a dingy T-shirt, sniffed, shrugged and put it on.

"I just want some information."

"Why?"

Why indeed. Deciding to put off the truth, I chose to go with a deception. "I'm doing research for a paper as part of an online class I'm taking."

"They teach how to be a drug dealer online?"

I blinked and somehow kept my jaw from dropping to the floor. "No. I chose it as a topic for my business class."

He shrugged and plopped down in a recliner. "Sit for a spell."

I sat on the edge of a brown and green plaid chair with a rip, revealing a foam pad with several cigarette burns. Jace pushed back in his chair and lit a cigarette. "So, what do you want to know?"

"I'm most interested in the distribution of drugs."

He stared at me with a blank face.

"How they get from where they're made to the end user."

"Some drugs are grown." He held up a plastic baggy with green leaves in it.

"Grown then. I assume you buy them from someone, instead of making...or growing them yourself."

"I get mine from Rhonda, but I don't pay money, if you know what I mean." He waggled his brows.

I swallowed the "eww" that rolled up my throat like bile. "Does she sell...for money, to others?"

Jace's eyes narrowed. "You won't use names in your paper, right?"

I shook my head. "I don't want to get anyone in trouble. I promise." I lifted my right hand like I had to when I testified in court during my dad's trial.

Jace relaxed into his chair. "She's the main seller around here now that Kyle's out. She sells some over in Potter's Cave and some of the other hollows too."

"Does she make or grow her product or get it from someone else?"

Jace barked out a laugh. "She can't even fry an egg, much less cook up meth."

"So where does she get it?"

He shrugged. "I don't know."

Really? All that effort for nothing?

"I do know she got a new source, though."

"A new one. How new?" I had no clue if or why this would be important, but I decided the more I could get Jace to talk, the more likely he might share something important.

"A week or so."

My brain started working overtime. Jace and Rhonda quit their jobs the day after Cullen was killed, nearly a week ago. Had he been their source? Had someone killed him to take over the business? I studied Jace but decided he probably wasn't ever coherent enough to swing a golf club without hurting himself. But maybe Rhonda was.

"Did you hear about Mr. Cullen?"

"Who?" Jace took a long drag on his cigarette.

"The guy who was killed at the airport last week."

"Oh yeah. I heard he was whacked with a golf club. Fore!" Jace broke into lunatic laughter.

I smiled, all the while wishing I could whack some sense into him. "There's a rumor he smuggled drugs into the area with his plane."

"I don't know anything about that. Rhonda might, though. She knows everyone who's anyone when it comes to drugs."

"Where is she now?"

"Don't know."

"Do you know when she'll be back?"

Jace shrugged.

I was about to give up when there were footsteps on the front deck followed by a rap on the door.

"Grand Central here today." Jace heaved out of the recliner. He wrenched open the door. "Yeah?"

"I'm looking for Rhonda."

I did a double take when I saw Mr. Fletcher standing in the doorway. I considered running and hiding in the bathroom, assuming I could find it. But then he saw me, his dark eyes widening and then narrowing.

"She ain't here." Jace held the door open.

"When will she be back?"

"Don't know. She's out doing delivery and collection."

Mr. Fletcher's eyes flicked toward me for a second before returning to Jace. Delivery and collection was more than Jace had told me. But more concerning was my correct assumption that Mr. Fletcher was a drug dealer and Rhonda was one of his distributors.

"But you can wait with Miss Sophie. Maybe you can help her with her paper."

Inwardly I winced. I hoped outwardly I appeared calm. "That's okay." I stood. "I can get help later."

"She's doing a paper on drug trafficking."

"Distribution," I corrected. I shook my head, because really, what was the difference?

"Is that so?" Mr. Fletcher stepped into the trailer, making the small space tinier.

I swallowed, wondering if my final resting place would be in Rhonda and Jace's yard.

"What sort of paper?"

"Ah…uh…business economics."

"Cool, huh?" Jace returned to his chair. "I might have finished school if it taught about drugs."

"You're writing a paper on illegal drug distribution for a business economics class?" Mr. Fletcher shut the door behind him. I was too afraid to look for the bulge in his jacket outlining his gun.

"Yes. It was either that or bananas." I was an idiot. But it was hard to think straight with death standing in the room.

"Bananas?"

I nodded, or I think I did. My body was so tense, I'm not sure anything could move. "Distribution of bananas. You know from South America to the end user." Did bananas even come from South America? God, I hoped so.

"And you came here for help?"

"Well…" I didn't know how to answer that.

"It's quite a coincidence, don't you think, Ms. Parker?"

I didn't like the accusation in his tone. "Yep. Yep it is."

"You know what I think?"

"No." I gulped down the fear that rose from my gut.

"Think about what?" Jace lit a new cigarette.

"I think you're poking your nose into Mr. Cullen's business. Why would you do that?"

Busted. I could keep with the drug distribution story, but I decided that might get me in more trouble. "I didn't kill Mr. Cullen or have him killed."

Mr. Fletcher's head jerked back and his brows drew together quizzically, as if he hadn't expected that answer. "So you're trying to clear your name?"

"Yes."

"By coming after me?"

"No." Did he think I was crazy?

"I didn't kill him either."

"That's good." I nodded and smiled. Now that that was out of the way, I could go.

"I have an alibi. The police have cleared me of suspicion."

Even better, he had an alibi, so there was nothing I could say to the investigators to hurt him.

"Besides, he was my importer. Why would I want him dead?"

"Good question."

"Who's dead?" Jace finally caught up to the conversation.

Mr. Fletcher studied me long enough to have me sweating, and then he turned to Jace. "Tell Rhonda to call me when she gets back."

"Sure thing, dude. Once she finishes handing off the collection."

"No!"

Even Jace jumped at Mr. Fletcher's booming voice. I nearly fell from my chair.

"She calls me first and she brings the collection to me." Mr. Fletcher reached into his breast pocket, revealing he did indeed have a gun holstered at his side. "Here's my card. You do this right, there's five hundred dollars in it for you."

"Whoop!" Jace bounded out of the chair and snatched the card. A knock on the door interrupted his celebration. "Oh man, I'm popular today."

Mr. Fletcher stepped to the side, almost like he was trying to hide in the shadows. I sat ramrod straight, hoping I might be able to bolt for the door and to the Bomber. Were Volvos bulletproof?

Jace opened the door. "AJ man. Watsup?"

AJ fist bumped with Jace, but his gaze shot straight to mine. "Not much. Rhonda around?"

"Nah, man, but get in line." Jace stood back and AJ entered. He flinched when Mr. Fletcher stepped from behind the open door.

"Crowded." AJ brought his gaze back to me. "I can come back later. How about it, Soph. Wanna take a drive up to Shiner's Crossing?"

"Ooh la la," Jace sang. "Two little love birds."

"I was just leaving." Mr. Fletcher stepped around AJ. He turned back to Jace. "Don't forget."

"Nah, man." Jace held up the business card. "Have Rhonda call."

Mr. Fletcher nodded and headed out the door.

I let out a relieved gasp.

"What the hell are you doing here?" AJ dropped to a crouch in front of me. It was hard to hear him because Jace was singing and doing a happy dance about Mary Jane and five hundred dollars.

"I'm ready to go."

He stood and held out his hand, helping me stand. "Wait for me by your car. I need a minute with Jace."

I was going to ask how AJ knew Jace and Rhonda, but then I remembered we were in Cooters Hollow, where everyone knew each other. Heck, they were probably related. So, I nodded and headed out the door. I breathed in the fresh Blue Ridge Mountain air and nearly dropped to kiss the ground to celebrate that I was still alive.

Several minutes later, AJ emerged. He took a deep breath too, but I imagine it was to clear his lungs of the stench in the house. He walked up to me, shaking his head. "It was too much to hope that someone else had an old brown Volvo."

I gave him a sweet, innocent smile.

"What are you doing here?"

"Probably the same thing you are. Trying to figure out if Cullen was killed because of his involvement in drugs."

"Who was the wise guy?"

I was surprised AJ wasn't going to give me the first degree, so I leaned against my car to tell him what I knew. "Mr. Fletcher. He and Cullen were partners in an import business." I used air quotes around "import."

"I told you about it the other night."

AJ looked toward the trailer for a moment. "Who knows when Rhonda will be back." He turned his attention to me. "Let's go for a walk. Follow me up to Shiner's Crossing."

I'd never been to Shiner's Crossing, named in the 1920s because it was a major route for moving moonshine north. But I knew it was lovers' lane for people in the Hollow. There were jokes made about how many hollow residents had been conceived there.

"We can talk there," he finished.

Apparently, there wouldn't be any necking for me.

He made his way toward his truck and Dutch's head popped up from the bed. "Let's go for a ride, Dutch."

Resigned, I got into the Bomber and followed AJ up the winding road to Shiner's Crossing. It had originally been named Clayton Crossing for the man who first passed from the east to west side of this part of the Blue Ridge back in the eighteenth century. I pulled off the road into the turnout. It had a Virginia Historic sign explaining the feat of Mr. Clayton, but no mention of bootlegging. I stepped from the car and admired the view. While the humidity cast a haze that reduced visibility, in the distance, the view was still spectacular.

"Come on, Dutch."

Dutch jumped from the back of the truck and trotted alongside AJ.

"There's a fire road that leads to Shiner's Rock. You can see both sides of the mountain from there."

I caught up to AJ and Dutch on the dirt road.

"So, what were you looking for on this visit?" AJ scratched Dutch's head.

"The link between Cullen, drugs and someone who wanted him dead."

"Did you find it?"

"Well, as far as I can tell, Cullen flew the drugs in for Fletcher. Jace said Rhonda was out doing distribution and collection. I guess that means she's the seller here in the Hollow."

"Maybe."

I cocked my head to the side. "Maybe?"

"Guys like Fletcher don't come to the Hollow. They use middlemen."

I wanted to ask how he knew so much about drug distribution but decided that wasn't as important as to who else might have killed Cullen. "So, why is he here?"

"I don't know. But I don't like it."

"You're probably right. He was adamant that Rhonda deliver the collection, which I'm guessing is money, to him instead of to her usual person."

AJ stopped and stared at me. "He talked about his drug business in front of you like that?"

I nodded. "But he speaks in code. And he told me he has an alibi."

"Jesus, Sophie." AJ raked his hands through his hair. "You asked him if he killed Cullen?"

"No. I'm not stupid. But he didn't buy my story about doing a paper on illegal drug distribution, so I told him I was trying to clear my name. That's when he said he had an alibi."

AJ put his hands on his hips and simply stared at me. In his eyes I think I saw, "are you crazy?"

"I think I believe him."

"Oh my God." AJ turned and started walking up the road. Then he whirled back. "You believe a drug dealer?"

I knew it sounded crazy. "He has a point. Cullen was the guy flying in the drugs. Why would he kill him? When I was at Maggie Cullen's house, he showed up and said he was supposed to meet Cullen that day. Cullen had some important papers or information or something. Plus, Jace said Rhonda had a new source of drugs and now Mr. Fletcher wants her to get in touch with him directly."

AJ stopped and looked out over the vast valley of the piedmont. "If Cullen was that new source, that gives Fletcher a reason to kill him."

I frowned. I hadn't thought of it that way. "He said the investigators cleared him." It was dumb to believe him though. Had Sergeant Scowl and Ethan really eliminated him as a suspect?

"We need to talk to Rhonda."

"What will you ask her?"

"If there has been a change of power in the drugs coming through the Hollow, she'll know about it."

"That's what Jace said." I frowned. "How do you know so much?"

"I grew up here." AJ shook his head and started to walk again. Dutch, who'd been off sniffing debris along the road, trotted up to join him. "She might be in danger."

"Really?" I didn't like that thought. Then again, wasn't that the nature of the beast? "Isn't the drug business inherently dangerous?"

"I suppose, but the Hollow would be a small part of that. No one would give Rhonda the time of day."

"Except Mr. Fletcher just showed up. She must be important somehow. Jace said she's also working in other areas. All the mountain towns."

"Rhonda is just smart and dumb enough to get into the middle of a drug war."

We walked around a bend, and the Shenandoah side of the mountain came into view. It was like standing on top of the world.

"How'd you know to see Rhonda?" AJ veered off the path to where a large rock slab was perched like special seating for the view.

"She and Jace worked at the Booty Burgo until last week. Apparently business changed and they no longer needed to work."

AJ motioned for me to sit. He sat next to me, and Dutch, after walking in small circles a few times, lay down behind us.

"Jace is a little young for her."

"I guess people don't notice age through a drug-filled haze."

AJ laid back, his head resting on Dutch. "What did you mean by a paper?"

I laughed. "I told Jace I was writing a paper for an online class on illegal drug distribution."

"He bought that?" AJ shook his head in disbelief.

"He did, but Fletcher didn't. Oh…also, did I tell you, Vivie had an affair with Cullen and she said she saw him with someone he called Fletch. He was upset after the meeting."

"All the more reason for you to not be talking to or running into that guy."

"I didn't mean to. It just happened." I leaned back too, hoping Dutch wouldn't mind me resting my head on her belly.

"Maybe he's the one who tried to run you down."

Finally. I wanted to talk to him about my near hit-and-run and assure him it wasn't me who suspected him, but I didn't know how to bring it up or even if he was mad about it. "Maybe he was."

He turned his head toward me. "It wasn't me."

"I know it wasn't. The investigators are the ones that came up with that idea."

"Did you tell them otherwise?"

"Yes." I sat up, incensed that he was mad at me about this. "You know why they think it's you, right?"

"Because you place me at the scene of the crime."

I turned to the side so I could see him better. "And it was your mother's car. How would someone get her car?"

He swore as he pinched the bridge of his nose with his thumb and forefinger. "I've been trying to get her to sell that thing for months. She doesn't drive anymore."

"So why does she have it?"

He sat up too. "She likes it available when my brother or sister visit, which is hardly ever, and they could rent a car." He shook his head in annoyance.

"Who would know the car was there not being

used?" Maybe I *was* going at this murder the wrong way. Perhaps Gwen had been right that the focus should be on the link between who had access to Liza Devlin's living facility and Jefferson Grove. It certainly should be easier to investigate my near hit-and-run than hunt down drug dealers for questioning.

"I don't know. I suppose anyone who lived or worked there would know. My mom is very social and forthcoming about her life."

That still limited the pool of suspects to people living or working at her living facility, and anyone who visited there. It seemed manageable if I could find an excuse to talk to them.

"You need to stay out of it."

Annoyance flared at his bossy tone. "I'm already in it."

He glared at me. "You know what I mean. You can't go around asking questions about murder. It's dangerous."

"I'm already in danger. Someone tried to kill me, AJ, and the investigators think it's you. Should I let them continue to think that? That's not safe for me or you."

He closed his eyes and let out a breath. "You're right. Sorry."

"I didn't hear you."

"SORRY!" His words echoed through the hollow below.

I started to laugh, but it got lost in my throat when I looked at him. He was sitting so close, I could see the pupils dilate in his intense blue eyes.

The palm of his hand rested on my neck, as his thumb brushed over my cheek. Electricity zapped through me at his touch, even as my brain reminded myself his touch didn't mean anything romantic.

"I'd never hurt you, Sophie."

I heard the earnestness in his voice and felt guilty for the few moments I'd doubted him. "I know."

His gaze drifted down to my lips and lingered. I licked them because, all of a sudden, they were dry. My throat felt like sandpaper.

"I don't want you to get hurt by anyone else, either."

Did he want to kiss me?

I swallowed. "I don't want that either."

Then his gaze lifted back to mine. He smiled and leaned forward. His lips pressed on my forehead. "We should go."

Idiot hormones! Disappointed, but not surprised, I nodded.

As we walked back to the cars, I stayed close to the edge of the road. So far today I was sure I was going to be killed by a smarmy drug dealer and then I thought AJ was going to kiss me. My emotions were now a mixed-up jumble and I needed a moment to pull myself together.

Dutch ran crisscrossing the road and, on occasion, down the slight embankment into the woods. Her joy in running free reminded me that I was safe and alive. At least in this moment.

Dutch ran down the wooded embankment, around a tree and stopped. Then she came loping back up the hill with a shiny object in her mouth.

"AJ, Dutch found something."

"Ah, Dutch. Leave the garbage alone."

Dutch trotted toward me and as she got close, I realized the item in her mouth was a golf club. "Do people in the Hollow play golf?"

"Only miniature golf." AJ joined me and he reached down to take the club.

"Wait. That's an expensive club."

His hand stopped short of grabbing the club. Dutch dropped it at my feet.

"It's the same brand as the wedge used to kill Cullen."

"What?"

The disbelief in AJ's tone matched my thinking. What were the odds that Cullen's clubs were here? Tossed like trash into the thick of the Hollow? I looked down to where Dutch had found the club. "We should go look to see if there are others."

"Sophie—"

"This is not a club for mini-golf, AJ. This club is only owned by people who live in Monticello Heights. Not Cooters Hollow."

"Maybe somebody stole it or bought it secondhand."

"Or maybe Cullen's killer got rid of them here."

He shrugged, but his facial expression said I was nuts. Maybe I was, but what could it hurt to look? We made our way down the slope, sliding in a few of the steeper areas. At first, all I saw was a bunch of junk—old tires, a rusted swing set and other stuff I couldn't make out.

"Is this the dump?"

"Sort of," AJ mumbled.

Finally, sticking out from under a rhododendron bush was a golf bag.

I whistled. "That's a three thousand dollar bag."

"What?" AJ's head whipped around to look at me.

"Don't touch it." I didn't think it wise for AJ's prints to show up on the bag.

He reached for a thick stick, using his hand to push the bush away, while trying to extricate the bag with the stick. "I got it."

"Does it have a name on it?"

"Give me a minute." He poked around. "Do you have a tissue or something?"

I opened my purse and rummaged around. "I have a gum wrapper."

"That'll work." I handed the wrapper to him. He reached down to pick something up. He held it for me to see. It was a silver golf ball marker with the initials JAC.

I SAT ON the rock where an hour before AJ had kissed me on the forehead. A group of cops were trudging through the woods looking through all the junk tossed there by residents of Cooters Hollow. They'd already taken the golf bag and club, which AJ and I had left on the side of the fire road. We decided there was no way the sheriff's people would believe I was trudging through the woods, so the only way for me to have found it would be if it was on the side of the road. That was my story, and I was sticking to it.

It was my idea that AJ not be around when the cops arrived. He'd balked, but I told him it would look bad for him that the clubs were found in Cooters Hollow. Then I suggested he go find Rhonda, which he reluctantly agreed to. That was when I called Ethan and told him about the clubs and bag.

"For the life of me, I can't figure out why you're wandering around an old fire road in a hollow." Ethan walked up to me.

"I was here visiting friends and decided to go for a walk. This view is famous."

He pursed his lips. "You have friends in the Hollow?"

I gawked. "Yes. I have nerdy friends too."

He winced, and I knew the comment hit the mark. "AJ doesn't live here."

"No. But some people from the Booty Burgo do." I turned away from him and looked out over the piedmont, even though I didn't really see it. I couldn't decide how much to tell Ethan. I wanted to spill my guts, but I was afraid something I said would somehow implicate AJ or me. The whole point of my effort was to exonerate us, not make us look more guilty.

"Who were you visiting?"

"Jace and Rhonda, but Rhonda wasn't in."

"Do they have last names?" He pulled out his notebook.

"Yes, but I don't know what they are."

"What was the reason for your visit?" He was in cop mode now. All signs of my friend were gone.

"Well...they used to be the bartenders but quit. I wanted to see if or when they were coming back. Personally, I hoped they weren't. I like bartending."

He studied me and I felt myself withering under his piercing stare. "Why don't I believe you?"

Ugh. "Because that's not the whole truth." Blowing out a breath, I explained running into Mr. Fletcher at Maggie's house and how Vivie had mentioned a Fletch when she'd been having her affair with Cullen. And finally, I told him how Fletcher showed up at Jace and Rhonda's trailer. I didn't tell him about the golf marker because I didn't want him to know I'd been snooping in Cullen's office at the airport.

By the time I was done, I couldn't read Ethan's expression. Annoyance? Anger? Whatever it was, it wasn't good.

"What makes you think you can do my job better than me?"

It was anger.

"Because I know neither I nor AJ killed Cullen and yet you keep focusing on us."

"No." He drew out the word in a way that suggested he was trying to rein in his anger. "We go where the evidence takes us. Right now, that's AJ Devlin." He shook his head as if he thought I was dense.

Anger erupted from deep within my belly. "You're misreading the evidence or are so biased you've missed some. You've completely ignored the drug angle, which doesn't make sense because aren't you the vice guy?"

He turned his head away and let out an expletive. His hands were on his hips, like my mother used to do when she was about to punish me. He finally turned back. "Fletcher didn't kill Cullen. He has an alibi."

So they *had* talked to Fletcher. A part of me was glad there had been some investigating of other options, even though Fletcher's alibi meant they weren't looking at the drug angle and instead were focused on AJ and me. "That's what he said."

"What? You asked him if he killed Cullen?"

"No, but he told me he had an alibi. I don't think he did it. But that doesn't mean he didn't have someone else take care of it. Or that he has a competitor who's trying to put him out of business. Aren't you the least bit curious about why he showed up personally to the Hollow? I think he came because someone is honing in on his business and he doesn't like it. He was adamant that Rhonda give him the collection personally."

"That may be, but it has nothing to do with Cullen's murder."

"You don't know that."

"Sophie." He barked out my name, making me flinch. "Do you think I haven't looked into Fletcher and Cullen's drug connections?" His tone was angry and defensive. I'd insulted him. "I have and there's nothing there. But Fletcher is dangerous. Poking around and asking questions is dangerous. I'm doing all I can to protect you and keep you out of jail, but you've got to stay out of it. Have you forgotten someone tried to run you down the other day?"

"No." I tried not to sulk, but he was right.

"You need to go home, do your coupons, or whatever you do, and let me do my job."

I drew back at his condescending tone. "I'm not some dumb little waif."

His tone softened. "No. But you're not a detective, either. Let me do my job."

I shook my head. "I have to protect AJ and me."

He huffed out a breath and turned his head toward the view of the valley. When he returned his attention to me, the tension in his jaw had relaxed a smidge. "I'm protecting you, Sophie." He stepped closer to me, glancing around him, presumably to see who might overhear. He leaned his head toward mine. "We don't think you're involved."

"You don't?"

He shook his head. "No, we don't."

I studied his face, looking for clues that would tell me if he was using his cop-deception skills on me. But I wasn't able to determine if he was lying or sincere. "Why not?"

He jerked back, his eyes widening in surprise. "Do you want us to suspect you?"

"No. But given all the questioning of me and searching of my house, I find it hard to believe you don't suspect me."

"We didn't eliminate you because of your stellar answers to our questions or the fact the clubs weren't found on the scene, as you keep pointing out. In fact, your continued interference and finding the clubs makes it hard to eliminate you as a suspect entirely."

"Then why did you say you don't think I did it?"

He stared at me for a long moment. "Because you never talked about Cullen with your father during your phone calls or visits. And there is no record of calls between you and AJ before the murder, or between AJ and your father at all."

I felt sick. That sort of sick from when you felt betrayed by someone you trusted. My rational mind reminded me that checking phone records was an investigative technique, but he hadn't just checked phone records. No. He said I'd never talked about Cullen with my father, which meant, my conversations were recorded. Of course, I knew prisoner conversations were monitored, but to have the proof of it waved in my face made me feel violated.

Ethan must have seen how repulsed I was at the idea because he reached out to touch my arm.

I pulled away. "You listened to my visits with my dad?" Was that why my father hadn't called? Had he heard about my troubles and knew that talking to me would increase suspicion I conspired with him and AJ to commit murder?

He inhaled deeply. "It's part of the job, Sophie. I

know it feels like an invasion of your privacy, but it's what I've used to convince Davis you're not involved. There's nothing in your conversations with your father that suggests you were conspiring to get revenge on Cullen. And there was certainly nothing in them that you should be embarrassed by my hearing."

"That's not the point." I could feel the tears forming, although I couldn't quite figure out why. His reasoning made sense. But emotionally, I couldn't help but feel violated.

He straightened, his body tensing and his facial features hardening, as if he was moving back into cop mode. "The point is, I have a murder to solve and I'll use whatever means at my disposal to solve it. It's distasteful sometimes, but murder isn't a cake walk."

I don't know how he did it, but now I felt guilty at making him feel bad. It couldn't be easy to deal with death and the uglier side of people.

I nodded and resigned myself to leaving. I considered taking his advice to stay out of the sleuthing business. "You'll let me know if you find anything?"

"I'll let you know what you need to know."

"Why don't I believe you?" I tossed his words back at him.

His features softened and he stepped closer to me. His hand came to my neck, his thumb brushing my cheek the same as AJ had done earlier in the day. But my hormones were quiet. "Believe that I want to keep you safe. Promise me you'll stay out of the Cullen murder."

Reluctantly, I nodded.

"Go home, Sophie. I'll call you later."

FIFTEEN

I WANTED TO climb under the covers and hide from the world, but Aunt Rose continued to hassle me about not being in touch, so I let her beat me at rummy and watched the marathon of *Deadly Women* on TV that night.

The next morning, I woke with newfound resolve and energy to get to the bottom of this murder. I was tired of AJ's protectiveness, Ethan's patronizing and Sergeant Scowl's belief I played a part in the murder. I was tired of Kyle threatening to fire me if I didn't keep my nose clean and of Randy's ogling. And I was done with my closest and only friends questioning my faith in AJ's innocence. While I'd considered keeping out of it, I couldn't sit back and hope the investigators stumbled on the real murderer, especially since they didn't seem to be looking at anyone besides AJ.

While I might not be a suspect, if what Ethan said was true, I was still a target for someone who wanted me dead. The investigators blamed AJ for that too, but I couldn't do nothing while the sheriff's office worked to pin a murder and attempted murder on him. I needed to see what *I* could find out. Ethan wouldn't like it, but all I'd promised him was that I'd stay out of the Cullen murder. I never said I wouldn't look for my attacker. Granted, they were probably the same person, but why mince words?

I had the day off and nothing until my coupon group that evening, so I decided to head to Charlottesville to see what I could learn from the assisted living facility. All I knew was that a man, dressed like a woman, took Liza Devlin's car from the facility she lived in.

The Brown Bomber made it to Charlottesville without a problem, although, since it was mostly downhill, I didn't anticipate any trouble until I went home. I parked in two-hour parking on the street and made my way into the building.

In my research online, I found out the facility was basically two types of residential living in one building. One part of the facility housed people in independent living. Apparently they needed some help and supervision but, for the most part, were able to function normally. The second was a traditional nursing home, in which patients needed more constant care. Liza Devlin was in the independent living section, although, according to AJ, she didn't drive and, in fact, he wanted to sell her car.

I stopped just outside the building's main entrance as I realized I didn't have a story for why I was there. I couldn't just say, "I'm looking for the person who tried to run me down." I blew out a breath and sat on one of the stone benches lining the path to the entrance.

Whoever tried to kill me had access to the building and knew his way around, which meant he'd been there before. Ethan had said the man, dressed as a woman, had told the lady in the front lobby he was a friend of Liza's. But Liza told Ethan she'd never seen the man and hadn't had any visitors except AJ in weeks. Did my would-be killer know someone else there? I deduced he had to, otherwise, why was he so familiar with the building and how did he know enough about the residents, or at least Liza, to take her car?

Whoever it was had it out for me, so he also had to have ties to Jefferson Grove. Until today, I hadn't been out of town since arriving nearly two months ago. Anyone I'd known from my life outside Jefferson Grove wouldn't have known about Liza. Plus, I couldn't imagine anyone from my past wanting to kill me.

So, whoever this guy was, he had to be from or have family in Jefferson Grove. And because he knew his way around the facility, perhaps he had family there too. I pushed aside the fact I still couldn't fathom who from Jefferson Grove would want me dead.

My next step was to figure out how to find out which residents were from or had family in Jefferson Grove. I suspected that sort of information was private.

I bit my lip and stared mindlessly up the street. There was a bakery across the street, two doors down. A priest exited carrying a pink box. It gave me an idea that I quickly dismissed. If I followed through, I'd likely go to hell. Still, my life was on the line. With a silent prayer of forgiveness, I stood and started toward the bakery. Once I'd crossed the street, I rummaged through my wallet and purse to find a couple of dollars. Hopefully it was enough to buy a few cookies.

I was able to afford five cookies, which I had placed in a pink box, instead of a bag, to make it look like I had more. Then I headed back to the assisted living facility. Walking in, I plastered a smile on my face and ignored my conscience that said lying and deception was a sin.

"Hello." I stepped up to the welcome counter. "I'm here from First Baptist in Jefferson Grove to make visits with the residents living here from our church. Unfortunately, Father Michael forgot to give me the list of residents."

The woman smiled, but her brows furrowed slightly. "I'm not allowed to give out that information."

"Oh no." Now what? "They'll be so disappointed. He told them I'd be coming. It's a special program we just started to visit our Jefferson Grove friends here so they know we haven't forgotten them. I brought cookies." I held up the box and gave her a hopeful expression.

The woman stared at me. I couldn't be sure, but I thought maybe she was having a tug of war within herself. Hold to the rules or break them so residents could have a guest and cookies.

"I really shouldn't do this, but once people get here, their family and friends often forget them. A guest and some cookies can make their month."

That was sad, and I felt even more guilt that I was a fraud. Unless I came back next month. Perhaps I could continue the program.

The woman tapped at her computer keyboard. "We only have three residents from Jefferson Grove. One is actually from Jefferson County. That's Liza Devlin."

I knew she didn't try to kill me, so I didn't need to visit her. The guilt stabbed again. I'd stop by and see her and give her a cookie.

"Then there is Alice Jenkins and Caroline Samuels-Wallace. They're both in our nursing home section. Ms. Jenkins is still fairly sprite, but Ms. Wallace has severe dementia."

"Oh, that's sad." What was even worse was I didn't know these women. I'd grown up in Jefferson Grove and, in a small town like that, even if you hadn't met everyone, you at least had heard of them. I remembered Aunt Rose mentioning Alice Jenkins and how she nearly starved until they got her here. But Wallace wasn't a name I recognized.

"Yes. Fortunately, her son still visits about once a month. Ms. Jenkins' daughter makes it a little less."

It was the visiting schedule I had to see my dad and brother. "Can you give me their room numbers?"

Holding the slip of paper with the names and room numbers in one hand, and the box of cookies in the other, I made my way to the nursing home side of the building. Since I knew Liza wasn't my attacker, I decided I'd stop by her room on my out. Ms. Jenkins' room was the closest, so I headed there. Along the hallway, residents were parked in wheelchairs, some sleeping, others staring into space. My heart sank at the sadness of it. These people once lived vibrant lives and now were set aside, essentially waiting to die. Did they know?

Refocusing on my task, I arrived at Ms. Jenkins' door. It was open halfway. I lightly knocked. "Hello?" I poked my head in.

"Can I help you?" A woman dressed in scrubs startled me at the door.

"Ah yes. I'm looking for Ms. Jenkins. I brought cookies." I held up the box.

"Oh, that's nice. But she's in physical therapy. She fell a few months back and recovery has been slow."

"Oh. I'm sorry to hear that."

The staff woman looked at her watch. "She should be back in twenty minutes or so."

"Oh. Okay. I'll check back."

I left the staff woman and headed farther up the hall.

"Hey, sweet cheeks." A shriveled-up man sitting in

a wheelchair pedaled his feet across the floor until he blocked my way. "Got some sugar for me?"

I stared at the man, trying to decide if he was being obnoxious or literal. "Want a cookie?"

"Sure."

I opened the box.

"Come to my room, and I can show you—" He waggled his brows suggestively.

"I've got an appointment." I didn't want to hear whatever he might offer to show me. I gave him his cookie, stepped around him and hurried to Ms. Samuels-Wallace's room.

Her door was halfway open as well. I tapped on it. "Hello."

I didn't hear anything, so I pushed it open enough to see into the room. "Ms. Samuels-Wallace?" I stepped in. There was a short hallway with a bathroom on the right. I had to enter the room farther to reach the main area that held a dresser with a TV and knickknacks, and her bed. Ms. Samuels-Wallace lay in the bed, snoring slightly.

I wanted to growl in frustration. I couldn't wake her up. That would be too mean, and I was already in trouble with the big guy in the sky for lying about coming from a church. I blew out a breath and decided to visit Liza after all. Maybe she'd remember something she hadn't told Ethan when he interviewed her.

I started to turn when I heard a noise from behind. A doughboy of a man in brown pants and a wrinkled button-down shirt emerged from the bathroom. He had a round baby face, but the fringe of hair wrapping around the sides of his shiny bald head suggested he was middle-aged.

"What are you doing here?" His mud colored eyes narrowed on me.

I stepped back, surprised by the venom in his voice. Did he think I was hurting Mrs. Samuels-Wallace? I held up my box. "Cookies?"

He glanced toward Mrs. Samuels-Wallace and then brought his beady-eyed gaze back to me. His left hand reached back and pushed the room door shut. The predatory gleam in his eyes sent a shiver down my spine. Fear made my mind work slowly. Why did the man look like he was going to hurt me?

"What are you doing?"

He took a step closer to me, a sinister smile on his face. He was enjoying my fear. "I'm going to kill you."

I stepped back, wanting to keep out of his reach. "I wasn't doing anything to hurt her." Who was this guy? And why did he want me dead? But those questions weren't as pressing as how was I going to get away. He was blocking the only doorway to the hall. My retreat brought me closer to the window. A glance out of it had me quickly realizing I was too far up for a window escape.

"You have some nerve coming here." He seethed, his breathing becoming shallow.

"I do?" I scanned the area looking for anything—a cane, a bedpan, anything to use to aid my escape.

"You're as bad as your father."

My gazed snapped to his. "My father? You want to kill me because of my father?" Then it clicked. "You're the one who tried to run me down with Liza's car." There was little satisfaction in achieving my goal of the day in finding my would-be killer. He clearly knew my father, but I still had no clue as to who he was.

"He took all her money." He nodded toward Mrs. Samuels-Wallace, but his angry gaze held mine. "She had a stroke when she found out. She hasn't been right since."

I glanced at her, wishing she'd wake up. I wondered if she could. Was she in a coma? Catatonic?

"I'm sorry." And I meant it. I hated that my father took her money. I felt bad if it was the cause of her stroke. But, I had nothing to do with it. "What my father did was horrible, and I'm so sorry he hurt you and…your mother." I guessed at their relationship. I blamed the fear for my slow thinking, but I was pretty sure I was being threatened by Ben Samuels, the man Aunt Rose had said wanted to string Cullen up by his balls. Apparently, he wanted to string me up too. Did he kill Cullen simply for being associated with my father as well? "I had nothing to do with what my father did. If I'd known what he was doing, I would have tried to stop him."

"You lived off our money. OUR MONEY!"

I flinched and stepped back as I realized how much closer he was getting. Only the bed separated us, but he was rounding it and there was no place for me to go. I was trapped between the window and the bed.

"Then that partner of his put me out of business."

"What my dad and Mr. Cullen did doesn't have anything to do with me."

"You have to pay!"

"Why?" I heard the high pitch of fear in my voice. I moved until the side table blocked me and I was stuck with nowhere to go. I was next to his mother, and I prayed he wouldn't do anything to me that could result in harming her too.

"Someone has to."

"My dad's in jail and Mr. Cullen is dead. Surely they've paid."

"I'm still broke."

"Killing me won't change that." I scanned the area again, hoping I'd missed a resource to aid in my escape. I looked at Mrs. Samuels-Wallace, willing her eyes to pop open and order her son to stop killing people. The steadiness of her snore told me I needed to be my own hero. An alert button hung on the side of her bed. I shot my hand out, grabbed the small device and pushed the button.

Ben lunged at me, his face red and bulging. My heart leapt to my throat. I dropped to the floor to avoid his meaty hand grabbing at me. From there, I could see under the bed and immediately slid under it, for once happy at my petite frame. I scrambled to the other side and focused my eyes on the door. The room hadn't seemed that large when I first entered, but now, cowering under the bed, the door looked a million miles away.

I started out from under the bed, but before I could stand, Ben was around it and lunging for me again. I slid back under to the other side. A large hand gripped my ankle. I screamed and kicked with my free foot. His hand lost its grip and I pulled my leg free.

"Get out from there!" His crazed eyes glared at me under the bed.

I shook my head. "I never did anything to you."

"I'm ruined."

"Killing me doesn't fix that. You'll go to jail, then who'll take care of your mom?"

"Don't talk about my mom." He rounded the bed, so

I slid to the opposite side, eyeing the door and trying to judge if I could outrun him.

"You've already killed Mr. Cullen and my dad is in jail. That's justice."

"Cullen deserved worse. So does your dad, but he's not here. You are."

"But I didn't hurt you."

"I don't care."

Just as I was about to make a run for the door, it opened and a nurse walked in.

"What's going on—?" She stopped as she took in the scene.

"Help me." I came out from under the bed and ran toward her. A large hand grabbed my shoulder.

"You're gonna pay!"

I ducked and twisted away, rounding and punching at him. I took a self-defense class in college, but mostly I was flailing my arms as fast and hard as I could. Fortunately, one punch caught him in his most vulnerable spot. He doubled over, cupping himself.

I ran toward the door. I was just over the threshold when I realized the nurse was still standing in the room.

"Come on." I hurried back, grabbed her arm and pulled her out the door. Then I let go and sprinted up the hall, yelling for help and asking someone to call 9-1-1. I couldn't do it because my phone was in my purse under Mrs. Samuels-Wallace's bed, along with the cookies.

ETHAN'S HEAD SHOOK, but his mouth curved up slightly, suggesting he was amused by my story. I was glad he wasn't mad, though I couldn't figure out why. "You sure know how to find trouble, Sophie."

"It finds me." I'd spent the last hour talking to the

local police, who apparently called Ethan when I told them about the hit and run attempt.

"What were you doing here?"

"Delivering cookies."

Ethan remained silent, as his cop eyes studied me. "I think I've mentioned before that you really should leave the sleuthing to professionals."

"How do you know I was sleuthing?"

"Because you told me you'd never been here before. Why would you come now, unless you were looking for answers to who tried to run you down? But that's what the professionals are for."

I jerked my gaze to his. "Except, the professionals aren't looking in the right place."

He shrugged and sat next to me on the wall. "You're right. He wasn't on our list."

"He was on Aunt Rose's." I made a mental note to consider that not everything Aunt Rose said was crazy.

"Maybe we should recruit her." He smiled disarmingly.

"Where's Sergeant Davis?"

"He's at the station interviewing Mr. Samuels." Ethan waited a beat. "How'd you figure out it was him?"

"I didn't. I just knew that whoever tried to run me down had to have ties to this place and Jefferson Grove."

"How'd you know which patients had this connection?"

"I brought cookies and told the lady at the desk it was for the residents from Jefferson Grove."

His brows drew together in a dubious expression. "And she just told you."

"She felt sorry that so many people here don't have visitors."

"So, how many cookies did you have to give away?"

"There are only three residents and one was Liza Devlin. She was in a class, so I didn't see her. And another was in physical therapy. So I went to see Mrs. Samuels-Wallace… I didn't put together the name… Samuels. Anyway, it was clear she wouldn't be talking to me, but as I went to leave, Ben came out of the bathroom. He recognized me immediately, but I had no clue who he was." I shuddered at the image of his murderous eyes and his large hands flashed in my brain.

"Why was he after you?"

"He said my dad took his mom's money and Mr. Cullen put him out of business. Apparently, jail and death weren't justice enough."

"So he wanted you?"

I nodded. "That's what he said."

Ethan took a deep breath. "Well, it's over now, Sophie."

"Thank goodness." My life before running into AJ and trouble had been boring, but I could do without all the excitement Ben Samuels brought.

"You know what that means?"

I looked at Ethan. I had no clue what he was alluding to.

"Want to have dinner tonight?"

"Tonight? I can't. I've got my coupon group tonight. And I can't skip it."

"How about tomorrow?"

I winced. "I'm back on nights at the Booty Burgo."

He nodded like he understood, but I got the sense he thought I was giving him the brush-off.

"I could do lunch sometime." I said it mostly because I felt bad at rejecting him. While I liked Ethan and appreciated his friendship, I really wasn't interested in moving into dating mode.

"I'll give you a call." He stood.

"Okay."

"Do you need a ride home?"

I shook my head. "I'm parked up the street. Oh God, I hope I don't have a ticket."

"I'll see what I can do to help if you do. After all, you helped stop a killer."

SIXTEEN

IT HAD BEEN a week since I flew with AJ and got embroiled in murder. It felt like forever. But while my life was still a struggle, at least I wasn't on a killer's hit list and I was no longer a murder suspect. Neither was AJ, because Ben Samuels had been caught.

Back from nearly being strangled under Mrs. Samuels-Wallace's bed, the only must-do on my list now was to cull my expired coupons and find new ones to bring to my coupon group that night. Thankfully, between the library visit and Dwayne's find behind the IGA, I was as flush in coupons as I'd ever been.

"Now that you're off the hook, it's time you acted right, Sophie." Aunt Rose waggled her boney finger at me when I got coffee for an afternoon pick-me-up before my coupon group.

"Yes, ma'am." I couldn't guarantee I would act right, but I thought she just wanted me to stay out of trouble, and I could do that. Or at least I could try.

"Tell me you're done with that AJ Devlin. Devlins are nothing but trouble."

"You don't have to worry about that." I was still smarting a bit at AJ's kiss on the forehead. I needed to work harder to push my schoolgirl crush aside. Maybe if I let that go, someone nice, like Ethan Taylor, would be more interesting to me.

"The girls in my canasta group told me to give these

to you." Aunt Rose handed me a stack of coupon inserts. "I don't know why you bother, but if it keeps you out of trouble, then okay."

"Thank you." I was actually excited. Maybe now that I had a good stash of coupons, I could trade for more than one or two good coupons during the group. "I'll be in my room."

I carried my coffee and coupons back to my room. I got my binder out of the closet and sat on the floor to spread out my coupon riches to see what I had. I'd cut out the last coupon I was willing to trade when Aunt Rose hollered at me.

"Sophie. The cops are here to see you. Tell me, girl, you're not in trouble again, are you?"

"Cops?" I groaned. I was done with them, wasn't I? Then I thought maybe Ethan was stopping by to arrange our date. "I'll be right there." I stuffed my coupons in my binder and set it on the couch.

As I approached the door, I'd plastered a smile to greet Ethan, except it wasn't him. "Sergeant Davis?"

"Yes, ma'am. I need to talk to you." He said it to me, but I could see his eyes were still focused on Aunt Rose. I couldn't blame him. It was always a good idea to keep one eye on Aunt Rose.

"We can talk on the porch." If Aunt Rose hadn't invited him in yet, she didn't want him in.

He nodded and stepped back to let me out.

"You're not in trouble again, are you?" Aunt Rose glared at me.

"I don't think so."

She shook her head and went back to watch her TV shows. I stepped out onto the porch and took a seat on one of the plastic resin chairs. "Do you want coffee or something?"

Sergeant Davis shook his head. "Ben Samuels didn't kill Joseph Cullen."

It was a good thing I didn't bring my coffee out with me or I'd have spilled it all over myself. My whole body jerked at his statement. "What? How was that possible? He said—"

"What did he say? Did he confess to you?"

I thought about the scuffle with Ben in his mother's room. Slowly I shook my head as I realized he'd never said he'd killed Cullen. "He said Cullen deserved to be dead."

"Did he say he killed him?"

"No. But—"

"He has an alibi for the Cullen murder. He was visiting his mother. It's on tape."

I closed my eyes and my head dropped back as the ramifications of what he was saying hit me. AJ and I were still on the list of suspects for Cullen's murder. My head popped up. "What about the golf bag?"

Sergeant Davis' eyes turned hard, reminding me of why I always thought of him as Sergeant Scowl. "It's Cullen's. No good prints, but it was found in Devlin's neck of the woods. We have a witness who puts him there the same day you were there."

His tone suggested he thought I'd left that out of my statement, which was true, but I wasn't about to tell him that. "It's also Rhonda and Jace's home. *And* Mr. Fletcher was there too. Certainly, he has more motive."

"He has an alibi for Cullen's murder."

Oh yeah. "So what now?"

"Rumor has it you saw AJ there, but I've read Deputy

building and how did he kno..

Whoever it was had it out for me,
have ties to Jefferson Grove. Until toda.
out of town since arriving nearly two month.
one I'd known from my life outside Jefferson.
wouldn't have known about Liza. Plus, I couldn't im.
ine anyone from my past wanting to kill me.

So, whoever this guy was, he had to be from or have
family in Jefferson Grove. And because he knew his
way around the facility, perhaps he had family there
too. I pushed aside the fact I still couldn't fathom who
from Jefferson Grove would want me dead.

My next step was to figure out how to find out which
residents were from or had family in Jefferson Grove. I
suspected that sort of information was private.

I bit my lip and stared mindlessly up the street. There
was a bakery across the street, two doors down. A priest
exited carrying a pink box. It gave me an idea that I
quickly dismissed. If I followed through, I'd likely go to
hell. Still, my life was on the line. With a silent prayer
of forgiveness, I stood and started toward the bakery.
Once I'd crossed the street, I rummaged through my
wallet and purse to find a couple of dollars. Hopefully
it was enough to buy a few cookies.

I was able to afford five cookies, which I had placed
in a pink box, instead of a bag, to make it look like I had
more. Then I headed back to the assisted living facility.
Walking in, I plastered a smile on my face and ignored
my conscience that said lying and deception was a sin.

"Hello." I stepped up to the welcome counter. "I'm
here from First Baptist in Jefferson Grove to make visits with the residents living here from our church. Un-

…el forgot to give me the list

…ed, but her brows furrowed slightly.

…d to give out that information."

Now what? "They'll be so disappointed.

…nem I'd be coming. It's a special program we

…started to visit our Jefferson Grove friends here so

…ney know we haven't forgotten them. I brought cook-

…ies." I held up the box and gave her a hopeful expression.

The woman stared at me. I couldn't be sure, but I thought maybe she was having a tug of war within her-self. Hold to the rules or break them so residents could have a guest and cookies.

"I really shouldn't do this, but once people get here, their family and friends often forget them. A guest and some cookies can make their month."

That was sad, and I felt even more guilt that I was a fraud. Unless I came back next month. Perhaps I could continue the program.

The woman tapped at her computer keyboard. "We only have three residents from Jefferson Grove. One is actually from Jefferson County. That's Liza Devlin."

I knew she didn't try to kill me, so I didn't need to visit her. The guilt stabbed again. I'd stop by and see her and give her a cookie.

"Then there is Alice Jenkins and Caroline Samuels-Wallace. They're both in our nursing home section. Ms. Wallace has severe dementia, but Ms. Wallace has severe Jenkins is still fairly sprite, but Ms. Wallace has severe dementia."

"Oh, that's sad." What was even worse was I didn't know these women. I'd grown up in Jefferson Grove and, in a small town like that, even if you hadn't met everyone, you at least had heard of them. I remem-

Taylor's report and don't see mention of it. He thinks you're innocent in all this, but keeping evidence from an investigation—"

"I don't have evidence."

"He was there."

"But he didn't have the golf bag."

"He could have tossed it earlier."

"I wouldn't know about that. You want me to tell you things that I don't have knowledge of."

"What do you know?"

I recounted my visit with Vivie, Maggie Cullen, and Jace, and finding the golf club. "That's it. Everything I've learned suggests Fletcher is involved. I never saw or heard anything that helps you."

Sergeant Scowl earned his name as his beady eyes stared down on me. I glared back, not willing to let him make me squirm.

"Did you ever see Rhonda?"

I shook my head. "As far as I can gather, she was doing work for Mr. Fletcher."

"Now she's at the morgue."

"What?" My stomach dropped to the porch floor.

"She's dead. Discovered not far from where those clubs were found."

"Overdose?" I hoped. Not that I wanted her dead. But accidental death would be so much better than murder at this point.

He shook his head. "Murder. Tell me, was AJ Devlin wanting to talk to her too?"

Oh God. Instead of answering that question, I gave him another suspect. "Mr. Fletcher was adamant about seeing her. He offered Jace five hundred dollars to make sure she contacted him."

He looked at me with pity. "He never got to deliver that message. Tell me, Miss Sophie. Was AJ Devlin wanting to find Rhonda too?"

I PULLED THE Brown Bomber in front of Lani's house, where our coupon group was being held this week. I thought my life was back on track, only to have Sergeant Scowl upend it again. I wanted to call or visit AJ, but I was afraid of how that would look to the investigators. Instead, I spent the afternoon ruminating over my next move. Why weren't the cops paying more attention to Fletcher? Sure, he might have an alibi for the day Cullen was killed, but that didn't mean one of his minions didn't kill him. Wasn't that how criminals worked?

I sat in the car wondering for the umpteenth time if I should just go home because my mind wasn't on couponing or should I join the group and act like all was normal. With a shake of my head, I grabbed my coupon binder and headed to Lani's front door.

"Hey, Soph." Lani's tone and expression suggested she was aware of the new wrinkle in the case. "I was going to call."

I shook my head. "Just as well you didn't."

"I really thought Ben was the killer."

"I did too. It's still not AJ or me."

"Of course not." She put her arms around me and squeezed. "Everyone else is here and talking about it. Are you going to be okay?" Her words whispered in my ear.

"Yeah." It wasn't like I hadn't dealt with worse with my dad.

She released me and studied me for a moment. I mustered a smile.

"Come on. I'll get you a drink."

I followed her to the back porch, where the coupon group was held in her home.

"There she is." Aggie stood and gave me a hug. "I swear, baby girl, you're a lightning rod for trouble, aren't you?"

"Apparently."

"Ben Samuels, of all people," Gwen said from the table. "Who'd have thought he had murder in him?"

I raised my hand. "I do."

"Sophie, this is Marla Naylor. She's a new neighbor of mine." Vivie introduced the woman sitting next to her.

I nodded and said hello, but I was more curious about how Vivie was going to act. I hadn't seen her since she'd let me in the gate and her home several days ago. Then I remembered Randy and his alibi. I pushed it all aside for the time being.

"Look at her coupon book." Vivie pointed to the thick binder sitting in front of Marla.

With a sheepish smile, Marla opened her binder. It was a wonder to see. If anyone deserved a couponing reality or talk show, it had to be Marla. It was at least four inches thick and each coupon was neatly slipped into a plastic pocket. She had some sort of contents or index in the inside cover. "My husband is always telling me I don't have to coupon anymore, but after struggling for so long, I can't help it."

"I think I can learn a lot from you." I took the drink Lani handed me.

"We weren't sure you'd come." Tracy entered the room with a plate full of food. "If it were me, I'd probably be hiding in bed."

"I guess I'm used to bad things happening."

"Well, at least Ben is off the street. But goodness, why are the cops having such a hard time finding Joseph Cullen's killer?" Aggie sat at the table next to Marla.

I'd shared my story with Ethan, but I could tell he didn't really buy my idea AJ was innocent. I knew Sergeant Scowl was targeting AJ as the murderer as well. And not just for Cullen, but for Rhonda too. I scanned the group of ladies of the coupon group. I know Aggie, Gwen and Lani thought I was naive to so quickly dismiss AJ as a murder, but they didn't know everything I knew. What would they think if I told them about my adventures over the last week? Would they have new ideas I was missing? Would I scare Marla off?

I put my coupon binder on the table and sat. "Over the last week I've met a big deal drug dealer and discovered Mr. Cullen's golf bag."

"No!" Gwen nearly did a spit take.

"Golf bag?" Vivie asked.

"Would you like to know all I've learned?"

In two seconds, all the coupon ladies were seated at the table, leaning forward and focused on every word of my tale. I included Vivie's mention of Fletch, ignoring her vicious glare when I did. I told them about Maggie Cullen and meeting Mr. Fletcher at her house and at Cooters Hollow. And finished with how AJ and I thought Rhonda would have information but now she was dead.

"You went to the Hollow?" Tracy asked incredulously. "You *are* brave."

"But what do you think?"

"AJ's guilty." Vivie opened her coupon book. "Can we swap now?"

"No," everyone, except Marla, who looked a little stunned, said in unison.

"This is a real-life whodunit." Aggie took a sip of her drink. "Why aren't they looking at that Fletcher guy?"

"He has an alibi for Cullen's murder."

"Maybe he hired someone?" Lani offered.

"Have you seen any reports on him?" I asked Lani.

She shook her head. "And you're right. Everything I hear around work is about finding evidence that AJ is behind this."

"See." Vivie's voice sounded victorious. "Just because you like him doesn't mean he's not a killer."

"And just because he's from the Hollow doesn't mean he is," I shot back.

"Maybe the new drug source killed your Mr. Cullen and Mr. Fletcher killed your friend Rhonda for doing business with him." Marla's soft voice cut through Vivie's and my arguments.

"Yes." I pointed at her. "Why aren't the investigators considering something like that?"

"I can't tell you about Mr. Cullen's murder, but one thing they are looking at on the drug angle is the money," Lani said.

"What do you mean?" I asked.

"In big drug operations, they launder the money, usually through a legitimate business. But the cops here can't find one. I know Ethan Taylor has busted his butt on it. But all the businesses they suspected, including Ben Samuels', are now out of business."

"So where do they think it's being laundered?" Gwen leaned forward, completely ignoring Vivie, who was trying to see her coupons.

"Somewhere out of town. Maybe it's going through one of Fletcher's out-of-town businesses."

"Yeah." I perked up at Lani's comment. "He told Rhonda to deliver the collections directly to him."

"But that was different than usual, wasn't it?" Aggie asked.

I nodded.

"But." Lani glanced at me with an apologetic smile. "They're also looking at the company AJ works for."

Ugh. There had to be another explanation. "What if whoever normally got the collections from Rhonda wasn't delivering it to Mr. Fletcher and he found out about it, so he asked her to give them to him directly." I frowned. "But it doesn't explain why Mr. Cullen or Rhonda is dead."

"And it still doesn't mean AJ isn't your phantom other drug dealer."

Sometimes I really hated Vivie.

"Maybe Mr. Cullen and Rhonda knew this mystery man wasn't delivering to Mr. Fletcher and he was afraid they were going to tell?" Marla offered.

The ladies nodded, and their brows knitted as they puzzled through the mystery.

"Do you think this Fletcher guy would kill someone for stealing from him?" Aggie asked me.

"Ethan seems to think so."

"Ethan?" Vivie asked. "You're on a first name basis? He better be careful, AJ might kill him too."

"He might kill Randy as well." Yes, it was mean, but I was tired of Vivie's snark.

"So you *are* sleeping with him!" She stood poised and ready to launch herself over the table to strangle me.

I shook my head. "No. But he does like to leer at me every night while I serve him beer after beer."

"Sophie." Lani's tone was asking me not to stoop to Vivie's level, but I'd had a tough week. It would be nice to have one place I could go where I wasn't having to guard or defend myself.

"Did you consider Randy could be the murderer? He just got the one business in Jefferson Grove that's booming."

"It wasn't Randy." Vivie and Tracy spoke up at the same time.

"How do you know?" I was on a tear and couldn't seem to help myself.

"Because Randy is a putz." Vivie waved the idea away.

"How do you know, Tracy?" Gwen asked.

Tracy looked at us and then Vivie. She shrugged, but there was guilt in her eyes. "Like Vivie said. He doesn't have it in him."

"He also doesn't have the ability to be a good husband."

I stared at Vivie, wanting to point out she wasn't a good wife. That whole pot calling the kettle black deal.

"Where were you last night, Tracy? Randy was out doing whatever and I tried to call you to come watch *Housewives* with me."

Tracy shifted. "I was out." She extended a coupon toward me. "You like nuts, don't you, Sophie?"

I bit my lip as it occurred to me where Tracy was or at least who she was with. Randy wasn't at the Booty Burgo last night, but he wasn't home either. I was pretty sure Tracy was Randy's alibi. Randy was sleeping with his wife's sister. Tracy was sleeping with her sister's husband. I shook my head, not understanding how deceitful people could be to the ones they were supposed to love the most.

Vivie appeared clueless. "If you don't want it, Sophie, I'll take it."

"No. I like nuts."

"Well, y'all aren't quite what I'd expected." Marla pulled some coupons from her binder. "I have some dollar off sausage if anyone is interested."

"Oh, sausage." Gwen rummaged through her coupons. "I've got dollar off tea or anti-aging skin cream. Which will you take?"

SEVENTEEN

WEDNESDAY NIGHT I entered the Booty Burgo, simply wanting to do my job. I didn't want to be leered at and teased by Randy. And I certainly didn't want to be hassled by Kyle. So, I worked my shift with a smile.

Just after Spike announced, "Last call," AJ appeared at the end of the bar.

"Hey." I checked to see if Kyle had noticed. Fortunately, he was nowhere to be seen.

"You about off?"

I nodded.

"We need to talk."

I leaned forward and whispered. "Did you ever find Rhonda…before…you know?"

He nodded. "After work. We'll talk. I'll wait for you in the parking lot."

"Why not wait here? Want a drink?" I knew Kyle would probably fire me, but we were about to close and the current customers weren't the type to care or even notice AJ was there.

AJ shook his head. "Dutch is in the truck."

"Parker. Kyle alert." Spike whapped me with a towel.

I jumped and looked up to see Kyle glaring at me. "After work," I told AJ.

He left the bar and I dutifully went back to work. I thought I was doing a good job avoiding Kyle and his glares, but at the end of my shift, he came up to the bar.

"Close up, Spike. My office, Parker."

He was going to fire me. He'd seen me talking to AJ, a murder suspect. Or Jace told him I'd been in the Hollow asking questions. Or maybe he'd heard about my finding Mr. Cullen's golf bag. All things that could bring dishonor to the great Booty Burgo name. If I wanted to keep my job, I'd have to beg. But as I turned to face Kyle, I couldn't muster the energy.

"I thought you were going to stay out of trouble."

I sighed and plopped down in the chair next to his desk.

"Well?" He remained standing, glaring at me.

I shrugged. What could I say? I reached over and picked up a paperclip on his desk, idly diddling with it.

"Do you want to be fired?" He stuffed his hands in his pockets, maybe to make himself look older or more powerful. But he still just looked like a kid to me.

"No. I want to work, not be accused of murder, and to not be attacked by my father's Ponzi victims. World peace would be nice too." I cocked my head to the side. "How do you know what I've been doing?" Who was tattling on me?

"Everyone knows everything about everybody's business."

That was true. Still. "Who'd you hear it from?"

He shifted slightly and his eyes narrowed. "I'm in this restaurant all day. I hear everything."

"Right." Public places were ideal for gossip.

"You're more hassle than you're worth, Parker."

"Well, that's not quite true. The regulars at the bar like me. Even Randy. He's had plenty of chances to fire me."

Kyle rolled his eyes. "He doesn't know the first thing

about this business. He just wants the drinks and to ogle the wenches." He pulled one hand from his pocket and fiddled with a coin.

His comment reminded me that Randy didn't do the books for the Booty Burgo, which was odd since he was co-owner and an accountant.

"He's a silent partner?"

"Yes. I run the business. You're not the only one with a college degree, Miss high-and-mighty-college-grad. I got an associate's degree."

"And look at you now. You're the manager of the Booty Burgo." It came out snarkier than I'd intended.

"I'm doing better than you." His cheeks reddened and he dropped the coin he'd been playing with. He glared at me for a moment and then bent to pick it up. His fingers gripped a silver golf marker with gold JAC.

My heart stopped. What was Kyle doing with Cullen's golf marker? I knew Cullen had been part owner of the Booty Burgo, but I'd never seen him here nor heard Kyle talk about him. But if Kyle ran the restaurant, they'd have met. Did Kyle play golf too?

There was a niggle in my head that told me not to ask. Or maybe it was Ethan's voice scolding me for poking my nose in where it didn't belong. The memory of Ben Samuels coming after me as I investigated my hit and run had me choosing to leave instead of questioning Kyle.

"So, am I fired?" I willed my voice to remain steady but wasn't sure I succeeded.

"Go help Spike finish up. Then I'll decide."

I hurried out, pulling my phone from my skirt pocket and calling Ethan. "You have to come to the Booty Burgo." I hissed into the phone when Ethan picked up.

"It's two in the morning, Sophie." He hadn't sounded asleep when I called, but maybe he was getting ready for bed.

"My manager has one of Cullen's golf markers."

"What?"

"Kyle has one of Cullen's golf markers." I looked over my shoulder to make sure Kyle wasn't behind me with an ice pick.

"Why does he have that?"

"I don't know. I distinctly remember you telling me not to ask questions anymore. Can you come?"

He grunted. "Yeah, sure. I'll be there in twenty minutes."

I checked my watch. We'd be done closing in ten and Spike would be gone. I remembered AJ was in the parking lot. I could wait with him. "Hurry." I poked off the phone, slipped it in my pocket and helped Spike finish closing the bar.

"Walk you out, Parker?" Spike put on his leather jacket.

"Yeah—"

"Parker." Kyle stood in the doorway to the kitchen. "Let's talk."

I looked at Spike. I wanted to ask him to stay, but I was probably being paranoid. Kyle was an opportunistic weasel, not a murderer. He probably found the marker and thought it made him look posh.

"I can wait."

I shook my head. "AJ is waiting for me."

Spike shrugged and headed out. I moved toward Kyle, ready to get my walking papers. At least that was what I was hoping. His having that golf marker bothered me.

"In here." Kyle held the door to the kitchen, not his office, open for me to walk through. I had a real bad feeling as I stepped inside. I was two steps through the door when I saw AJ sitting on the floor, slumped against the walk-in freezer. I whirled around right into the butt of a gun held by Kyle.

"What did you do to him?"

"He's just out for a bit. He'll have a headache from where I hit him, but he's not dead."

"How'd you get him in here?"

AJ had to have thirty pounds on scrawny Kyle.

"I told him I had food for that giant mutant mutt he has."

If this was a kids' movie, this would be the point where Dutch would barge in and save the day. Too bad for me. "What are you doing, Kyle?" My heart was racing and I couldn't pull in a breath, but I knew I needed to stay calm. Ethan was on his way. All I had to do was keep Kyle from killing us until Ethan arrived.

"I'm going to kill you both, once I find out what you know."

He waggled the gun, motioning me farther into the kitchen.

I scanned the area, looking for something to protect myself with, but what could I use against a gun? "I don't know anything."

"Cut the dumb ditz act. It might work on others. It won't work on me."

How strange that for so long I thought Kyle underestimated my smarts. Turned out, I underestimated his. "You killed Cullen?"

"That's right. How'd you figure it out?"

"When you pulled a gun on me just now." I made

my way to the center workstation. Several heavy-duty pots and pans hung above, but I'd never be fast enough to grab one and hit Kyle with it.

"Why were you in the Hollow? What did you tell Fletch?"

I shook my head. "I was visiting Jace and Rhonda. I like being a bartender, so I wanted to know if they were coming back. I don't know Fletch."

"Liar." He jabbed the gun toward me.

My breath hitched as I waited for it to go off.

Instead, Kyle moved closer to me. "Don't tell me. Doesn't matter. Once you and Devlin are dead, it's all business as usual."

"I have no idea what you're talking about." I continued to move away until I was near the sink. I saw a large frying pan and my brain did a tug of war on whether or not I should risk using it to defend myself.

"When I heard you caught that nutcase Ben Samuels, I was sure I was in the clear." Kyle moved toward me. I recognized the murderous gleam in his eyes and his sinister smile, because it was the same that Ben had sported. What was it about murderers that they took a sick pleasure in their killing?

"Since I don't know what you're talking about, you're still in the clear." I positioned myself so the pan handle was at my hip.

"Come on, Sophie. Don't play dumb."

"I'm not dumb." I grabbed the handle and swung the pan, hitting his hand with the gun. He cried out and the gun clattered to the floor. Kyle held his hurt hand, bending forward slightly. Before he had time to gather himself, I swung the pan again, this time catching his cheek with a loud clang. He dropped like all the bones in his body had liquefied. I scrambled to get the gun and ran over to AJ.

"AJ? Are you okay?" I patted his face. "AJ!" I glanced over at Kyle, who was moaning and slowly rolling over to his side.

AJ's head lolled to the side, but his eyes fluttered. "Soph?"

"Yeah. AJ, are you okay? Help is on the way."

He looked toward Kyle still laying on the floor. Then AJ's glassy eyes turned to me. "You did that?"

I nodded.

His lips widened into a goofy grin. "My hero."

I laughed, although my voice still shook from the endorphins. "Yeah, well. Don't forget it."

The kitchen door swung open and I immediately raised the gun to the intruder.

"Whoa, hey, Sophie." Ethan put both his hands up, one of which held a gun.

"Ethan, thank God."

He walked over to me. "What's wrong with him?" He nodded toward AJ.

"Kyle said he hit him."

"Is that your work?" Ethan glanced over at Kyle, who was now on his hands and knees.

I nodded. "I whapped him with the frying pan."

Ethan flashed a grin. "Tough cookie. Maybe you should give me that." He reached a hand for the gun I was holding.

"We're okay now, AJ." I handed Ethan the gun.

Ethan smiled at me, but it wasn't the affable friendly smile I'd come to know. It was eerily reminiscent of Kyle's and Ben's; sinister and scary. "You should have listened to me when I told you to stay out of it." Ethan pointed the gun at me.

"You've got to be kidding me." It probably wasn't the right reaction, but I was seriously perturbed.

"Get up, Kyle." Ethan walked over to the now-standing Booty Burgo manager and gave him back the gun I'd just beat off of him. "I tried to protect you, Sophie. Kyle here wanted to kill you days ago."

"Why? I don't know anything."

"You know more than you think. You just haven't put it together. But your boyfriend has, haven't you, Devlin?"

AJ winced as he tried to sit straighter. He took my hand, probably to reassure me, but it didn't work. What were the odds we were going to get out of this mess?

"What do you know?" I asked AJ.

"You found out most of it. You figured out Cullen was most likely murdered because of drugs. And you believed Fletch when he said he didn't do it."

I nodded. "He said Cullen was supposed to meet him that day to deliver information to him."

"Cullen was going to out the other partners in this drug ring," AJ said.

"Other partners?" I glanced up to Ethan, who smirked, as if he were entertained as I figured out what the heck was happening.

"Let's just kill 'em." Kyle pointed his gun at me. He still had a big red mark on his face, but he seemed to have gathered his wits or, in this case, all his crazy.

"Patience. Let's at least let them know why they're dying." Ethan was enjoying this way too much.

"You're part of the drug ring?"

"We're the head of it." Kyle lifted his chest and I thought he might beat it like a gorilla.

"What about Fletcher?" I asked.

"What he doesn't know won't hurt him," Kyle said.

"But he already suspects." I bit my lip as the pieces came together. "He knows someone has been cutting into his territory."

"Not quite, but almost." Ethan's tone reminded me of a teacher telling me I was wrong but to try again.

I thought back to what Fletcher said in the trailer. "He wanted Rhonda to bring him the collection…the money, directly to him." I looked up at Kyle as Lani's comment about the investigators trying to find out how the money was being processed came back to me. "You were laundering the money for him through the Booty Burgo. But he realized that he wasn't getting it all. You've been taking it."

"That's how it started." Kyle smiled like a kid who'd just won the class spelling bee.

"But they wanted more." AJ lifted his hand to his head and winced again. "They started cutting Fletch out of the deal in the Hollow. It was his drugs being flown in by Cullen, but they weren't paying Fletch for them. When they heard Fletch was asking for the money straight from Rhonda, they knew she'd turn on them. So they killed her and planned to pin the missing money and drugs on her to put Fletch off of them. She knew it was coming, too. She was trying to run when I finally found her."

"That's what she told you?"

"She wouldn't give me names, but when I told her I'd take her to the sheriff's office, she freaked out. That's when I figured one of them was involved." AJ nodded toward Ethan.

My gaze jerked to Ethan. "I told you about Fletcher's message to Rhonda." Guilt rose like bile in my throat that I was responsible for putting her in danger.

"Thank goodness you did. It made up for Kyle's mistake in not better disposing of the golf bag." Ethan glared at Kyle.

"What was in the bag?" It was the one thing I still didn't understand. Why take the bag?

"Drugs. And, of course, the accounting sheet that showed the money we'd taken," Kyle said.

"So Cullen was working with you but changed his mind?" At this point, I didn't really care anymore, but I figured if they kept talking, maybe AJ and I could find a way out of this mess.

"Fletch caught Cullen siphoning some of the drugs. So he decided to make a deal. He was going to tell Fletch that not only were we siphoning drugs but money from the laundering as well."

"But you killed him before he could meet with Fletch." It all made sense now.

"Couldn't have Cullen outing us," Kyle said. "I tried to talk him out of it. But he was afraid of Fletch. He should have been afraid of me."

"So you were at the airport when AJ showed up to repo the plane." I remembered the truck parked behind Cullen's car at the airport.

"That was the beauty of this whole thing. You two made it so easy to pin it on you." Ethan had been leaning against the counter but finally, he walked toward AJ and me, huddled on the floor in front of the freezer.

"That's why the sheriff never caught Cullen with the

drugs. You protected him." A new thought came to me. "You were the one in the third car. The one that pulled up as we took off."

"How do you think the sheriff's deputies arrived so quickly?"

If I had that pan, I'd have used it to wipe the smug grin off of Ethan's face.

"Did you clear Fletcher too, so he wouldn't suspect you were one of the ones stealing from him?"

"You got it." Ethan pointed the gun toward us.

"Sophie." AJ squeezed my hand.

I was shaking so hard it was a wonder I couldn't hear my bones rattle. I looked at AJ. I didn't want to die, but if I was going to die, I wanted the last thing I saw in life to be AJ.

A loud bang rang through the room and I squeezed my eyes shut as I waited to feel the piercing of the bullet.

"Hold it there, Deputy Taylor."

I peeked one eye open. Sergeant Scowl and three other cops burst into the kitchen, the swinging door slamming against the metal counter. To my relief, they were holding guns on Ethan and Kyle.

"We'd have been here sooner, but there's a dog the size of a dinosaur at the front door."

"Dutch." AJ and I said in unison.

"It's not how it looks." Ethan held his hands up. "I'm undercover."

"No. You're under arrest."

In that moment, I wanted to kiss Sergeant Scowl.

EIGHTEEN

WITH KYLE AND Ethan behind bars, I thought my life would settle down, but for the next week, it was still crazy. I was able to see AJ for a few minutes in the hospital, where he stayed a day for a concussion, but after that, I spent most of my time being interviewed by sheriff's deputies or the media. I could understand the sheriff's interest. Sergeant Scowl, a term I use endearingly now, grilled me on all the conversations I'd had with Ethan over the course of the investigation, with special focus on what was said in the kitchen of the Booty Burgo the night he and Kyle tried to kill AJ and me. Like me, Sergeant Scowl wanted to figure out what he'd missed.

Boy, had we missed a lot. I'd been right to question Ethan's intentions. What I'd been wrong about was why. I thought he was trying to trip me up to say something that would incriminate me. Instead, he was a drug dealer, using the power of his position to protect Fletcher, Cullen, Kyle and Rhonda from being caught. I felt sick and stupid for being duped.

"If it makes you feel any better, I think Ethan really was trying to protect you. Had you stayed out of it like he asked, you probably wouldn't have been in danger." Sergeant Scowl didn't do sympathy very well, but I appreciated the effort. Not that it made me feel better, because it didn't. The choice between remaining a murder suspect or becoming a victim wasn't a great choice. Sure, I'd rather go to jail than die, but still… I'd rather not do either.

Of course, Sergeant Scowl felt duped as well.

"How'd you know to come to the Booty Burgo?" I asked him during our first interview.

He gave me a sheepish smile. "There was a call about a wild animal stalking outside the restaurant. But as I was getting ready to head out there, something just clicked in place."

"What?"

"The only business of Cullen's that was making any money was the Booty Burgo. About a year ago, the profits really picked up."

"That's about when Ethan came back to town."

Sergeant Scowl nodded. "The income was pretty steady for about eight months, then a few months back, they dropped. Not too much, but enough that it was noticeable. Deputy Taylor suggested it was the natural ebb and flow of business."

"But you didn't think so?"

"Well, I'm not a business man, but even I know spring and summer are the peak seasons for businesses around here. That's when we have the most tourists."

I mulled over his comment. "You think that's when Ethan and Kyle started embezzling from the money being laundered through the restaurant."

Sergeant Scowl tapped his nose to indicate I was spot on. "Deputy Taylor was working extra hard to keep me focused on AJ and away from Fletcher and the drug angle."

"Not that hard." I grumbled.

"When I saw Deputy Taylor's car in the parking lot

of the Booty Burgo, it was all I needed. Well, that and your statement."

"How'd you get past Dutch?"

"Peppermint candy. That dog has to have the fresh-est breath of anyone in Jefferson Grove."

THE BOOTY BURGO was closed the week following Ethan and Kyle's arrest, partly due to it being a crime scene, but also, Randy needed a new manager and accountant. I figured he'd handle the latter himself. I was unhappy when he hired Vivie for the former. Fortunately, she said she would only work a few hours in the morning, so I was committed to only working nights. Promising not to tell Vivie about him and Tracy insured I could have whatever schedule I wanted.

The big change for me was instead of being a freak show for having a father in jail, I was a celebrity for helping solve a murder and bringing down a local drug ring. Granted it was a small ring. But getting rid of Kyle and Ethan meant Fletcher didn't have a dealer in the area. And with Cullen gone, he didn't have a smug-gler here either. Sergeant Scowl said Fletcher's drug business was plenty big in other areas of the state, so he would probably stay out of the area, at least for a little while.

It was nice to go out in public and not have people whisper about me. Instead they congratulated me and asked if I was afraid when I whapped Kyle with a fry-ing pan.

I also finally got a call from my father, who indi-cated he hadn't called because, after being interviewed by Sergeant Scowl and Ethan, he determined contact-ing me could make me look guilty. I told him some of what transpired but left out the part where I was nearly killed. He didn't need to know that.

The best news was the call I got from Mrs. Wayland offering me the job assisting the children's librarian. It was only part-time, which meant I had to continue at the Booty Burgo for the time being. But Mrs. Wayland said that after a probation period, I might be able to get more hours.

A week after the incident, I walked back into the Booty Burgo just before the dinner rush. I took a chance that with my newfound celebrity, I wouldn't need to wear the wench uniform and instead wore a white T-shirt and black shorts. Just to make sure I wasn't pushing my luck too much with Randy, I wore a red choker necklace that had little gold coins decorating it. That was sort of pirate-like, right?

I'd anticipated there'd be more customers in the restaurant since it had been a crime scene. People had a strange interest in the macabre. But I didn't expect the cheers and congratulations that erupted when I walked in. Of course, after about two seconds, Spike was barking at me to get to work. Which I did with a smile.

At two thirty in the morning, the restaurant and bar were closed. The waitresses had already left and it was just Spike and me.

"Now would be a good time for you to invent a drink, Parker." Spike tossed his bar rag into a laundry bag.

"Really?" I looked up from putting the last washed beer mug away.

He nodded. "You're famous. A Sophie Parker signature drink would be a great promotional ploy."

"I'll get right on it." I already had an idea of drinks

that paid homage to my beloved fairy tales, starting with a drink called the Poison Apple.

"Let me walk you out."

I wasn't in danger anymore, I hoped. But it still made good sense to have a big guy like Spike around at two in the morning in the middle of a deserted parking lot. I stopped short when I saw AJ's truck parked next to the Bomber. AJ sat on the tailgate with Dutch lying next to him.

"You alright there, Parker?" Spike nodded toward AJ.

"Yeah. Thanks, Spike."

"See ya." Spike strode off toward his car.

I stared at AJ, wondering what he was doing here. "Why didn't you come in?"

He slid from the back of the truck. "I didn't want to hurt your newfound celebrity. Once a Devlin, always a Devlin in this neck of the woods."

His comment hurt and annoyed me. "I don't care about that." And to be honest, I wasn't sure anyone in town really cared about it either. Sure, people talked, but it wasn't always bad.

"No. You never did." He tugged on one of my stray curls and watched while it bounced back into place.

"What are you doing here?"

"I have to go out of town for a few days."

"Okay." I hoped my voice sounded nonchalant, even though on the inside I was disappointed. I was just getting used to having AJ back in my life, but now that Kyle and Ethan were in jail, and he wasn't a suspect in murder, there was no reason for him to come around Jefferson Grove.

"I've got a repo in Texas."

I smiled, genuinely happy he was working again. "Gordo took you back?"

AJ nodded. "It will be nice to fly again."

"I bet." I took a deep breath to prepare for my next statement. "So, you're here to say good-bye?"

He cocked his head to the side. "Just for a couple of days."

"Then what?"

He put his hands on his waist and turned his head out toward the view of the valley. Of course, it was dark and not much could be seen. When he turned back, his brows were pinched together. I couldn't read his expression, but it made me uneasy anyway.

"Sit for a minute. I've got something I need to talk to you about." He motioned to the tailgate of his truck.

In my experience, those words never amounted to anything good. The last time I heard them, my father was telling me he was in legal hot water and would likely end up in prison.

I stared at AJ for a moment, wishing I could read in his expression if I was misunderstanding. But since I was no mind reader, my only hope to know what was going on was to sit and let him tell me whatever he needed to say. He put his hands on my waist to help me up. He let go of me, but he remained close, and, of course, my hormones went haywire. I wondered if they'd ever settle for liking AJ as a friend.

"Is everything okay?" I pushed the flutter in my belly down and looked into his eyes. I didn't understand his behavior and it worried me.

"Yeah. Great." He stared at me and I couldn't stop myself from shifting in my seat from the intensity of his gaze.

"What's going on, AJ?"

"I was thinking, when I get back, maybe we can get together."

"Sure. That'd be fun." Why was he being weird about that?

He gave a small laugh and shook his head. For a moment I thought he looked nervous. "I mean a date, Sophie."

A date? "Oh." My belly did a flip and my heart raced like Secretariat in the Belmont. The combination stalled my breath.

"Yeah, oh."

I studied his face, for what, I'm not sure. Maybe to see if he was sincere. Or maybe I was misunderstanding. His expression seemed more baffled. As if he was surprised by his own statement.

"Like a date date?"

He laughed. "Yes, Sophie. Unless it's too weird. I know you see me more as a big brother—"

"No, I don't."

"You don't?"

"I've tried to because…well…you see me as a kid sister."

"No, I don't."

"You don't?" I frowned. "Then why are you always trying to protect me and boss me around?"

"Because I care about you. And I don't boss." He stepped closer to me, and every nerve ending on my skin sizzled to life. He shook his head. "I think you're a smart, fun, brave, loyal woman."

My insides melted. I grinned, hoping I didn't look like a loon. I didn't need him knowing my heart was doing cartwheels.

"And I'd like to take you on a date, unless you have a problem being seen with a Devlin."

I frowned. Actually, I got mad. "If I had a problem with being seen with a Devlin, I wouldn't have agreed to go flying with you and end up being a suspect in a murder. And I wouldn't have snuck around with you so we could solve the murder. And I wouldn't be sitting out here with you in the Booty Burgo parking lot in the middle of the night."

"So, that's a yes?"

"Yes."

He grinned, watching me for a moment. His head cocked to the side as one of his hands cupped my cheek. I'm not sure if it was his touch or the intensity of his gaze, but my breath hitched and the world stopped.

"Can I have a kiss before I go?"

Well, duh. My head bobbed. His smile widened into the cocky one that had always made me swoon. Then he leaned toward me and gently pressed his lips to mine.

At the end of *The Princess Bride*, the movie, not the book, there was a description of the perfect kiss of all time between Wesley and Buttercup. My kiss with AJ was better. It was everything a woman who loved fairy tales would want and more. When he pulled away, he rested his forehead against mine.

"I thought about doing that on your eighteenth birthday."

My head jerked back. "You did?" Was it possible AJ had had more than friendly feelings for me back then?

"I did." He gave me one more quick kiss. "I should go."

I nodded and hopped off the tailgate of the truck. AJ took my hand and walked me the few steps to my car.

I looked at our joined hands, thinking how surreal but totally awesome this new situation was.

    "Try to stay out of trouble while I'm gone."

    I smirked. "You're my only trouble, AJ."

    He grinned. "It's a good thing you like trouble."

    "Good thing indeed."

* * * * *

JENNA HARTE LOVES to write about crime and passion. She is the author of the Valentine Mysteries, the first of which, *Deadly Valentine*, reached the quarter-finals in Amazon's Breakthrough Novel Award in 2013. She also has a three-book romance series, Southern Heat, is currently working on a traditional cozy mystery featuring a fairy tale loving, coupon clipping sleuth. When she's not telling stories, she works by day as a freelance writer, blogger and online entrepreneur.

In her free time, she loves coffee, chocolate, books, and YouTube. She is an empty-nester living in central Virginia with her husband, and a nutty cat.